## Praise for *Arctic Rising*

"If you count on good thrillers to be told in clear, engaging prose and made up of interesting psychology, state-of-the-art research, and [illegible]ing plots, you couldn't be i[illegible]

—[illegible]ed

"An intimate techno-thr[illegible]v-down in an ice-free Arc[illegible] weekly



"Buckell focuses as much on action-thriller set pieces as he does on teasing out a plausible future, placing the novel somewhere around the intersection of Michael Crichton and William Gibson."

—*Kirkus Reviews*

"You might as well strap yourself in for the ride."

—Suzanne Johnson, author of *Royal Street*

"A gripping and convincing near-future scenario that is composed of many beautifully machined speculative parts, which all cohere into a stirring, verisimilitudinous portrait of our world circa 2050. Additionally, [Buckell] provides a thriller-style plot worthy of Hitchcock or Neal Stephenson."

—*The Barnes & Noble Review*

"This commercial sci-fi thriller has a premise that should interest ecologically minded Canadians."

—*Winnipeg Free Press*

"A very good classic spy thriller set in an exotic location. A location that exists only because of the drastic changes in our planet's climate."

—*The Denver Post*

"A first-rate SF thriller." —Rich Horton, *Black Gate*

[illegible]

"[illegible] in a better place."

—NPR's *All Things Considered*

"[illegible] thriller about an ecological [illegible]"

—*Publishers Weekly*

[illegible]

# ARCTIC RISING

TOBIAS S. BUCKELL

1 3 5 7 9 10 8 6 4 2

First published in the US in 2012 by
Tor at Tom Doherty Associates, LLC
Published in the UK in 2013 by Del Rey,
an imprint of Ebury Publishing
A Random House Group Company



The Random House Group Limited Reg. No. 954009

Addresses for companies within the Random House Group can be found at: www.randomhouse.co.uk

A CIP catalogue record for this book is available from the British Library

The Random House Group Limited supports The Forest Stewardship Council® (FSC®), the leading international forest-certification organisation. Our books carrying the FSC label are printed on FSC®-certified paper. FSC is the only forest-certification scheme supported by the leading environmental organisations, including Greenpeace. Our paper procurement policy can be found at www.randomhouse.co.uk/environment

Printed and bound by CPI Group (UK) Ltd, Croydon, CR0 4YY

ISBN 9780091953522

**For Karl and Paolo**

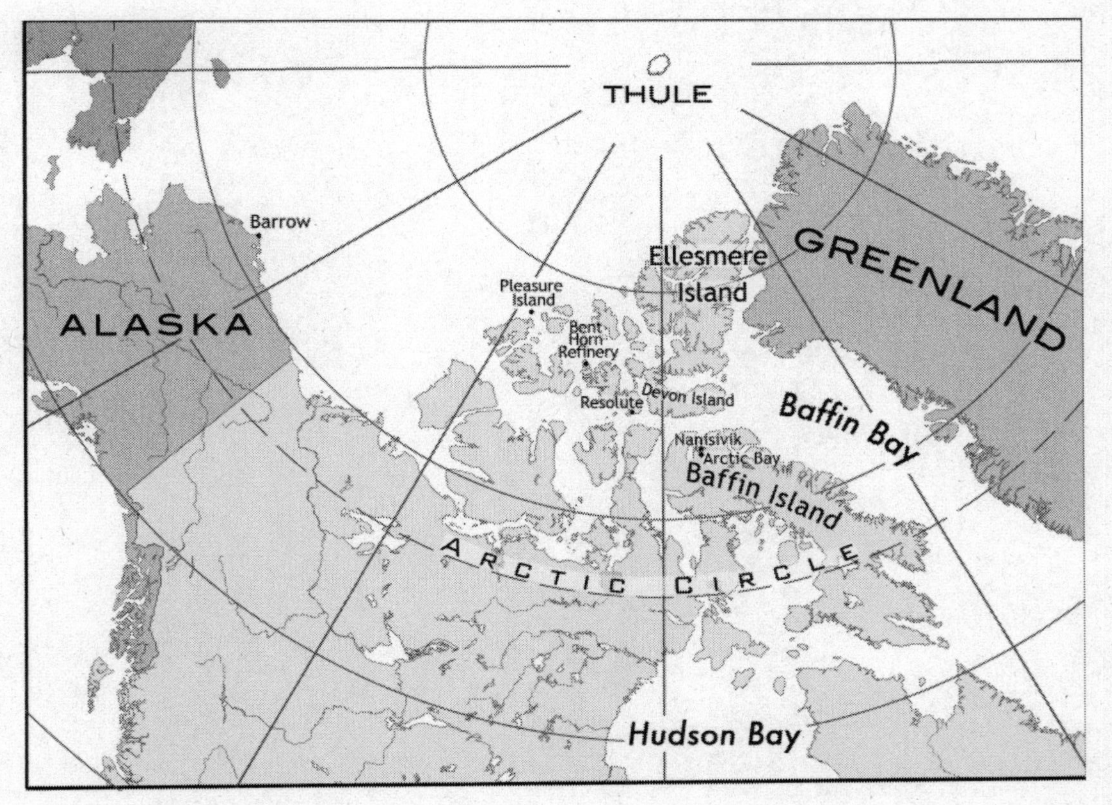
THULE
Barrow
ALASKA
Pleasure Island
Bent Horn Refinery
Ellesmere Island
GREENLAND
Devon Island
Resolute
Baffin Bay
Nanisivik
Arctic Bay
Baffin Island
ARCTIC CIRCLE
Hudson Bay

# ARCTIC RISING

# 1

Centuries ago, the fifty-mile-wide mouth of the Lancaster Sound imprisoned ships in its icy bite. But today, the choppy polar waters between Baffin Island to the south of the sound, and Devon Island on the north, twinkled in the perpetual sunlight of the Arctic's summer months, and tons of merchant traffic constantly sailed through the once impossible-to-pass Northwest Passage over the top of Canada.

A thousand feet over the frigid, but no longer freezing and ice-choked waters, the seventy-five-meter-long United Nations Polar Guard airship *Plover* hung in a slow-moving air current. The turboprop engines growled to life as the fat, cigar-shaped vehicle adjusted course, then fell silent.

Inside the cabin of the airship, Anika Duncan checked her readings, then leaned over the matte-screened displays in the cockpit to look out the front windows.

The airship's cabin had once held twelve passengers, but was now retrofitted with a bunk, a small kitchen area, supply closets, and a cramped navigation station. Tourists had once sat in the cabin underneath the giant gasbag as the airship glided over New York's tallest buildings. After that tour of duty, the United Nations Polar Guard purchased it well used and very cheap.

Airships didn't use much fuel. They could put observers into the air to monitor ship traffic for days at a time, wafting from position to position with air currents.

It saved money. And Anika knew the UNPG was always struggling with a lean budget. It showed on her paycheck, too.

"Which ship should we take a closer look at, Tom?" Anika asked.

She'd unzipped her bright red cold-sea survival suit and rolled it down to her waist, as it was too hot for her to wear fully zipped up as regulations required. She had her frizzy hair pulled back in a bouncy ponytail: a week without relaxant meant it had a mind of its own right now. She'd consider letting it turn to dreads if she could, but the UNPG didn't approve. And yet, she thought to herself, they expected her to sit up in the air for a week without a real shower.

Someone once told her to just shave it. But she *liked* her hair. Why hide it? As long as it was tied up, regs said she could have longer hair.

Now Thomas Hutton, her copilot, was all about the regs and then some. He had his blond hair millimeter short. Shorter than required. But even *he* wore his survival suit halfsies.

It was one of those balancing acts: if they kept it cold enough in the airship's cabin to wear the suits zipped up, using the tiny, cramped toilet was torture.

Particularly, Tom said, for the guys.

"Tom?" she prompted.

"Yeah, I'm looking, I'm looking." He walked back from the nav station, the top half of his suit floppily smacking along behind him as he peered down through the windows along the way.

Four ships were funneling their way into the Lancaster Sound from the east, where Greenland lurked beneath the curve of the horizon. The ships looked like bath toys from up at this height. Three of the ships had large wing-shaped parafoils hanging in the sky overhead. The parafoils, connected to the ships by cables, reached up to where the strong winds were blowing to drag the ships through the water.

"I want to take a closer look at that oil burner," Tom finally announced.

"You are getting predictable," Anika said as he slid into the copilot's seat. Though one of the things she liked about Tom was his easy predictability. Her own life had been chaotic enough before coming so far north. It was a different pace up here. A different chapter of her life. And she liked it. "It *is* supposed to be a random check?"

He pointed at the black plume of smoke trailing from the stacks of the fourth ship in the distance. "That one sticks out like a sore thumb. Hard to say no to."

Anika tapped the scratched and well-worn touch screens around her. She pulled up video from one of the telephoto-lens cameras mounted on the prow of the cabin and zoomed in on the fourth ship.

Thirty meters long with a bulbous-prowed hull, flaking rust, and colored industrial gray, the ship was pushing fifteen knots in its rush to pass through the sound.

"They seem to be in a hurry."

Tom glanced over. "Fifteen knots? She hits a berg at that speed she'll Titanic herself quickly enough."

The Arctic still had an island of ice floating around the actual Pole. It was kept alive by a fusion of conservationists, tourism, and the creation of a semi-country and series of ports that sprang up called Thule. They'd used refrigerator cables down off platforms to keep the ice congealed around themselves despite the warmed-up modern Arctic, a trick learned from old polar oil riggers who'd done that to create temporary ice islands back at the turn of the century.

It was an old trick that didn't really work anywhere else but near the Pole now. But even the carefully artificial polar ice island that was Thule still calved chunks, some of which would get as far south as Lancaster.

Hit one at the speed this ship was going, they'd sink easily enough.

"Shall we get closer to him and sniff him over?" Anika asked. "Remind him to slow down."

Tom grinned. "Yeah, their credentials should come through shortly. The scatter camera's up. Let's see if this ship's radioactive."

The neutron scatter camera, mounted on a gimbaled platform right next to the telephoto cameras, hunted for radioactive signatures. Port authorities had been using them to hunt for potential terrorist bombs for decades. But what they found, over time, was a secondary use for the scatter cameras: catching nuclear waste dumpers.

At the turn of the century, after the tsunami that washed over East Asia, UN monitors found themselves contacted by East African countries about industrial pollutants washing up on the beaches. People had been falling sick after approaching large, well-insulated drums washed up from deep in the ocean. People had also been showing statistically high rates of cancer near coastlines throughout countries where standing navies and coast guards just didn't exist.

Toxic waste, including spent nuclear fuel, was clearly getting dumped off non-monitored coasts by commercial shipping.

The gig started when a shady company got the lowest bid for safely storing fuel or industrial waste. Ostensibly, they were transporting it out of country to another location.

In reality, once offshore of some struggling African country with no navy, they'd dump it.

Even so-called "first world" countries weren't immune. A statistical study of waste-transporting merchant ships thirty years ago showed a higher number of merchant ships "sinking" in the deeper Mediterranean.

Charter an old leaker, stuff it with barrels full of whatever the host country and its businesses didn't want. Take the big payout, head out to sea, and then experience difficulties. Instant massive profit.

The African and Mediterranean dumping had

faded with the EU and East African naval buildups and public outrage. More dumping was going on off Arabic coasts these days. The post oil-boom nations were too busy trying to destroy each other for what little black gold was left to have the capability to worry about what was going on off their coastlines.

But now the Arctic was also seeing dumping. With the whole Northwest Passage open and free of ice, merchant ships could cross from Russia to Greenland, on through Canadian polar ports, and then to Alaska. Which also meant they crossed over some very deep Arctic water.

As nuclear power boomed across Eurasia and the Americas, with smaller corporations offering small pebble-bed nuclear reactors to energy-hungry towns and small cities demanding an alternative to oils needed in the plastics industries, the waste had to go somewhere.

Somewhere was more often than not . . . out here where Anika patrolled.

Hence the old, repurposed UNPG spotter airships with scatter cameras. Anika and her fellow pilots hung above the Northwest Passage helping monitor ship traffic that came from the world over. But mainly, they were hunting for ships with radioactive signatures.

The program had proven effective enough. Word had gotten out, thanks in part to a major UNPG advertising campaign online. For the past seven months Anika's job had become rather routine.

Maybe even a little boring.

Which is why, for a moment, she didn't notice the sound of the scatter camera alarm going off.

# 2

Anika gunned the turboprop engines to shove the airship down toward the choppy ocean.

"Do you have an ID on the ship?" she asked. The ship could be nuclear powered, she guessed. There were plenty of bulk carriers that were. But this one felt way too small for that.

Tom had a tablet in his lap and was paging through documentation.

"The transponder onboard claims it's the *Kosatka,* registered out of Liberia. Papers are in order. She cleared herself in Nord Harbor." He looked across at her. "She's already been cleared by Greenland Polar Guard. We shouldn't even be paying attention to her. If we hadn't left the camera on, we would have just pinged the transponder and let them through."

They'd dropped a couple hundred feet, and the *Plover* picked up speed in the still air as the four engines strained away.

"Is there anything about radioactive cargo when she cleared Greenland?"

Tom shook his head. "She's clean on here. Do you still want to get in closer?"

That was Tom, following the letter of the law. The rules said the ship was cleared, that someone had checked it over in Greenland. They didn't need to run a second check.

"Someone in Greenland could have slipped up," Anika said. Or, she thought silently, been bribed. She picked up the VHF radio transmitter and held it to the side of her mouth. This was weird enough to warrant a closer look, either way. "*Kosatka, Kosatka, Kosatka,* this is UNPG 4975, *Plover,* over."

Nothing but a faint crackle came from the channel.

Tom waved his tablet. "Says here it's a private research vessel operating out of Arkhangel'sk."

"So they are registered in Liberia for convenience," Anika said. "But operating out of Russia. And they're studying what?"

"It doesn't say."

"Search around online, see if you can find anything."

"Already on it."

Anika piloted them down through the black plume of smoke in the air behind the Russian vessel. They were catching up to it.

Once abreast, she would run the scatter camera again. This would get them better data for Baffin Island. This way whoever was doing this couldn't then claim the camera flagged a false reading. Even if the ship dumped its waste, Anika could prove it had been carrying something obviously radioactive.

Then the gunships would get involved. And boarding parties.

But that wouldn't be her problem. Which was why Anika liked flying. Back in the Sahara, after she'd put Lagos well behind her, she'd flown as a spotter for the miles of DESERTEC solar stations out in the middle of nowhere. High over the baking sand, she'd run patrols looking for trouble.

Like a god looking down from the clouds, she'd directed guards out to the perimeter to make sure Berber tribesmen weren't really disguised terrorists looking to blow up the solar mirrors that ran most of North Africa and Europe.

Anika throttled back as she matched speed with the *Kosatka* and glanced portside, down at the ship. It was a few hundred feet away. She could see the silhouettes of figures behind the glass panes of the cockpit windows looking over the ship's decks. The gasbag of the *Plover* had blocked the sun out for *Kosatka*. Surely the bridge crew had noticed her by now.

They had. Two men opened a rusty door on the side of the bridge and looked at her, shading their eyes as they did so.

They ran back inside.

"Well, they're paying attention now," she laughed.

*Kosatka* was a beater. Rust showed everywhere, and where it didn't, it had been sanded away and covered in gray primer. Patches of the stuff blotched the entire ship.

"*Kosatka, Kosatka, Kosatka,* this is UNPG *Plover* off your starboard side, over."

"Case of beer says they're dumping," Tom said, standing up and looking over her to the ship.

"What kind of beer are we talking about?" Anika asked as she fired up the scatter camera again. She backed the readings up to a chip and slipped them into a pocket on her shoulder. Old habits. Hard copy trumped all. Half the equipment on the airship broke down, and she didn't want to lose the data. Dumpers deserved nothing more than to rot in jail, she figured. And she'd be really annoyed if some slipup of hers let one of them slip through. "If it is that cheap 'lite' beer you had at your barbecue last month, I don't want to win a bet with you."

Tom looked wounded. "Jenny picked that out, not me. I was stuck in the air with you all that week, remember?"

"I remember." Anika looked over at the radio. Still static.

"What kind of good Nigerian beer should I bet, then?" Tom asked, sitting back down and looking up his results for the search on the ship.

"Guinness will do."

"Guinness?"

"Number one in the mother country," Anika said. "Someone told me they sell more of it back home than in Ireland." She tapped the picture of her and her father sitting on a blanket on Lekki Beach just outside Lagos. Each was wearing a crisp white shirt, holding a pint. Big smiles. Hot sun. Cool ocean.

"No shit?"

"None at all." Anika grabbed the mic. "Let's see if we can raise them and get them to heave to, okay? Next step: we call in the nearest cutter and get this over with. The camera still thinks they are hot."

Before she could call again, a heavy Russian voice crackled over the radio. "Yes, yes, hello. You are United Nations Polar Guard. Correct?"

Anika sighed. "The crew doesn't know how to respond to us on the radio properly." She keyed the mic. "*Kosatka,* switch to channel forty-five, repeat, four-five. Over."

She waited for confirmation, but none came. She was considering switching to channel forty-five when Tom tapped her shoulder. "What's that?" He sounded as if knew, though, but just couldn't believe what he was seeing and wanted confirmation.

Anika glanced over. The two men had pulled a small crate out onto the metal deck around the bridge. Anika squinted at the contents, but spotted the distinctive and familiar long tube of a shoulder-held rocket-propelled grenade launcher.

No time to react, no time to think. She yanked on the joystick and gunned the turboprop engines to maximum. The massive, lighter-than-air machine banked hard to the left as she flew just fifty feet over the old ship's superstructure.

Crossing to the other side of the ship would force those men to move the RPG over, Anika thought. That'd give her a minute. And it would get them further away as the airship struggled to accelerate toward its top speed of seventy miles an hour.

This was bad, Anika thought. Probably worse than Nairobi.

Definitely worse than Nairobi.

"Is that what I think it is?" Tom shouted at her over the roar of the engines.

"RPG." Anika yanked her survival suit up over her shoulders and zipped it up.

"Jesus Christ," Tom said. "Jesus Christ."

Anika snapped her fingers to get him to look at her instead of back at the ship. "Hey. Stay calm. Zip up your survival suit. And grab the controls."

He fumbled at his suit with one hand and held the joystick loosely with the other. She left him to hold their course and raced back down the cabin.

She kicked a large plastic chest open with one booted foot and pulled out an old Diemaco C11 assault rifle packed inside. She slapped a clip in it, shouldered it, and stood up in front of the rear window.

Some small part of her wanted to join Tom's mantra of "Jesus Christ," over and over again, but she knew that was the sort of useless shit that got you killed. You needed to take action.

She flicked the safety off.

They'd pulled clear of the ship by several hundred feet. The two men had moved to this side of the bridge, and one of them got the RPG launcher up onto his shoulder and was aiming at the *Plover*.

Anika's heart raced as she yanked the rear window down. She could hardly focus as she aimed and fired a burst from the Diemaco, hoping she was in time. The ear-bursting chatter shocked her. It drowned out the engines.

A flare of light burst on the *Kosatka*'s bridge as the RPG launched and flew right at her. Anika scrunched low and winced. This was it.

The entire airbag over the cabin shivered, but didn't explode.

"Did they hit us?" Tom shouted back at her.

"I think it punched through the bag but didn't explode. It just kept going. Check the bag's pressure."

"We're losing gas and lift," Tom yelled.

Anika propped the Diemaco up on the windowsill and tried to get a better shot at the men on the ship, forcing them to take cover in the bridge with their launcher. Waste-dumping *bastards*. An RPG? This was the Northwest Passage. They were just north of Canada, not in some war zone.

The *Plover* slipped slowly out of the sky as the *Kosatka* churned on past.

Up front, Tom got on the radio. Over her quick bursts of fire, Anika could hear him calling for assistance, his voice suddenly sounding pilot-calm as he followed a routine. "Nanisivik Base, Nanisivik Base, Base this is *Plover,* we've been hit by an RPG. We're under fire. Repeat, under fire. We need assistance by *anything* in the area."

Anika kept the men pinned inside the bridge with her rifle. But now another man with a launcher appeared down on a lower deck. Anika swiveled to shoot at him, but he fired first.

She kept firing just ahead of that flash of fire, trying to intercept the insanely fast blur of the rocket leaping at her airship.

The rocket struck the bag and this one exploded as it hit a structural spar inside. Melting fabric rained down around the cabin. Alarms whooped from up front in the cockpit. "We're going down!" Tom screamed.

Anika could feel it: her stomach lifted toward her chest. The *Plover* dropped out of the last fifty feet of air in a dignified, fluttering spiral that gave Anika enough time to make sure her survival suit was zipped and to make sure that she had braced herself against the corner of the cabin.

Outside, the waves became choppier and more defined with each split second as they rose to meet the airship.

The *Plover* smacked into the Arctic Ocean with an explosion of spray and flaming debris as the burning gasbag overhead collapsed and draped itself over them with a fluttering sigh.

# 3

The world darkened. Electronics sparked and fizzed, then blew out for good. Painfully cold water slapped Anika's face as it poured through the shattered windows, shocking her.

The Arctic might be ice free, but it was still damn cold.

"Tom? Can you hear me?" Ruined equipment and a buckled ceiling blocked her way forward. "Tom?"

"Anika? I can get out, are you okay?"

"I can get out through a window. Get clear of the debris, I'll swim around to you. Okay?"

He paused for a moment. "Yeah. See you on the other side."

He sounded relieved.

The cabin's natural displacement had kept the wreckage floating somewhat, but she knew it was starting to settle and would soon get to sinking. Anika didn't have much time.

She swam clumsily along to the back window and took a deep breath. There was helium in the gasbag, that was why the first rocket had gone clean through without igniting a massive explosion.

But she didn't want to take a big gulp of helium while swimming through the remains of the gasbag and end up passed out, facedown in the cold water.

She ducked briefly underwater and swam free of the cabin.

But there was nowhere to surface. The heavy fabric of the gasbag sat on the water.

Lungs bursting already, Anika kept moving along, looking for light.

There.

She burst free and up out of the water. The wind stung her face, but she'd never been so glad to see the gray clouds overhead.

Shivering, almost convulsing despite the survival suit, she pulled herself on top of the floating debris and looked around.

"Tom!"

She pulled herself up over a large spar attached to a pocket of fabric, still filled with helium and listlessly floating just above the surface, hoping to spot Tom and orient herself.

Instead, she found herself staring at the bow of the *Kosatka*. It had turned around and was now bearing down on the remains of the *Plover*. A massive bow wave piled up in front of the *Kosatka,* rippling through the debris of the fallen airship and scattering it even further.

Water surged through the mess, soaking Anika.

The ship shoved its way through like an old icebreaker, leaving a mess of even smaller pieces of airship behind it. The mounds of cloth, broken spars, and helium and air pockets underneath that kept the mangled wreck still afloat, slapped up against the side of the *Kosatka,* screeching against the old, barnacled hull.

Anika watched its bubbled and rust-pitted bulk sweep past her, a giant moving wall of metal. After it pushed its way through the worst of the debris, the engines coughed back to life, thrumming so powerfully her chest ached. They'd coasted through with them off to protect the propellers.

The churning water threw Anika around, doused her, and then just as abruptly, the water calmed a bit, broken by the ship's passing. Anika floated in the quiet, listening to the fizz of disturbed air bubbling around her.

It was so damn cold, it was almost all she could think about.

After a moment she fumbled around inside her suit and pulled out the EPIRB. It was the size of a small flare in the palm of her gloved hand. She broke the seal on it and then put it back inside a zippered pocket.

The tiny radio beacon inside the device activated, and it began to pip audibly to let her know the distress signal was going out. She lay back, still shivering, and yanked the suit's inflation strings.

The survival suit filled with air and bobbed on the surface.

Anika yanked the hood as tight around her face as possible, pulled her legs up to her chest as best she could, then wrapped her arms around her chest and waited for rescue.

So damn cold.

# 4

A ferry skidded on hydrofoils over the dark ocean, floating almost magically on the air above the waves. When it slowed, the foils sank deeper into the sea, unable to hold it up. The ferry's hull slowly settled down into the water, until it looked just like any other ship.

High above the ferry a parafoil hung in the wind. The taut cables beneath it vibrated and sang as the kite-sail began to dance a figure-eight pattern overhead, allowing the ferry to slow down enough to meander through the debris.

Anika tried to sit up, forgetting for a second where she was. The movement sank her, and cold water washed over her face and dribbled down the sides of her cheeks. It even got inside the suit a bit, down her neck and onto her shoulders.

As the ferry picked its way through the debris of *Plover,* Anika waved weakly at it. "Over here!"

Someone on the deck spotted her and the ferry changed course.

An orange life preserver hit the water a few feet away. Anika clumsily paddled over to it, then pulled it on underneath her arms.

Three burly men in plaid shirts and blue coveralls hauled her out of the water and over the railing, grunting as they helped her onto the deck.

The contrast of sudden heat from the ferry cabin and the cold water she'd been pulled out of started her shivering again, her teeth pressed against each other so hard they felt like they would shatter. Her muscles spasmed, like she was having a seizure.

One of the men threw a first aid kit on the dirty metal floor in front of her.

"Come on, we gotta get this off you," said another man behind her, yanking at the strings she'd pulled so tight.

They stripped the survival suit off her, and then someone grabbed a pair of scissors and cut her wet uniform away. Someone else wrapped a dry thermal blanket around her.

The warm air between her skin and the survival suit disappeared, and that sent her into another round of deep, bone-shaking shivering.

"Tom," she told them, teeth chattering. "Tom." She wasn't sure if they could understand, and she kept repeating it as best she could.

"We're looking for him," someone said into her ear as they rubbed her arms.

A thermometer beeped, and Anika felt pressure against her ear release. "The shivering's okay," the voice behind her said. "Means you're alive. Your temp's a bit low, but you're fine. Keep shivering and moving and rubbing your arms."

Anika took an offered cup of warm water.

"Sip it," they told her. "No gulping."

She almost dropped the cup, but with focus and determination, she managed to bring it shakily up to her lips and sip. She hunched in place on the floor, listening to the thermal blanket crinkle and crunch every time she shifted.

"Got him!" someone shouted.

A few minutes later they dragged Tom in, dripping water, and the whole routine repeated itself. Only Tom didn't look so good. His uniform was sopping wet; the survival suit hadn't gotten zipped quite properly.

His lips were blue, Anika saw. Tom was almost translucent, a pale man almost tailor-built for living in this polar world. But it didn't matter to the cold water.

A redheaded man with a long beard held up a satphone as they wrapped Tom in a thermal blanket. "UNPG's five minutes out by helicopter. Jen? They want you to drop the parafoil."

A short, wind-burned woman in her late fifties with a ruddy face and straw blond hair walked out into the cabin. "Five minutes? Shit. Hey! Everyone on deck, we're pulling in the sail!"

The redhead remained bent over Tom, checking his temperature. When he sat back and glanced at Anika he didn't have to say anything. It was in the posture. Anika saw. Tom was in bad shape.

A minute later a large amount of parachute-like material dropped to the flat back deck where the crew of the ferry grabbed it and rolled it up.

As the parafoil was being packed away, she could hear the *thwap* of rotor blades approaching.

Two UNPG search-and-rescue men dropped out of the sky on ropes and hit the deck. They conferred with the redhead, shouting over the noise of the hovering helicopter.

Then, consensus reached, they hauled Tom out on deck, fastened him to a basket, and all disappeared back up in the air.

"They're low on fuel. They said they've been in the air since your mayday call, all the way from Nanisivik. They'll send another helicopter for you," the redhead said, appearing in the door.

Anika leaned back against the steel bulkhead behind her. "I understand. Does anyone have a satphone that they can lend me?"

Jen, who Anika took to be the ferry's captain, had a thick, plastic-covered phone with a whip antenna: all functional and weatherized. The logo GAIA and a smaller TELECOMMUNICATIONS was stamped into the side in raised letters with a globe in the background. Anika slowly punched the numbers in to dial Nanisivik Base.

"Claude here," replied a smooth, but slightly tired-sounding Québécois voice on the other side.

"Commander, it's Anika Duncan," she said through jaws still clenched from the cold.

"Anika! A second chopper's about fifteen minutes out from you," Commander Michel Claude said quickly. "Are you okay? They said you were okay. They said Tom needed to be flown back right away."

"Yes, yes, I'm doing fine," Anika reassured him. "They were right to leave me if they were low on fuel." She didn't want to be responsible for her rescuers getting themselves in danger as well due to something as simple as running out of fuel.

She could hear Michel let out a deep breath. "We have two cutters headed out at top speed for the area. We've put out an alert for the *Kosatka*. Five airplanes, two airships, and the Canadian Navy and U.S. have been updated. We're looking over a recent satellite scan of the area. We *will* find and catch up to these assholes."

"Thank you, sir. If you hear anything more about Tom, please call this number back."

She handed the satphone back over, and Jen exchanged it for some faded blue jeans, a garish neon yellow t-shirt, and a thick, beige Carhartt jacket. "You're about five eleven?" Jen asked.

Anika nodded. "Five ten . . ."

"Those'll fit you well enough." She shook her head. "You're damn lucky we were out here."

Anika pulled them on, loving the feel of warm cloth against her skin. They'd almost died. Then almost been rammed. Then frozen. She felt numb, not just physically, but mentally.

And exhausted.

But she had enough energy now to remember to ask for her uniform. She unzipped the shoulder pocket and found the backup from the scatter camera. She slipped it into her new jeans.

The ferry was on its way to Thule's floating assemblage of old tankers, barges, and laced-together ice islands at the Pole. There they'd offload goods in the hold and workers for Gaia, Inc., a multinational company with interests in carbon mitigation. For now, though, they'd remain in place until help could get to Anika.

Fifteen minutes later she was out in the whipping cold of the rotor wash of another helicopter, into the rescue basket, and then being winched up.

As one of the chopper crew busied himself getting an IV in her arm, Anika stared out at the gray sea and the bright evening sky to the west of them.

That's where the *Kosatka* was, somewhere out there over the curve of the horizon.

Another chapter of her life had just slammed shut, Anika realized, as anger gelled inside of her. A chapter of routine, calm, and knowing what each day would hold. A peaceful chapter. A good chapter.

But that was over.

# 5

Tom's wife, Jenny, leapt up from a padded bench near a nurse's station at the Nanisivik Hospital and grabbed Anika in a fierce hug. Her small hands gripped the back of Anika's jacket. "Oh my God," she said. "They said you were okay. I kept thinking, if Tom's spent the same amount of time in the water as you, maybe they weren't telling me everything."

Anika squeezed her back. Having Jenny as a friend was like having a hyperactive, overly eager-to-please, little white sister. But it was okay. Jenny and Tom were the closest things Anika had to family out here in the Polar Circle. Anika was slow to make friends, a casualty of the last ten years spent hiring her services out as a pilot. She kept to herself and kept others at a distance, as she was going to leave anyone she met in a few months when she hopped off to a different job. And maybe a part of the fact that being distant came so naturally to her was due to the violent early years before she earned her first chances to pilot. Back when she'd always had to carry a gun. "I think his suit got water in it. I got off easier."

"I'm so glad you're okay."

They hugged again. Anika got a mouthful of Jenny's blond curls. Then she pulled back and looked Jenny in the eye. "And Tom?"

"He's peeing into a jug right now, made me leave the room," she said.

"He's awake? He's okay?" Anika felt the hundred pounds of anxiousness that had been clinging to her drop away.

Relief prickled at her.

Jenny nodded. "He's really tired. But he's talking." Her translucent green eyes teared, and she wiped at them with a sleeve. "I'm sorry."

Anika shook her head. "Sorry? You have nothing to apologize for."

Jenny rubbed her upper arms nervously, her sweater sleeves flopping about. "I don't understand how you can be so calm. Anika: they shot you down."

"Calm?" Anika thought about it. She wasn't calm. She was still running on adrenaline and shock, that's all. None of this had penetrated that outer wall, a pilot's levelheaded ability to run through a checklist while something was going wrong.

Anika had been through some tight spots. She knew the shakes came later. She wasn't sure what was going to happen once she wrapped her head around everything that had just occurred.

Jenny knocked on the door. "Are you done in there?"

"Yeah," a familiar voice said. A husky, scratchy, and frail-sounding Tom.

"Okay, we're coming in then," Jenny said cheerfully.

Anika followed her, wrinkling her nose again at the smell of hospitals. She didn't like them. She associated them with dying relatives. There was nothing worse as a child than being forced to go visit and make small talk to family members whom she only occasionally saw. They were always hurting, tired, and scared in hospitals, and that put her off.

But this was Tom, and she felt angry at herself for those childish memories.

He looked pale. And tired. He was wrapped in warming blankets, with a slightly bent container of urine hanging off the side of a bed rail.

"I guess I owe you a case of beer," he said when he saw Anika step around the curtain with Jenny.

Anika smiled. "I'll let it go. Just this once."

He reached a hand out, and she took it, shook it firmly, and then he pulled back into the blankets, shivering. "Christ, it's like I can't ever get warm anymore."

"Worse than Polar Bear Camp . . ." Anika agreed.

They both nodded. Every new UNPG pilot who arrived on base got initiated by being taken to "camp." In reality, it was a large icy lake near some dramatic foothills not too far from Nanisivik.

You had to jump into the ice-cold water and swim a single lap. If you refused, they'd toss you in.

But afterward they'd gone to the hot tubs along a wooden platform near the road to the lake and drank.

That had ended well, Anika thought. This hadn't.

Tom looked up at her, apparently coming to the same conclusion. His smile had faded. "They fucking shot us out of the fucking sky, Anika." There was wounded outrage written across his face now.

Anika felt the same thing. "I know. I don't . . ." Actually, she wasn't sure what she wanted to say next. She hunted around for words. "I can't figure it out. They have to know they're being hunted. Where can they go?"

"Guess we'll find out soon enough," Tom muttered.

Half an hour later, Anika stood outside the hospital, blinking up at the bright Arctic night. They'd had it darkened inside.

From outside, the hospital looked like the world's largest Quonset hut. A giant aircraft hanger. Arctic architecture chic, according to some Montreal designer who'd stamped his mark on what seemed like every public building out here. The hospital itself was basically a smaller building inside the giant hanger, which let them keep small gardens and trees in the lobby year round.

The buildings in the deep Sahara Anika had lived in when she'd worked for the DESERTEC project used the same principle: create a large space of protected air in a dome, then build a small piece of the world you'd come from inside of it.

They were like space stations, she thought, but sitting on the pieces of Earth's land that were too alien for anyone to survive in.

Her Toyota ran out of power three miles up the gravel road from base housing. She walked the rest of the way, jacket pulled tight, hugging herself, her breath billowing out into the air and then being yanked away by the wind. She'd go back for the car in the morning, push it the last flat miles, and hook it up to the charger.

Inside her square prefab, one of the hundreds all splayed out across the Arctic gravel in spiral patterns, she turned the heat up even further and shucked off the stranger's clothes.

She considered a bath. The appeal of soaking in warm water until she'd chased every last chill from her bones was strong. But she was tired enough that she feared she would fall asleep in the tub.

Instead she took a shower so hot it felt like it would burn the top layer of her skin away.

Then she crawled into the thick sheets and comforter under the gaudy poster of an airship advertising an old Nollywood movie.

For once, the beams of light from around the corners of the shades didn't bother her. She fell asleep the moment her head hit the pillows.

And what felt like seconds later, she sat up.

The house phone rang again, and she rolled over and picked up the old headset.

"Nika!" said the scratchy voice. "Is that you?"

She hadn't even gotten in a fuzzy hello. Her father sounded scared, hopeful, nervous, and angry, all at the same time.

"Father . . ." She blinked against the light streaming in around the darkening blinds. Hearing his voice, even if transported from so far away, made her feel better.

"I cannot believe you did not call me. Here we are, hearing this news that says an airship was blown out of the sky near Baffin Island, and you have not even called us to let us know you are okay, or even sent us a message? I called your phone over and over and over again. Then your aunt says to me that she has another number for you and that's how I finally reached you. I almost died from the worry."

Anika braced herself against the headboard from the onslaught of clipped, angry words from her father as he lectured her. "I fell asleep," she said, rubbing at her eyes. "And yes, it was me they shot at."

"I . . . what did you say?" Her father lost his train of thought.

"They shot me down. Me and the other pilot."

A long silence dripped from the other side of the phone. Then finally her father collected himself. No more yelling now. "Are you okay, Anika?"

Anika slumped forward around the phone. "I don't know. I haven't thought about it all yet. I am just . . . still thinking over what happened. And trying to figure out why."

"But you're not hurt?"

"No." Suddenly she now wanted to hear him drone on about her cousins, and who was pregnant, and what was coming into season in the markets. She wanted to hear about the air conditioner that kept breaking down in the window of his Lagos apartment and hear him complain about the heat. All those mundane details of life back home, that she usually wanted him to skip on past, now sounded like delicious nuggets of familiarity and normalcy.

"I thought you flew normal patrols," her father said. "I don't understand. I thought you had taken on a *less* dangerous job. This isn't the Sahara."

The phone beeped. Anika looked at the incoming

call. Commander Michel Claude, the phone blinked. "I thought so, too. But I have to go," Anika said.

"You should call your mother," he said quickly. Anika sat, letting the words roll past. "You are close enough to *visit* her. Whatever our pasts, she will have heard the news story. She will want to know her daughter is safe."

Anika pursed her lips. "It was good to hear your voice. But my commander is calling. I have to go."

"Well, be careful, Anika," her father said. "And think about it."

"I will," Anika promised. Then she switched to the incoming call. She took a deep breath. "Commander?"

Michel sounded tired, his voice scratchy from lack of sleep. "Anika . . . I'm very sorry about this. . . ."

Anika's stomach lurched. This couldn't be good. "Commander?"

"I know you were just with him, but Tom passed. I'm so very sorry."

Anika closed her eyes and bent over on the side of her bed. "I was *just* there. He seemed okay to me. He made jokes."

"I saw him as well, Anika. But it happened."

She gripped the phone and heard a piece of plastic in the case crack. There was no going back to bed. No time for curling up and waiting to process what had happened. "We need to hunt down these assholes who did this to us, Commander. They need to pay for what they did. I want to come in and *do* something; I don't think I can sit here by myself."

Michel paused for a moment. "You sure about that? You up for flying out to Resolute?"

Anika sat up. "What's in Resolute?"

"They've found the *Kosatka,* trying to hide in the harbor with other ships. The U.S. Navy has a patrol boat there, and the local police have the crew in custody. Can you fly our Investigations Unit guys out there to participate in the interrogation? They might use you to ID any of the guys. If you can."

"Of course I'll do it." She stood up.

"There's a light jet being fueled up right now," Michel said. "They'll be waiting for you."

# 6

Resolute hadn't changed much in the last three months. It was still a mess of boxy prefab mini-skyscrapers. They all cluttered around the sloping gravel leading to the harbor, which jutted out of the boundary of rock and sea.

Another port deep in the Arctic Circle. Another island detached from the mainland of Canada, like Baffin. Just farther west. Most of these places were barely presences at the turn of the century. Forty years later, they were bursting with prefabs and activity. When the ice left, the Canadian North opened up. Once-tiny towns exploded, particularly once shipping traffic began to stream through the Northwest Passage, and ports rapidly built themselves up. Places that were actually on the Canadian mainland, like Bernard Harbour, Coppermine, Gjoa, and Taloyok, had become powerful economic and demographic engines that made Canada the lead of the so-called "Arctic Tiger" nations that benefitted from the warm polar oceans. The megalopolis Anchorage turned into had made Alaska one of the more powerful states in the U.S.A.

Anika stood for a moment on the helicopter deck on the back of an old U.S. Navy destroyer. Her blue UNPG flight suit kept her warm against the bitter wind.

She spotted the familiar bulk of the *Kosatka* at anchor among four other larger ships.

Her lips quirked. There it was. Like a shark hoisted out of water. She remembered why she feared it, and she remembered the attack. But now it was just this inert, still thing. It was nothing more than a ship at anchor.

The two very serious-looking UN Polar Guard special agents that she'd flown out to Resolute paused as they noticed her looking. Yves and Anton. French and Russian. Mirrored sunglasses. And not a smile between the two.

"Real fucking mess, no?" Anton said, taking off his glasses to reveal bright blue eyes.

Anika nodded. "Can we go inside to see them now?" Standing up here stewing about what happened wasn't what she wanted to do. She needed to keep moving and to keep busy. To not think about Tom. Not think about Jenny, sitting on that bench in the hospital.

Yves pulled a cell phone down and pointed to a pair of uniformed Americans waiting for them. Yves, Anton, and Anika had been let aboard the destroyer, but in the time it had taken to fly out here, the whole thing had become some sort of jurisdictional mess, and they were stuck on the helicopter deck as everyone tried to figure out if they were allowed belowdecks.

The Americans had found the *Kosatka* trying to hide in the harbor. But the Canadians said it was their port the *Kosatka* was inside, and that the men should be handed over to them for charges. And of course, the UNPG wanted a piece. After all, it had been Anika and Tom shot of the sky.

Her special agents, usually used to internal investigations and smuggling prosecution, had spent the whole flight out making calls and arguing with people on the other side, trying to penetrate the international layers of bureaucracy involved.

"We can go in," Yves said, nodding at the Americans. "We can interrogate, we can record. We cannot move prisoners."

Anton swore in Russian, then gently grabbed Anika's elbow. "You can stay out here, if you like. You don't have to come inside. But it would be helpful for our cause if you ID them."

He looked hopeful, but understanding at the same time. Giving her space to come to a decision of her own. No pressure here, said his body language. And yet, there was some tension. He was angry and keyed up. The attack on Anika was an attack on him.

Brothers in arms. The uniformed tribe. Anika suddenly had a lot of pissed off fellow guardspeople in blue wanting to lash back at whoever had done this.

Anika turned toward the pyramid-shaped stealthed superstructure of the destroyer and nodded. "I'm ready."

. . .

A short man with a silvering mustache stepped out and waved them through. “Captain Martinez,” he said, introducing himself and quickly shaking hands. “Glad you were able to get out here. Come with me.”

Then it was down into the tight confines of the corridors. Everything gleamed: polished and clean. Shipshape navy. Hardly a speck of dirt, grease, or anything of the sort.

Anika stepped sideways past a seaman on his hands and knees, polishing a kickplate on a bulkhead door. Salutes were exchanged between the Americans in passing, and the group continued on through the metal warren, footsteps echoing on down ahead of them.

“My superiors view this as a justification of our presence,” Martinez was explaining to Anton. “Critics aren’t happy about diesel-burners chewing up fuel rations for force projection up here in the Circle, they think the fuel’s better kept in reserve. In case we ever do end up in a major conflict, we can’t afford to use it up.”

“That is what UNPG is for,” Anton grumbled.

“Yes, and the Canadian Guard, and Navy.” Martinez grinned back at us. “But brass thinks you guys are undermanned and the Arctic is a real Wild West sort of area: Northern Europe and Russia to Canada and Alaska smuggling, new drug trade routes, loosely monitored offshore drilling operations, ecoterrorists.”

“So your brass thinks, Alaskan coast is not enough, no?” Anton said. “Wild, Wild West gets your attention?”

"Yee-haw," Martinez agreed.

"And you, what do you think?" Yves asked the captain.

Martinez scratched his beard and slowed down. He looked back at them. "I'm just trying to explain to you why you had such a hard time getting permission to come aboard and talk to the *Kosatka*'s crew. One sailor shot at is just the same as any other to me, understand? I'm glad to burn fuel and hunt for the bastards, after what they did."

Then Martinez narrowed his eyes and stabbed his finger to make a point. "But I want to make sure you understand that this is also a PR coup for the people who gave me the orders to go hunt for the vessel. They're trying to justify keeping ships like mine operational. Normally a ship like this, we coast around, trying to sip fuel as best we can and patrol some area. We usually leave the fast-moving interception and hunting to nuke-powered steamers and the sailships."

And, Anika wondered, was that also a sign of the Americans overcompensating for the unexpected rise of Canada's strength throughout the polar region, and as a result of those riches, the world?

There were Americans rioting about the cost of their military. And the American naval fleet would be testing combined maneuvers soon with other G35 navies as a way to possibly make cuts in its fleet. No wonder this captain's superiors wanted the usefulness of their ships proved. It'd get that much harder for the UNPG to keep order in the North if the Americans started drawing down from the Alaskan bases because of the cost of the Polar Fleet.

Maybe Canada would step up.

Anton nodded. “We just want to talk to the sailors of the *Kosatka*. No pissing match, Captain. We won’t try to take them back with us.”

Martinez smiled sadly. “It’d be nice if we could prove the value of keeping these ships around, enough to justify the expense of converting them to nuclear power.”

Anton and Yves nodded sympathetically. They were both former sailors, now deskbound. They understood a captain’s desire to work hard to keep a ship going.

Martinez stopped in front of a locked room with two men on guard outside of it. “I doubt they’ll tell you much more than we found out already. We already passed on everything they said.”

“Yes,” Anton replied as he waited for the door to be opened. “But it’s always best to do your own interrogation, I feel. Look into their eyes and see what is there, yeah?”

The thick metal door swung open.

“Knock yourselves out,” Martinez said.

Six grubby men sat on a long bench, their backs to the gray-painted metal bulkhead. Two of them had their faces in their hands, elbows on their knees.

Anika locked eyes with the man wearing the blue woolen cap.

“That’s the man who fired the rocket at me,” she said.

# 7

Anika's attacker had been about to stand, as were some of the other men on the uncomfortable-looking bench.

They were, she realized, quite young. Very early twenties, maybe late teens. Hardly more than boys. One of them had a patchy beard.

This crew wasn't a group of hardened drug runners, as Anton and Yves had passed along to her. That was what the *Kosatka*'s crew told the navy they were, after they'd been captured.

The U.S. Navy said they'd most likely weighted and sunk their evidence after ramming her airship in the water, then ran for it, because there was nothing in the *Kosatka*'s holds when they found the ship. And the U.S. Navy didn't buy the whole seasoned criminals thing either.

"A bunch of young punks, most likely first timers, who panicked," Yves said. "That's what everyone seems to think."

Now Anika felt like a tightly wound spring that had snapped, pieces scattering everywhere. She'd come here taut and angry. Self-controlled, but sadness and anger torqued tight and deep within her.

These . . . kids, she thought.

Just scared kids.

Anton and Yves sat down on small metal chairs in front of the five drug dealers and started asking questions.

"You're . . . you're not the lawyers, then?" one of the young men asked. He looked scared.

Yves shook his head and leaned forward. "Terrorists don't get lawyers on a U.S. Navy ship," he said softly. "Terrorists don't get much of anything at all."

One of the young men leaned forward and threw up.

Anika turned around and left the stink of fear behind her.

Half an hour later Yves joined her, leaning against the rail, looking out at the *Kosatka* again. "Okay?" he asked.

"They're younger than I expected," she said.

"Young drug dealers. Young murderers." Yves lit a delicate thin cigarette and drew in a deep breath of smoke. Exhaled. "You know . . . drug dealers on a street corner, they can be any age. They are still deadly people, yes?"

Anika looked over. "I've seen enough fourteen-year-olds with automatic rifles, Yves. I know. I was just surprised."

Maybe she thought she'd left some of that behind in the desert. Lagos was built up. Like any other city in the world, it was its own little country deep in the canyons of its skyscrapers and municipalities. Not what foreigners thought of when she said Nigeria when they asked where she'd been born.

But up north . . . Up north it was all still tenuous country in scattered places. Religious tension. Riots. Broken landscapes and desperate people.

Kids with weapons.

She'd been a city girl with Nollywood-inspired dreams of becoming a pilot. To fly out from the depths of city and noise and packed people outside in the heat.

And she'd flown into a part of Africa that she'd only ever seen in news reports or Western-made movies.

"If they were running drugs, then how come my scatter camera went off?" Anika asked, turning and leaning her back against the cold metal rail. "Are drugs radioactive now?"

Yves grinned briefly around the edge of his cigarette. "They are not. But, you know, it is good you asked."

"Why is that?"

He took another long drag. "Your airship transmits flight data via satellite continuously. Your scatter camera logged nothing on this flight. I think maybe there was a mistake?" He looked meaningfully at her.

"The scatter camera went off. We went in for a closer look."

"Maybe you heard the wrong alarm," Yves suggested. "It's been seven months since your last event.

That's a long time. Combine that with the trauma of the attack . . ."

Anika stared at him. "We went in closer and got further readings. There *was* something on that ship."

Yves looked uncomfortable for the both of them. "Maybe something went wrong somewhere?" he suggested. "Bad data?"

"Maybe. I have a physical backup of the data at home. Pass that back to our superiors. When I get back I can prove this wasn't just about drugs, and that they're lying." Anika rubbed her temples. This sort of mess was why she always made sure to cover herself. Her father had always warned her about bad equipment and bureaucracy. "I don't want to talk about that anymore, Yves. What's next?"

"Next?" Yves mulled the word over. "Next." He folded his arms and looked out over the dark harbor water.

She followed his gaze, turning around to face the rail again. "The boat."

Yves nodded. "*Kosatka,* yes. Understand, it is just routine, yes? But I like the poking around. There's a dinghy waiting for us."

"Routine?"

"We have the *bastards* who did this to you," Yves said. "We have their confessions. You identified them."

"And then that's it. . . ." Anika said.

"That's it," Yves said.

Except it wasn't. They were lying about being drug runners. And why lie about something bad unless you were covering something worse?

"Let me come with you," Anika asked.

Yves moved his head back and forth, as if considering. "We just needed you to identify the crew. You are not needed for this part."

"You need me to fly you back, though, right?" Anika said.

"You wouldn't!" Yves protested.

"You leave me here on this ship to go out there, I'm headed for the airport," Anika insisted. "After a day like this, do you think anyone would be willing to formally discipline me?"

The dinghy that took them out was a twenty-foot-long semirigid inflatable, a fiberglass flat-bottomed hull that sliced through the waves and that had inflated pontoons around the edge.

Anika bit her lip as they slowed down and approached the rusted-out bulk of the Russian ship.

It loomed, shoving everything else out of her mind, replacing it with the implacable metal bulk thundering, surging through the water at her.

She gasped and grabbed the rope running along the pontoons, sitting down and looking up the side of the giant wall.

"Coming up?" Anton pointed at the rope ladder dangling down from the rails up above. "Are you good?"

She waved him away. "Lost my footing. I'll be right there." Yves was already attacking the ropes, swarming his way aloft.

Anton nodded, and then awkwardly starting pulling himself up.

The fresh-faced seaman who'd piloted them over walked forward. He tied them to the ladder, and waved her up.

Anika leaned forward and touched the hull. Paint and metal flaked off and fluttered down into the space between the dinghy and the ship.

The dinghy slammed against the *Kosatka*. For a second Anika was worried about falling into the water, following the flakes she'd disturbed. But she got a hand on the ladder, and then a foot.

"Got a good grip?" the seaman asked.

"Yes."

"Then I'm going to pull back a bit, so we don't rip the sides apart on this hull. It's rusty as hell, ma'am." He gunned the outboard engine in reverse, the water boiling around the dinghy as he pulled away.

Nowhere to go but up. Anika scrambled until she reached the rail, then swung onto the deck.

Her boots hit the metal surface with a clang.

She was on the surface of the enemy, the ship that had tried to kill her.

# 8

Yves waved her down. "Coming into the belly of the beast, *Ms.* Duncan?"

The holds had been opened; the maw of the ship was wide open to the overhead sky. Light spilled into the cargo hold.

"They found her with the holds open," Yves said. "The cranes had been working overtime. Dumping whatever it was they were carrying, yes? They ran for the harbor after that, didn't even bother closing back up."

They walked around, footsteps echoing loudly off the metal deck and empty hold back at them. Anton was videotaping the hold with his phone, narrating what they were seeing in a low mutter.

And what they were seeing was nothing but a dirty, dusty hold, with several piles of rusted chains scattered around.

Eventually Anton folded up the camera and slid it into his pocket. "That's it," he announced.

"That's it," Anika repeated.

"That's it," Yves confirmed.

They all stood at the bottom of the hold for a moment. Then, as if on a telepathic cue, Yves and Anton turned and started up the metal stairs together.

Anika followed. The echoes of their steps got higher and higher pitched as they got farther up.

Then she stopped.

A faint glimmer. In the corner of her eye.

Anika frowned. She climbed onto the rail, careful not to look down at how far she'd fall to the metal floor if she slipped. Then, balanced, with one leg on a lower rail for stability, she reached up for the faint glint, stretching until her stomach ached.

It was a fist-sized, transparent globe. And it was floating. Like a tiny balloon, it had drifted up into a nook in the ceiling along the side of the cargo hold.

Back on the stairs now, Anika shoved it inside her flight jacket. Anton and Yves considered their work done.

Maybe she could find something out.

She was more convinced now that the *Kosatka* had not been carrying drugs.

Back through the harbor, onto the streets of Resolute again. Fake igloo architecture for the tourists. Large blocks of city buildings, the square tyranny of super-fast construction the world over, only here, like in the tropics, they favored bold, bright colors. Purple façades and pink pastels fought back against the constant Arctic gray and the blear of the perpetual sun.

Anton drove. Anika sat in the back of the cramped car with the constantly fogging windows, looking out at the buildings.

Something dinged, indicating a message received. Yves glanced at a wristband that lit up, and then tapped it. "Your commander, Claude, he'll be expecting that hardcopy when you get back to base," he said.

"Sure."

The old Honda light jet had been turned around and refueled. It sat under the protection of a wireframe hangar with sheet metal skin painted some shade of fuchsia. Yves followed Anika as she did the walk around of the small jet.

"What did you find?" he asked, as they both passed around a wingtip.

"I am sorry?" Anika kept walking toward the back of the craft.

"Back in the cargo hold. You got up on the railing. You put something in your pocket. Please tell me, what did you find?" Yves looked at her mildly.

Anika got up on her tiptoes to look at the small GE jets on the tail, their outlets stained with miles and miles of smoke. For a while the VLJs like this Honda had gotten their engines swapped out with engines from an outfit that used some biofuel, but they'd failed a few times, forcing emergency landings. UNPG brass used the VLJs a lot, so a lot of them had had the engines swapped back to the originals. And it looked like this was one of them.

"Anika?" Yves asked.

She sighed. She didn't want to give up her find and share it, but she had to. She reached inside her jacket. "Don't let go of it. Whatever it is, it floats."

Yves turned the globe over in his hands. "What is it?"

"I don't know. I was going to find out. It sounded like you were all done back there. I thought maybe I could look a little harder."

"Of course." Yves sounded apologetic. He always sounded apologetic, Anika thought. He took his phone and held the small globe up in front of it.

After he'd captured a few seconds of video, he looked down at the globe. "I have to keep it. I apologize. My superiors, they see that we have these assholes in custody. They're happy. Everything has been tied up, no? But all physical evidence, it has to be tagged and stored in the appropriate place. I cannot let you keep it."

"I understand," Anika said. She held up her phone and snapped several pictures of the globe before Yves could react. Better to ask forgiveness than permission here. "You both would have walked right by it and never known."

"I should make you delete those," Yves said.

"Try," Anika told him.

Yves smiled. "Don't think you can lead an investigation of your own. Let us do our jobs, Anika. Tell us anything you stumble across. We will, of course, send everything we can share to your commanding officer."

"I promise you, I will not be causing you any trouble," Anika lied. "I found it. I'm curious. You would be curious as well, yes?"

Yves smiled. "You have your picture. You've earned at least that and probably more. And I promise you, I will keep you notified about anything we learn."

Right. Anika scratched her ear. "And once they're behind bars, wherever they end up, how much time will you spend on seeing what else you can find out about them?"

"Well, that is the problem, *Ms.* Duncan. *Ce qui est* UNPG? I answer you this way: What we are is understaffed. We suffer with old equipment from ten different agencies from around the world who gift us their old castoffs. Every year the Pole, it gets warmer, and there are more people up here, and I get more busy each month, not less. But I will not forget you."

Anika felt slightly guilty. "I'm sorry, Yves. It is a hard thing to stop thinking about."

He shrugged. "Come. The rest of your life, it is waiting."

She watched him climb into the jet.

The rest of his life, she thought, hadn't fired a rocket at him lately. "Yves?"

He looked back down at her. "Yes?"

"When that boy fired the RPG at me, I reached for the rifle and returned fire. I did not even think about it. Do you know where I got those instincts from?"

"Not training for UNPG?" Yves guessed.

"I used to be one of those kids with a gun you talked about. I ran away from Lagos. I dreamed I would pilot an airship, like the adventurers in the movies. But before anyone would let me fly, I sat in an open door of a gondola with a very large chain gun. I was fifteen. My job for two years was to make sure bush fighters were scared of us. I made sure of it. I don't run away from a fight, Yves."

Yves spread his hands. "We already won the fight."

No. This was just a small battle of a larger war; Anika felt it in her gut. Something was going on. And maybe it was stupid to pursue it. But she felt slighted. She'd walked away from the rough life of a security contractor. She'd been little more than a mercenary pilot for so long, and the UNPG had been a chance to head in a new direction. And this violence snapping at her, it offended her. She wanted to turn around and kill it until she was sure it was never going to reach into the orderly world she'd made for herself here.

Or, she wondered, maybe there was nowhere in the world you got to have that life, where you knew you were safe every morning when you woke up, and knew exactly what to expect. She'd lived that in Lagos, growing up. Then ran away from it all for excitement. And after a decade of excitement, she treasured her life here.

Maybe, just maybe, mulling over all this kept her from having to think about Tom. Or his wife.

She was going to have to go see Jenny at some point.

Anika wasn't sure she could face her.

Not without feeling guilty that she was still alive, still talking to her loved ones.

Anika slipped the phone back in her pocket.

This was far from over.

# 9

It was midnight when she got home and changed out of her uniform blues. For a moment she stood in her underwear, considering her next move.

Go comfort Jenny?

No. She couldn't face Jenny. Anika felt like she'd let her down. She couldn't face that and keep herself held together right now.

Anika pulled on weathered jeans and a purple turtleneck, an old leather jacket, some gloves from the wicker basket near the door, and found her Oakleys.

She pulled the data backup out of the other jeans and slid it into her pocket. Now that she knew it was the only copy, she wasn't letting it out of sight until she handed it over to Commander Claude.

She was still thinking about the fact that the *Kosatka*'s crew had claimed to be drug runners. It didn't make sense, and it gnawed away at her. And, she thought, she did know someone who could help answer a few questions about drug running. She let her hair out of a tight bun. It sprung loose, a halo of comfortable brown kinks she was happy to see again.

It went against her nature to go ask someone for help. But she was sort of looking forward to this trip, she had to secretly admit.

If she could arrange transportation.

She walked next door and banged on the screen door. "Karl!"

She banged again, until Karl's blond curls appeared at the window, and then at the crack of the door as it opened. He was wearing a towel around his waist, tufts of coarse, dark hair running up from his belly to his chest, covering a fairly fit physique. "Jesus, Anika, what?"

"I need to borrow your bike, if it is charged."

Karl rubbed his eyes and looked up the road. "Oh, come on, Anika. You ran your damn car down *again*?"

Anika didn't answer that, but cocked her head. Karl sighed and reached over to the hooks screwed into the wall by the door, then handed her the keys. The key fob was made of paracord, six feet of it woven into a five-inch decorative plait. Useful. She kept telling herself she needed one. The bike's "key" was actually just an RFID chip in a decorative logo casing that didn't need to be inserted into the bike. As long as Anika had the keys within ten feet of the bike it would start up with a press of a button. "Make sure you plug it back in when you're done," he growled.

"Thank you, Karl."

"Fuck off. It's late," he grumped. "I'm going back to bed."

"It's not like I'll get any sleep with you having a visitor over. These thin walls. Is it still Chief Evisham?"

He closed the door. They had a good-natured sort of blackmail arrangement. She borrowed his bike and kept shut about fraternization.

Though Anika was pretty sure he'd let her borrow the bike anyway.

The bike's rear tire spat gravel as Anika wobbled her way out of the drive, and then she got her balance as the bike sped up. The wind snapped at her loose hair.

Out past base housing she turned onto the paved Nanisivik highway. The bike's motor whined as she gunned it, sucking juice for a sudden burst of speed that left a long strip of rubber down the fresh asphalt.

At seventy miles an hour she eased back, letting the rhythm of the bike and the road's dips canter underneath her. The whine fell away, leaving her with the just the sound of the constant hurricane of wind ripping at her.

This felt good. She was releasing something buried deep inside.

Now that she was off the gravel and on pavement her Oakleys finally connected wirelessly to her phone. A map appeared in her field of vision, showing her location and turn-by-turn directions.

It was an hour's ride, and a fun one. She wound her way around the bases of the peaks overlooking Nanisivik. She crossed over the valleys carved out by now-extinct glaciers in the mountainous hump of the semi-peninsular Nanisivik.

A dip into a valley again, then slowly back up, and she was coming down toward an icy shoreline. Houses began to appear again, dotting the hills overlooking the sea.

It was a spare landscape. Rock. Snow. Moss. What little green there was struggled to live in the cold, constant wind. It was as much a desert as any she'd seen in Africa.

And it was all changing.

Baffin Island was some eight hundred miles long. North of Quebec. West of Greenland. And eight hundred miles farther south on Baffin Island the older folks shook their heads when they talked about how things were. They had vegetable gardens, now. And farms! They only remembered ice.

Greenland was growing more and more of its own food. And Canada's grain lands, once in a thin band of land just above the border with America, now extended ever farther north, while First Nations villages relocated farther south as the ice their villages once sat on disappeared into an ever-warming Arctic Ocean.

She gunned the bike along toward the core of Arctic Bay, where the neon lights flashed along with the dim, distant Northern Lights, barely visible in the ever-constant twilight.

The Oakleys guided her through downtown and back to where the neon flashed the most garish. Now Anika knew she could take the glasses off, because all she had to do was follow the brightest lights and the noise to her destination.

. . .

The Greenhouse was jumping tonight. Superbikes and fast cars cluttered the street, and the bike racks were packed and looking like brightly colored metal shrubs.

People spilled out onto the sidewalk, their breath puffing out in the cold air. Bright colored jackets, leathers, and look-at-me hairstyles. Someone inside had the bass jumping, and even on the street people were unconsciously tapping out beats with their toes or nodding their heads.

Anika locked Karl's bike up to a lamppost and joined the line at the velvet rope.

Five stories tall, The Greenhouse was exactly what the name implied. In the past it was used to grow fresh greens here in Arctic Bay, but as the roads and shipping got better, and the farms in lower Baffin started up, it had been abandoned.

So it had been repurposed as a club.

Anika pulled out a plastic card and showed it to the bouncer, a vaguely Eastern European bodybuilder with black-light tattoos of wildlife on his forearms that fluoresced with the grow lights that had been jacked into a computer running them through some Fibonacci sequence.

He looked it over. The Greenhouse didn't use RFID tags, or social technologies, or your phone, as a pass. They actually printed up these physical membership badges once they "adopted" you. Very retro. Very coveted if you wanted to jump the line.

"You're one of those Smurf pilots, yah?" the bouncer asked. The Eastern Europeans called anyone in the UN military Smurfs, thanks to the damn blue helmets and please-shoot-me blue uniforms.

Anika nodded as he handed back her badge and she slipped it into her jacket. He looked her up and down, clearly not liking her sense of fashion, but sighed and waved her in anyway.

The wall of noise being delivered by locationally targeted speakers aimed right at the foyer just about knocked her off her feet, but she took a few steps to the right, into a virtual corridor of dead silence created by reverse noise-canceling zones.

Three feet to the right, people were jumping into the air to the music. Others walking the corridor of silence nodded wryly at her, a sort of instant bond between those who liked the clubs, but couldn't handle the distorted sound.

She stepped out into the atrium and glanced up. The twilight trickled in, boosted by mirrors and grow lights. And everywhere in the niches and nooks and crannies tropical plants bloomed and grew. Banana trees, rich with green clumps ripening away. The smell of mangos and nutmeg drifted around, intoxicating for their exotic smells so far from the tropics.

Flowers and fruit of every color was all the decoration The Greenhouse needed.

Since she'd discovered it, Anika had been coming here for the smell of something like home. Not all the trees and fruits were things she recognized. She'd never been to South America, or the Caribbean. But there were things in common.

And the tropical heat, partially generated by the sweaty dancing bodies constantly inhabiting The Greenhouse, made her feel more at home than sitting in her tiny box on base with the heat turned up to max. Because at base those drafts of cold air still seeped in through the cracks and mixed with the heat like oil and water, caressing and chilling her, reminding her where she was even while she was slick with sweat.

A couple of girls wearing jackets with large Chinese flags on the back were feeding meat to a pitcher plant in one of the nooks along the stairway. Anika walked past them up to the second level and along the railings to the bar.

From up here, away from the coherent sound speakers targeting their music at specific spots on the floor with sound, the dancing masses on the ground floor looked like an insane, but eerily quiet mob.

Anika stopped at the second floor bar, which was framed by bird-of-paradise flowers and hibiscus threaded through self-watering and self-feeding glass-tube trellises.

A lean, but whip-muscular older First Nations man with wolf eye contacts and deep creases around his eyes, a look gained from a lifetime lived outside, leaned over the polished mahogany. "What do you want?"

"Vy."

He straightened up and folded his arms. "Who's asking?"

"Anika."

An arm draped itself across her back, and Anika stiffened. "Hello there, little Smurf," Vy said into her ear, then nodded at the bartender. "It's okay, Eric. Two Belladonnas?"

"I don't need a drink," Anika said, still facing the bar. There were hundreds of bottles, all shades of liquors, catching the grow lights against a back mirror, sparkling and dazzling the air.

"Oh, you need a drink," Vy said. "Heard what you've been through. You really, really need a drink. You'll like this, the pineapple juice in here is fresh squeezed, made right here in The Greenhouse."

Anika could see herself in the mirror behind the pyramids of bottles, her hair haloed out around her face, the black jacket loose and unzipped, and Vy slipping onto the stool next to her.

Vy had a strong jaw and Midwest girl-next-door features. Her impossibly straight blond hair hung loose just above her chin in a pageboy cut. Anika almost suspected she had pompoms in a closet somewhere, and that until the recent cut, her hair was kept back in a ponytail.

There was a short, bubbly cheerfulness to her that seemed at odds to the crisp Armani suit and executive look she had right now. And it also seemed at odds with the fact that Violet was the biggest drug dealer in Arctic Bay.

# 10

The Belladonna, all real fruit juice and rich, expensive rum, settled over Anika like a faint haze. She grabbed Vy by the crook of her arm and guided her to a couch in a niche dominated by tiny palm trees in large plastic tubs.

So Vy had already scanned the news. She rubbed Anika's shoulder, concern in her eyes. "I'm glad you're okay. Some of us were worried about you. They're saying the navy hunted the bastards down, right?"

Here in the niche, in the humid air, silenced from the outer party, Anika relaxed.

"They had me fly out to take a look. The Americans do have the people who fired at us."

Vy grinned. "U.S.A. for the motherfucking win!" Vy was from somewhere in the southern United States. Anika had heard the accent in her voice the first time they'd met, when Vy had been drunk. Her slurring had strange cadences to it that weren't there when she was sober and alert.

"But there's something that doesn't make sense," Anika said. "They said these guys were running drugs."

"Really? What kind?"

Anika leaned forward and buried her face in her hands, frustrated. "Shit, I didn't think to ask."

"Well, they're not moving weed, not by ship. Anywhere in the Canadian Polar Circle, it's all grown locally. Look at me: I have a license to sell. Pay taxes. I mean, you can think of me as the CEO of a very lucrative series of farms and pharmacies here in North Baffin. No sense in shipping it when you can grow it. The harder stuff, that usually comes smuggled up from the States, via the Midwest. That's how I got my start, actually."

"What gets shipped, then?"

Vy frowned. "Not much. Counterfeit pharmaceuticals, sometimes? Opiates from Afghanistan. But they usually ship them with regular shipments. Stick a container in the middle of a crapload of other containers. Smuggling via anonymity. It's pretty awesome at getting your stuff where it needs to be."

"So this chartered drug boat stuff, it's bullshit."

"I don't know for sure. But my guess is: yes, it's bullshit. I mean, I'm not hearing about it. It's ridiculous, risky, expensive, and totally pointless. Particularly now that the UNPG has such a strong presence."

Anika finished up the Belladonna and set it on the small table catercorner to the couch. "Okay. Thank you. I guess . . . I owe you? I'm not good at this sort of thing." She stood up.

Vy sprang up next to her. "You're not going to stay, are you?" She sounded disappointed.

Anika looked over at her. "I can't."

Vy's eyes flicked around, and then she smiled ruefully. "You look determined. I won't press it." Then she leaned over, grabbed Anika's hand and kissed the back of it. Anika closed her eyes for a second. "Well, I'd tell you that you know where to find me but it's been two months since I last said that and you came to visit. Take my card."

She slipped a piece of actual cardboard with contact information printed on it into one of the pockets of Anika's jacket. The action reminded Anika of when Vy had slipped her the pass that let her into The Greenhouse.

"Vy. I can't take your card. It would cause me trouble."

"Sweetie, you're out here asking me about how drugs are smuggled. You're *already* in trouble." And with that, Vy slipped back off down toward another niche where a pair of very large men with shaved heads waited for her.

Anika whipped the bike out of town, passing cars tooling their way along too slowly for her. She had a two-thirds charge still left in the batteries. That was plenty to allow her to race back home.

She'd gotten what she'd suspected: proof that things didn't add up right. But did she have to come all the way out to Arctic Bay?

No. She had to answer that honestly to herself. She'd driven down to see Vy as much as anything. After everything she'd been through, she'd wanted to get back to Vy. To see if she was still at The Greenhouse. To see if she was still . . . interested in her?

Anika had first come down to The Greenhouse several months ago in a van full of pilots looking to blow off steam. Vy had tracked her down, picking her off from the pack.

There'd been something there. A sparkle in the smile. A knowing glance between them.

But that's as far as it had gone. Because Anika couldn't date a dealer. She wasn't going to risk her pilot's license.

Not that other flyboys weren't doing similar things, or worse. But Anika knew it would come down heavier on her if her higher-ups found her involved with a dealer. That's just how it was. Women didn't get the same latitude. While boys would be boys, *she* would lose her airship.

And she wasn't giving up a lifetime's dream. Not on a fling. Not after everything she'd been through.

Yet it still hurt to make that decision, to turn away from a path.

There was a car behind her. The lights grew brighter as it pushed closer.

The bike had slipped down to half the speed limit as it groaned up the hillside. Anika moved aside to let the car pass. But as the headlights almost blinded her, she sensed, like a rat about to be hit by a striking snake, that the car was veering off to hit her instead of passing by.

At the last second before it struck, Anika whipped the bike left, crossing the centerline as the car clipped her instead of running her down.

The bulk of the vehicle rushed past, buffeting her and slamming into her leg. The mirror smacked into the small of her back and a wheel caught the back of her tire.

She wobbled, fighting to control the bike, then let it slide as gracefully as she could manage out from underneath her.

Anika hit the road on her left thigh, the bike now sideways and skidding on the asphalt with her. Sparks flew, metal screamed and groaned, but due to her low speed, the slide was manageable.

The bike spun off the road into the shoulder and up the hill, catapulting and smacking into a boulder.

Anika slid to a stop, bouncing into scree and dirt, cursing half-remembered childhood Igbo and Hausa phrases, and then finally English again as she realized she'd scraped to a stop.

Her leathers were ruined. A patch on the left thigh had come clean off; the skin underneath was ripped and shredded. Her left palm ached; she might have sprained the wrist, she thought. But after a second of flexing, she decided it was just badly bruised.

Now she was angry, not scared. She looked at the car. It was a BMW, with tinted windows, that skidded to a stop down the highway.

"What the hell do you think you are doing?" she shouted.

The driver got out. A muscular, tall, dark-haired man in a gray suit. He had a gun, which he raised over the roof of the car and pointed at her.

Anika bolted for the large rocks and scree, using them as a cover.

Three puffs of dirt and cracked rock exploded from the ground around her, near misses, as she zigged her way deeper into the natural maze of large rocks.

She was out here, very alone. And with no sidearm of her own.

That very large guy in the cheap suit was going to hunt her down. She was sure of that. She had a limp, she was tired, and he had the gun.

Anika kept moving, her mind racing, as she scrambled over loose rock and raced for bigger boulders to use as shields. She wasn't going to be able to keep running much longer, though. She needed a weapon.

She picked up a fist-sized rock, square-ish, with some sharp points. But bashing his head in would require getting close. And with that gun the chances of doing that were low.

She pocketed the rock and doubled back, circling around him as quietly as she could.

Her pockets had nothing but the rock, Vy's business card, and the phone. No one she could call would get here in time to save her.

Then she felt the rope key fob.

The paracord that made the fob was just six feet of standard parachute cord, thin and strong. It was knotted up into a compact little rectangle that took a few seconds to tug loose as she crouched her way from boulder to boulder.

A long time ago, a cousin of hers taught her to build slingshots to bring down birds on a dusty plain out in the countryside. For a Lagos girl, it was like a foreign land, a slice of her own country that seemed to leap out of the history books.

She never got the hang of making a sling, but she could wrap the rope into quick, half-remembered knots around the rock.

Now, with a crude mace built on the run, she found a spot where she'd make her stand. She walked back along her footprints in the dirt and gravel, letting them look as if they led off behind another large boulder, then she hid behind the other. She grunted as she jumped sideways toward it, trying not to give herself away. Then she waited.

It didn't take long. She could see her attacker's elongated shadow cautiously skirting toward her. "Tell you what," the man shouted in a strong German accent. "It doesn't have to be like this. Give me the data backup and I'll leave you be."

Anika began twirling the rock. Softly at first, as she didn't want it to make a sound yet. He was lying. If his first move was to try to run her down, he still wanted her dead even if she made the trade.

He stepped into a valley between two smaller knee-high rocks. He looked at her trail, and then stepped forward.

Anika gave the rock an extra burst of speed with all her upper body strength. The rope made a whooping sound, and she aimed it right at his head.

He glanced over, at that moment, sensing the movement out of the corner of his eye. He wasn't quick enough to block her attack, but he instinctively pulled the gun up to aim at her. The large rock just grazed his head and smacked into his gun hand.

"Fuck." He fired, the bullet kicking up dirt and rock, but the impact knocked the gun out of his hands.

Anika yanked the bloody rock back to her, swung it under her arm, and spun it twice around her head and then let it go again.

He'd instinctively stooped to try and pick the gun up, but now raised his cracked, bloodied hand to block the rock arcing toward his head. He only partially managed that; it hit him hard in the temple, staggering him back.

Anika yanked on the rope, retrieving the rock for another go, but now he charged her. There was blood in his right eye, so it was a clumsy tackle, but when he collided it knocked the air out of her.

She gasped, but didn't spend any energy trying to fend him off. She could hear the words *shitshitshitshit* being hissed, and she wasn't sure if they were in her head or if she was saying them out loud. He punched her in the gut, forcing her to try to double up, but she couldn't. His weight kept her pinned down, the rocks digging into her back, her ribs creaking from the weight. His hot breath filled the air around her as they grunted and struggled.

Anika freed her arms as he repositioned himself astride her to strike again and swiftly wrapped the paracord twice around his neck, got it looped three times around her hands, and pulled as hard as she could.

His eyes bugged out and he reared back, trying to pull at the thin, slippery cord as she choked him. The bloody rock tied to the one end dangled and slapped her arm as he struggled.

He bucked back again, so hard and far that he lifted her upper body off the rock as she gripped the paracord for all her life.

Then he stopped trying to pull the rope off and fixated on her. He threw her back down against the rock, smacking the back of her head against it.

She didn't let go. He punched her sides, but lying on top of her, he couldn't get much of a swing in. It hurt, fuck it hurt, but she was still choking him, and the punches got weaker.

Then he rolled off her, throwing himself around to try to break her wrists free of the rope.

Anika wasn't having it. As battered as she was, she understood deep down that only one of them was walking away from this encounter. And the only way for it to be her, was for her to keep the cord wrapped around his throat.

He was dragging her along the rock as he tried to pull free, and she managed to get on his back, pulling on the rope from behind like she was a jockey.

For the first time she could take a full breath.

Her sight returned, and she felt dizzy. But she pulled even harder on the rope. They toppled over together.

They were lying side by side in the dirt, moss, and scree, like spooning lovers. She had her knee in the small of his back, pushing herself out away from him, her rope-knotted hands just behind his neck, her triceps straining from pulling so hard. Blood stained the sides of the rope and skin peeled off her palms.

It was as if she were trying to pull the rope *through* his neck.

The man had one last burst of energy in him. He stood up again, yanking Anika along with him on his back. He staggered toward a rock, then spun and threw his back, and Anika, at it with all his strength.

Pain burst through her spine and up her skull, and

she screamed but held on, wrapping her legs around his waist and pulling tight with every bit of strength left to her as he did it again.

But this time, after throwing himself against the rock in reverse, he slumped forward.

Anika, wrapped around him, rope pulled tight, just hung on and waited.

She could feel the bruises and throbbing pain slowly washing over her. There wasn't a limb, a muscle, or any part of her that didn't scream for mercy.

There were tears of fear and relief to be alive coursing down her cheek and onto his neck. The sweat on her skin began to cool, and the cold air made her shiver.

For another ten minutes she lay there, making absolutely sure her attacker would not move again, and then she let go and flopped onto her back.

There were rope burns on the palms of her hands. The red lines and blood ran from the chewed-up brown of the back of her hands to the pale of the front.

She held them up in the air in front of her face and stared at them, and then at a single star up in the twilight summer sky of the Arctic.

# 11

Eventually the pain subsided enough that Anika could sit up, but with a gasp. Unsteadily, on her hands and knees, she crawled over to the dead man.

Who knew about the backup? She'd told Yves. He'd reported up the chain while they were in Resolute. Commander Claude knew, of course.

With shaking hands she checked the dead man's pockets to see if she could figure out who he was. No wallet. She found his holster underneath his left shoulder. There was no ID in that either.

None of the suit pockets had anything in them.

But his left trouser pocket had a small business card, a small phone, and several hundred euros cash. She looked at the silver money clip holding the cash, but it was blank.

She kept the cash, and then flipped the business card over to read it.

Michel Claude's name was stamped over the United Nations Polar Guard seal. And it was his contact info.

"What does this mean?" Anika muttered, sitting back down abruptly. "What . . ."

She ran a hand through her dirtied hair. Take a deep breath, she thought. Slowly. It could just mean this man talked to the commander.

Or it could mean Michel had wanted her killed.

Right?

Someone had cleared the *Kosatka* in Greenland, and if Tom and Anika had checked their data first, they wouldn't have bothered to train the scatter camera on the ship. Anika had assumed it was a bribe. But maybe someone inside the UNPG was involved in this, somehow.

Maybe that's why her scatter camera data had gone missing. And why people were hunting for the backup.

"Oh shit," she whispered. Maybe Tom hadn't died of exposure. Maybe he'd been killed.

Someone didn't want people to know that the *Kosatka* had been shipping something radioactive.

She had to be really careful, now. It was going to be best to take this information to the police. Someone not in the UNPG.

Only someone with a contact in the UNPG could have known that she had the data backed up, so she couldn't trust anyone there.

She patted herself down for her phone, while wondering what it was the *Kosatka* had been carrying. Just nuclear waste? Was that enough to kill someone for? This felt bigger, somehow.

There had been a few stories about people killed over illegal dumping activity, caught up with the wrong people. But that was overseas and far away. But going after UNPG pilots? Whoever was doing this was willing to risk a lot.

Well, they picked the wrong UNPG pilot, Anika thought.

She pulled her phone out. Pieces of screen and plastic shell fell between her fingers onto her lap. The electronic guts spilled out.

Where was the phone she'd taken off the dead man? She found that.

Jenny. She needed to talk to Jenny.

"Jenny? It's Anika, I need a minute."

"Anika?" Jenny asked on the other side, her voice tiny and cracked in such a way that it hurt more than Anika's current pains.

"What happened? We were talking to him."

"He collapsed later. It was too much of a shock for his heart, they said."

Anika bit her lip for a long moment. "This might sound weird, but, did you know the doctors and nurses in the room?"

"That . . ." Jenny also paused. "Are you okay, Anika?"

"I'm okay. I'm sorry. I know it's weird to ask you. I know you volunteer there sometimes."

"Yes, I knew them all. They all took it very hard." Jenny lapsed into quiet crying again.

"I'm so sorry," Anika said. "Listen, Jenny, someone tried to run me off the road and kill me. I don't know who, or why, but I think it has something to do with why Tom and I were shot at. I promise you,

I'm going to figure out who did this to us, and I swear I'm going to make them pay. Somehow."

"Oh God, Anika, just be safe. Be safe. I don't want any more people to die. I don't think I can handle that."

"I'll be okay," Anika promised, before she hung up. "Don't worry about me."

Tom hadn't been murdered in the hospital. That was a small relief. But the men who'd arranged all this had something to do with the attack on their airship, and that had ultimately killed him. They were still responsible.

Anika took a deep breath and limped her way around the rocks she'd used as cover back down to the road.

Karl's bike lay upside down, front wheel mangled, the frame bent.

For some reason that left her feeling helpless and broken. Karl had always been good about lending the damn thing to her whenever she let her car lose its charge. She almost depended on the damn thing.

Nothing she took for granted as stable in her life even existed anymore. The bike: mangled. Tom: dead. Jenny: broken. Michel: maybe involved in trying to kill her.

In a short few days, everything had just been yanked away from her. The entire life she had built. Like it didn't even matter.

And for what?

Some goddamned nuclear waste?

Now that she wasn't distracted by fighting for her life she started shaking from delayed fear. She leaned over a boulder and threw up. Bright fruit juice and rum splattered against gray rock.

She'd never drink a Belladonna again, she thought, wiping her mouth with the sleeve of the torn-up jacket.

Leaning against another rock to steady herself, she considered dialing emergency services, then decided to call Karl and apologize for the bike.

It was something she had to do, she felt.

"Karl? Karl, it's Anika."

There was a long silence on the other side. She guessed he was waking up, slow to understand what was going on. It was three in the morning, after all.

But then Karl exploded. "Jesus, Anika, Jesus, there are people over at your place ripping it apart."

Anika slid down into a crouch against the boulder. "What?" she whispered. "Tom?"

"They say they're UNPG MPs and that you're in some sort of trouble," Karl said. "Please, let me hear you say it's bullshit."

"It's bullshit," she repeated numbly.

"I figured. They're being tight-lipped and following orders from somewhere else. I don't know the details. The commander wants to talk to you. They got here fifteen minutes ago. Where the hell are you anyway? I didn't tell them you were on my bike. Probably not smart, but, shit."

"The bike," she said, looking across the ground at it. "Karl, I'm really sorry about the bike. Someone just tried to run me over."

"Run you over? Forget it," he said. "We can fix it later. Where are you?"

Anika pulled the phone away and looked at it. Was it too paranoid to assume they were being listened to? Or just paranoid enough? She put the phone back to her ear.

"That rope braid on your keychain?" Anika said.

"Yeah?"

"It saved my life. Thank you." She ended the call. If her commander was caught up in this, or someone in the UNPG was out for her, going back to her place or reporting in for duty was off the list of options.

She groaned as she stood up, steadied herself, and then staggered toward the BMW. The driver's side door was still open, light spilling out onto the highway. The key fob dangled from the parking brake between the front seats.

A car passed, then slowed down and pulled over ahead of her and the BMW.

A heavyset woman leaned out the window and looked back. "Hey, was there an accident? Are you okay? Do you need me to call for help?"

Anika coiled up the rope, with the stone still on the end, and tossed it onto the smooth leather passenger's seat. "Yes, the man in this car tried to run me over," she called back to the concerned woman.

She was thinking about the time she had ejected over some Cameroon rain forest during a training flight. Akinjide, her copilot, had broken a leg landing three miles south of her. She'd lashed him to a travois and dragged him through a hundred and fifty miles of muddy jungle until they'd stumbled across a logging camp with a working radio.

That had been a test of her will. Every day, dragging Akinjide's useless weight along behind her. Not daring to eat anything she didn't recognize, fearing it would poison them. Drinking muddy water.

She wasn't about to be broken. No, the Arctic hadn't thrown her yet.

But she was thinking that maybe, just maybe, she should have listened to her dad and tried to get a job flying sightseeing tourists around New York. They have airships there, he'd said. Why go to the cold?

Why?

Anika slid gingerly into the driver's seat of the BMW and adjusted the chair forward.

"Are you stealing that car?" the woman asked. She had gotten out of her car and was standing on the side of the road.

Anika found the window controls and rolled the passenger side window down. "Yes. You should call emergency services," she shouted, and pulled out onto the highway, leaving a very confused-looking good Samaritan alone on the road.

She had a destination firmly in mind: Commander Michel Claude's home.

# 12

Commander Michel Claude looked exhausted as he entered the door of his little base cottage along with a gust of cold air.

He hung his coat up and ditched his gloves in a bin on a stand near the door. Removed his holster and gun, car keys, and a wallet, and set them in a large terra-cotta dish on the stand, and then he made his way to the small kitchen.

The fridge light filled the cottage with an eerie glow as he grabbed a soda, popped it open, and then moved to the couch.

He sighed and began unlacing his boots with one hand, pausing only for an occasional sip.

Until the faint sound of Anika cocking his own gun made him freeze.

“Commander,” Anika said softly. “I don’t want to use this. I’m really sorry, but . . .” she dropped the paracord, now minus the bloody rock on the end, over his shoulder.

"What do you want me to do with this?" he asked.

"Please tie yourself up."

They faced each other over his coffee table, the gun dangling off her hand in her lap, resting on the shredded leathers.

"You stepped over a line," he said softly, holding his bound hands up to point at her. "There's no going back. Pointing a gun at a superior officer is not something you get to undo! You understand that?"

"Someone ran me off the road and tried to kill me. Before that, someone tried to shoot me out of the sky. I don't care about *my job,* or going to jail, right now, Commander. I want to know who got my copilot killed. And I want to know who is trying to kill me right now because I have that scatter camera data." As she said that she carefully set his business card down on the table.

He looked down at it and frowned. "What's that?"

"Your business card." Anika tapped it for emphasis.

"Yes. But why are you putting it on the table?"

"It was on the guy who tried to kill me."

Anika raised her eyes up from the table and met the commander's. She didn't blink or look away until he frowned and looked back down at the card. When he slowly blinked and looked up at her, she wondered what he saw on her face. Sincerity? Or could he not see past his situation? Did he think he was looking at the face of someone who'd snapped?

Or was he surprised to see the face of someone he thought would be dead by now?

She couldn't help but assume he wasn't involved. He was the damned commander, after all.

"Do you understand what I am asking you?" she asked, crisp and steady, enunciating each word like her old English teacher.

"All you had to do was come to us. If you truly think people are trying to kill you, all you had to do was come to me. We'd protect you."

Anika sighed. She was beaten up, bruised, and exhausted from exposure and lack of sleep. "Commander, whoever is doing this is *inside* the Polar Guard."

He glanced back down at the card. "It's not me. Anyone could get my card."

She gingerly pulled her legs onto the couch. She felt like she could just sink right on into the soft material and keep on sinking. A deep, hungry gulf of tiredness threatened to drown her in sleep. It was all she could do to remain alert, his gun in her hand. Stabbing pain, from the road rash, from bruises in the fall, where the assassin had punched her and slammed her against the boulder, from the chafed palms of her hands where she'd clung to the rope, all of it built up into a crescendo of hurt that left her shaking.

"Commander, someone cleared the *Kosatka* in Greenland, and I'm starting to think that was so that none of our spotters would think to give it a second scan for radiation," she said. "I should have thought to try and get to a computer with clearance to follow that piece of the paper trail, before I went to Resolute. And then there's the fact that my scatter camera data shows the radiation, but the readings backed up by satellite in the main UNPG database say something different. And then, tonight, someone tried to kill me for that scatter camera data."

Claude sat for a long moment.

"Look," Anika said, holding up her arms and raising her shirt under the jacket. "I didn't just wipe out on my bike, someone tried to kill me tonight."

"So you want me to help you find out who cleared the *Kosatka*?"

"That's it, then I leave."

He held up his hands. "If you'll let me stand up and get to my laptop, I can look up who cleared the ship for you. But you realize what you've done here? There is no more UNPG for you. This will be reported to the police."

"I can't trust anyone right now." Anika pointed to his hands. "I won't be untying you."

He shrugged. "I'm a hunt-and-peck typist anyway."

The laptop was in a leather satchel, and Claude carefully set it up on a small table in the middle of the kitchen.

It hurt to stand, Anika thought. She leaned against the table as Claude slowly logged in, typing with both hands bound and one finger extended.

"Do you have any painkillers?" she asked.

"Left drawer, facing the microwave." Claude's face was underlit by the bluish glow of the screen.

She turned to look in that direction and Claude jumped at her. He knocked the gun aside with his clubbed fists. It smacked the tile floor of the kitchen and skittered across the floor.

He shoved her back against the fridge, and Anika felt raw panic. Stupid mistake. He was going to kill her. He hadn't been interested in looking anything up, he'd just been buying time.

Anika kneed him in the groin, and as he collapsed, she fought free. But he recovered and tackled her feet. Her cheek slapped the tile as she fell, dizzying her.

The kitchen briefly contracted to a point in her vision, and she sucked air as she tried to yank away.

"Don't fight, damn it, Anika," he grunted as she kicked him in the face.

She didn't waste air on words, but grabbed the edge of a cabinet to pull herself onto the carpet. This was another fight-or-die situation. She was going to fight.

He yanked her back onto the tile by her feet. She was too bruised, too tired, to really stop him. She reached deep into her physical reserves, but all she could do was jab at his throat as he yanked her around and into a choke hold.

She flailed and kicked to get free, but his arms were bound. Once he had them around her, all he had to do was hang on.

He was going to kill her in much the same way she'd killed that other man tonight.

Slowly, Anika stopped kicking his shins.

And then, the stale air in her lungs overwhelming her, she slipped off into the painless dark.

It felt good, in that last second, to stop fighting and just surrender. She'd never done that before.

# 13

The smell of ammonia bubbled, then ripped through Anika's sinuses to sledgehammer her awake.

She gasped and sat up, coughing and spitting, her eyes watering, shoving the small capsule someone had underneath her nose away with her hands.

Both her hands, she realized muzzily, because they were handcuffed.

A Polar Guard MP unwrapped a blood pressure cuff from her upper arm and folded it back into a small emergency medical kit he had on the floor of an SUV.

"Where am I?" Anika asked, her voice husky. She put her handcuffed hands up to her throat, feeling the bruising and tenderness where she'd been choked.

She took a reflexive, deep breath of cold, sweet air, and watched it puff out with all the apparent satisfaction of a smoker hitting a first puff early in the morning.

"On this fine morning, you're on your way to lockup," the MP said. Anika realized that the vehicle was in motion. She sat up with a grunt. All those bruises and pulled muscles screamed at her.

The road underneath changed from paved road to gravel. A familiar-enough transition. Anika could see the tips of base housing units.

"You're getting court-martialed, at the least," Claude said from the front of the SUV.

Anika pulled herself a bit higher, using the backs of the seats. "What about the attempt on my life for the data?" she asked. "And Greenland? Did you find out who cleared the *Kosatka*? I don't care what happens to me, just please don't drop this."

The MP driving the car looked over at the commander. "Damn. She sounds sincere, sir."

"I know." Claude's voice sounded tired.

"Do you want to wait and let the big guys toss her place, or you still want to check it out?"

"Keep driving," Claude said, and he pointed out the window. "There."

They turned down the road and slowly approached Anika's home, gravel crunching under the tires, and then stopped.

"What are we looking for?" the driver asked, as he opened the door.

"I don't know." Claude glanced back at Anika, then stepped out. "But we need to make sure she isn't working for someone, or with someone."

Anika rubbed her face. What was Claude up to? If he was genuinely not interested in killing her, then all this made sense. Or it could be he was looking for the scatter cam data.

She'd already made so many mistakes. She needed to think darkly, to assume the worst. And to plan for the worst.

What if he were planting something, and trying to get her locked up to get her out of the way?

And what was she going to do about any of it from the back of the SUV with handcuffs on?

Michel Claude and the driver opened the back of the SUV. "Come on, Addison," Claude grunted, waving out the MP who'd acted as her medic. They kept their distance, and they had their guns in hand.

It wasn't like Anika was going to be able to fight her way out through three armed men.

Particularly not in her current shape.

She watched the MP crawl out and stretch as he stood on the gravel, and saw the driver hand him his gun back. They were being very careful around her.

They shut the car door on her and walked off.

There were no handles on the inside to open it. Anika looked out. The three men were spreading out, one going around to her back door. Commander Claude and the driver approached her front door, guns ready.

Anika crawled out of the back of the SUV over the rear bench seat, grimacing in pain with every movement, and checked the doors. Unsurprisingly, no latches again. And there was a metal grid bolted behind the front seats.

On her back in the seat, she thought for a second.

If she escaped, or tried to escape, it made her look guiltier.

But then, she didn't know whether her commander was trying to lock her up for life or just following the book.

She gritted her teeth and kicked at the window.

Nothing happened.

Again, she tensed and kicked with her heels, and thought she heard a faint cracking sound.

She took a deep breath, and as her feet struck the glass again the world exploded in pieces of glass as every window in the vehicle blew out.

For a split second she didn't understand. Then the waves of heat roiled through the vehicle and debris started raining down, plinking off the roof of the car like a spatter of hail in a quick, brief storm.

When she sat up she saw the fiery frame of her house slump slightly. Debris smoldered, scattered out onto the road and several rows of houses back. Shattered windows slumped in frames, some tinkling to the ground well after the explosion.

Off-duty base people were stumbling out of their doors and looking around.

Anika reached out and used the outside door handle to open the door and step out. Something squished under her feet and she looked down.

It was a severed forearm, white bone sticking out of the bloody end, ropy muscle fibers limp on the gravel.

She stumbled forward, falling to her knees.

"Claude!" she shouted. "Commander Claude?"

This was nearly incomprehensible and apocalyptic and, somehow, even worse than some lone gunman trying to kill her on the highway. And she realized now that Claude hadn't intended her any harm. He'd been following the book. A good man had walked right into a mess left for her.

Someone had rigged her home with explosives.

God. She repeated that to herself: someone had rigged her home with explosives!

Those "MPs" that Karl told her had been here previously.

"Claude!" she shouted again. He'd been standing behind the one MP, the driver, when she last saw him. Covering him.

She heard a groan, maybe a whimper, from somewhere nearby.

On her hands and knees, Anika scrabbled her way over to the remains of her front door and pulled it off Claude. She gasped. There were burns everywhere, the man was hardly recognizable.

But the pale eyes recognized her.

Someone crunched across the gravel. It was Karl. He was in boxer shorts, sandals, and a simple white shirt, his breath puffing in the air as he ran over. From the expression on his face, it was clear he was in just as much shock as she'd been. "Anika?"

"It's the commander," she yelled at him. "Call an ambulance! Now!"

Karl hesitated, looked down, flinched, then ran back to find a phone.

Anika turned back to the badly burned body of the commander. Claude was going to die, and it was going to be her fault. There was no way people weren't going to think she did this.

"Commander Claude, what was the name of the man in Greenland?" she asked, staring right into his eyes. "Did you look it up?"

His breath was raspy and irregular. He stirred, and then groaned. No doubt the pain was unimaginable. Anika found tears in the corners of her eyes for doing this, instead of leaving him to die in peace, but she leaned in closer. "I'm begging you, sir. Greenland. For both our sakes."

He kept panting for a long moment, until finally, his lips moved. Anika leaned in until they were almost touching.

"Braffit," Claude hissed.

Anika waited for more, but it became clear from the faint gurgling in the back of his throat that this was all Claude could manage. She pulled back. "Thank you," she whispered. She reached into her pocket and pulled out the flat shard of plastic the scatter camera data was on. His good hand curled around it as she pressed it there.

If he lived, then maybe he could put it to good use. If he didn't, then the world would assume she killed him, and not even the scatter camera data was going to do her much good.

He closed his eyes, and the whistling breathing slowed.

There were sirens in the distance.

Anika stood up and shielded her face with her handcuffed hands, approaching the burning remains of her home. She found the scorched, ruined, limbless body of the driver. The smell of burned flesh left her nauseous, the heat from the fire crackled and licked at her.

But she found the keys to the SUV on the man's belt.

They burned her fingers, but she yanked them clear, gritting her teeth, and staggered back to the vehicle.

The hot keys turned the car on just fine, despite the handcuffs. After a moment of leaning over to awkwardly yank the shifter into drive, she accelerated out. She saw Karl in the rearview mirror, watching her leave.

She tensed and lowered her hands to the bottom of the wheel as she passed the emergency crews whipping their way down the road toward the base. But they paid her no mind, trying to get to the pillar of smoke as fast as they possibly could.

# 14

She didn't see another batch of police until she reached the stretch of road where she fought her would-be assassin. They stood around the edge of the road near the track marks of the car she'd stolen from him.

Lights from the ambulance rapidly strobed against the back of her eyeballs as she glanced up in the rearview mirror of the MP's SUV.

But no one even looked up or back at her, not bothering to wonder why there were no windows in the SUV, why her hair was being blown all over the place. She steered into what felt like a gale, a storm of her own making, but was just the unprotected blast from driving nearly fifty miles an hour. No one wondered why she was shivering and hunched over the wheel.

Ten miles down the mountain from them, Anika slowed and pulled to a stop along the shoulder of the road.

She took a deep breath, as if she were trying to inhale the entire vehicle out of existence, shuddering from the effort. She placed a hand against the door pillar to brace herself.

Well, here it was, she thought. She was on the run for real now. A suspect. Innocent men had been killed.

All because she wanted to double-check the port-of-call clearance on an old freighter.

"Shit!" She punched the wheel with both of her handcuffed hands. Then she punched it even harder, ignoring the stabs of pain from bruises. "Shit! Shit."

She smacked her head against the back of the headrest. Why hadn't she listened to Tom? Why bother with a double check if they were already cleared?

Why not just sit up in the sky and take it easy.

Why had she had to push it just that much further?

She let go, then kicked the brake pedal, and the car lurched and stopped again.

She screamed up through the open sunroof at the stars, a yawp of frustration, rage, lost choices, and fear.

Then Anika looked around until she found the phone she'd taken from the dead man's pocket. It had been put in an evidence bag by the shifter.

"Vy . . . I'm sorry to call you so early in the morning, but I need your help," she said in a flat voice, pulling her elbows close to her sides to try and warm herself up, but still shivering.

Vy had her come around to the back of The Greenhouse. A large Russian bouncer, Chernov, let her in through a service door and pointed at an industrial lift in the gloom, surrounded by boxes of alcohol. It was eerie to be in The Greenhouse and not hear music thumping. "Come with me," he said. He glanced down at the cuffs, but didn't say anything. None of his business.

The steel floor of the lift shuddered as it rose. Gated doors passed them slowly by as they ascended through to the fifth floor.

Chernov slid the gate aside, and they walked down a corridor. He opened the last door for her, and Anika stepped into Vy's private office.

Unlike The Greenhouse, Vy's office was plant-free. Wood panels darkened the whole place, and a large, computer-free desk dominated the center of it. Small leather couches were scattered around, carefully positioned in front of the desk and facing it.

In a meeting in this room, it would be clear who was in charge.

There were no personal effects. No pictures, no motivational posters. What kind of decoration would a semilegal drug dealer choose anyway? Anika wasn't sure.

"Where's Vy?" she asked. Chernov had taken up a position near the door, hands folded in front of him, a blank stare on his face.

"Soon," he grunted. He smiled at her. "Violet, she likes you very much, I think."

Anika sat on one of the couches, then leaned back into it and sighed. "Why do you say that?"

"You are not buying or selling from her, and she still lets you into the office. And you are very pretty, yes."

The door opened. "Chernov, be quiet," Vy said. Anika struggled to stand, but Vy pulled a small ottoman over and sat in front of her. "Jesus on a Popsicle stick, you look like shit."

"I'm sorry," Anika said.

Vy reached for the handcuffs and held her hands. "Don't apologize. Chernov, get the damn bolt cutters, what are you waiting for, a formal invitation?"

Chernov shrugged and walked out the door, hulking his way down the corridor.

"Who did this to you?" Vy asked. "I have a few more Chernovs I can round up. We can fuck whoever did this up, they won't ever want to lay a hand on you again."

Anika squeezed Vy's hands. "He won't be a problem anymore," she said. "I killed him."

Chernov coughed from the door. They both looked at him, and he held up the bolt cutters.

Vy looked back at Anika. "Chernov'll keep his mouth shut."

Chernov grinned as he got the bolt cutters' bottom blade in between Anika's wrist and the first cuff. "It's wax in my ears. Violet always yelling at me, yes? Do this. Do that. Don't you hear what I am telling you, big stupid man."

The cuff cracked apart, and Chernov grunted in satisfaction. He turned his attention to the other hand.

Vy kept holding Anika's hands as she looked at the Russian bouncer. "Chernov smuggled himself to Baffin aboard a sealed shipping container with a shitload of scuba tanks to keep him breathing. He was trying to reach Alaska, but he miscalculated; the crew of the ship luckily heard him banging. He jumped overboard a few days later in some survival gear he found and floated to Baffin, where some friends of mine fished him out of the water. He's been following me around like a puppy ever since." She ruffled his hair.

"Woof." Chernov smiled as he freed Anika's second hand, and held up the mangled pieces of the handcuffs.

"Make those disappear," Vy ordered, "and come back up with a doctor who'll work for cash and owes us a favor."

"There's med student, um . . ." Chernov frowned. "Edward. He's home from Montreal. Yes. He will do."

And then the Russian ambled off to make arrangements.

Vy had some oxycodone and gave two to Anika with a bottle of water. By the time "Edward the med student" showed up, out of breath and blinking, the worst of the pain had receded into the background. Anika was struggling to stay awake.

Edward, still a bit pale and sweaty, no doubt from only having had left The Greenhouse a few hours before, swallowed. "I really shouldn't be doing this," he said as he sat on the ottoman Vy had pulled up to the couch.

Vy sat on her desk, feet folded, watching them. "It'll be cash."

Edward licked his lips and looked back at Chernov. "I could get in a lot of trouble practicing without a license . . ."

"You have bigger trouble if you refuse," Chernov grumbled, folding his arms. "We solved problem for you. Remember that problem? Now you solve problem for us. This is how it works."

Edward brushed a stray blond hair back behind an ear and leaned forward. Anika looked at his green eyes as they flicked over her, taking in the bruises. He took her hands in his, examining her torn-up knuckles.

Then he was looking at the scrapes on her thighs. Had her breathe in and out while he listened, ear flat against her back, then her chest.

She hissed when he pushed at her ribs, one by one.

He leaned back. "Bike accident, then a fight?"

Anika nodded.

"I'd hate to see the other girl," he said.

She didn't bother correcting the automatic assumption in his statement, but she saw Chernov quirk an uncharacteristic smile.

Edward focused on the marks on her neck. "Someone tried to strangle you, too." He frowned. "This wasn't a bar fight, was it?"

"No." Anika rubbed her neck.

Edward's demeanor shifted. "Listen, if this is domestic abuse, you need to report it."

"It wasn't domestic abuse," Anika said. She swam in a world of near sleep due to the painkillers. She wished Edward would hurry up.

Edward didn't believe her, but turned his attention back to her ribs. "I don't think anything's broken. Bruising, strains, maybe a slightly cracked rib—either way the advice is the same. I'd take it easy. Get to a doctor as soon as you can, get some X-rays. What painkillers do you have, Violet?"

Vy rattled a fluid list of names and finished with, “She’s already had some oxycodone.”

“That’s more than necessary. Make she sure takes something anti-inflammatory as well. Ice the ribs. Rest. Above all, she needs to take it easy. The abrasions aren’t too bad, I can clean them off. Get some antibiotic cream on them. If there’s anything too deep, bandage it. I don’t see anything that needs stitches.”

“So she’s okay?” Vy asked.

“She’s going to hurt tomorrow, but yes, she seems okay. But she really, really needs to visit a real doctor. Understand?”

“We’ll clean her up.” Vy nodded at Chernov, who grabbed Edward’s shoulder.

“Time for us to leave,” Chernov said, and led Edward out.

The door closed, and Anika heard Vy moving about. But the sludge of painkillers and exhaustion spun the room slowly around her. Anika lay back into the folds of the couch, sinking further and further into it.

Vy crouched next to her, whispering into her ear. Light glinted from a pair of scissors. “You know you’re in a safe place, right?”

Anika nodded.

“Good.”

Vy’s hands slid down the sides of Anika’s leathers, and then she started snipping them with the scissors, avoiding the road injuries, carefully pulling strips of cloth away as Anika fought sleep.

In brief snatches of lucidity, she summarized everything that had happened, unsure how much it was making sense. "I have to get to Greenland," she said. "I have to find Braffit."

"Okay," Vy said. "But for now, just rest."

Anika's legs and forearms had been cleaned up, slathered in antibiotic cream. She realized, suddenly shocked, that her jeans had been entirely cut away. But even as she realized that, and looked for the energy to object, Vy draped a large, soft blanket on her.

Anika woke up and found Chernov sitting in a chair by the door watching a movie on his phone with earphones turned up loud enough she could hear mosquito-like explosions and screaming.

He saw her moving and turned it off. "*Dobry 'veche*," he said.

"What?" Anika fumbled around, and Chernov rushed forward, handing her a handful of pills and a bottle of water.

"Here is more oxy," he said, "and for inflammation, take as well."

Anika downed everything, wrapped the blanket around her, and limped toward a door in the back behind the desk. She needed to pee so badly. "Please, is that a bathroom?"

Chernov nodded.

After washing her hands, Anika filled the sink and plunged her face in. Invigorating. But mostly painful.

She dried herself off with a wad of paper towels, and found that Vy waited for her outside when she opened the door.

"You may not remember, but we had quite a chat last night while I was cleaning you up," Vy said.

"I told you what happened," Anika recalled. "I told you what Commander Claude found. I need to get to Greenland, to find Braffit."

"Yes, and I can help you get to Greenland. . . ."

Anika, standing by Vy's desk with the blanket wrapped around her waist and legs, her hair flying every which way, a halo of brown around her face, interrupted. "Why?"

"Why am I helping you?"

"Yes." Anika stared at her.

"Jesus. You have to ask that?" Vy looked hurt.

"Do you want a pet Polar Guard pilot? Another person who owes you a big debt? I have to understand what I'm getting into, Vy. Because there's a lot that's happened to me lately."

Vy softened. Somewhat. She sat down in her chair and put her legs up on her desk. "Chernov?"

"Yah?"

"Will Anika owe me anything for my getting her to Greenland?"

"No. This is not business," Chernov said. "This is personal favor. This is because we like you. This is because, when we were in The Greenhouse that night, Vy thought you looked interesting. She wanted to get to know you better."

Anika shuffled her way over. "I don't know how to repay you. . . ."

"Just let it be," Vy said softly. "I can't get you all the way down to the Polar Guard station in Nuuk. That's where you told me you wanted to get to, this morning. But I can get you to Upernavik; it's up the coast a ways. And you'll need to avoid getting picked up."

"Because I'm wanted?" Anika asked, grateful to be talking about something else.

"Greenland's got this guest worker obsession. You can fly into Greenland and automatically get a three-month-long pass to wander around the island and even do temporary work. The diamond and ruby mines are always hiring, and the more the ice melts, the more they can drill. Greenland doesn't have enough workers for the interior, so the state-run concessions are always bringing in guest workers."

"Oh, yeah. Right." The Greenlanders were mostly First Nations people, with some Danish background. They'd encouraged First Nations peoples to emigrate from Northern Canada, Alaska, and Russia. But as the glaciers receded and Greenland's interior released a bounty of natural resources, there was more work than people in Greenland. Companies had to reach out to find workers, and they trickled in from Africa, the United States, and Northern Europe.

There had been protests and some strikes by international workers who ran out of their three-month stays, demanding to be treated fairly and given a chance to apply to become Greenlanders, but the Greenlanders didn't want to become minorities in their own country. And they were First Nations peoples. They'd seen the rush to Northern Canada's newly opened and ice-free land displace enough Inuit there. They knew history. They were nervous, and as a result, Greenland remained obstinate about the three-month stay.

Pay was generous enough, they noted, that one could work for three months, then come back the next year, and still make a yearly salary.

"They spend good money to run background checks on everyone's ID who enters the major ports," Vy said. "And have the best counterfeit detection systems I've come across. So it's less risky to smuggle you into Upernavik. We'll give you a fake passport to flash once you're inside Greenland, but if they pick you up and actually run it, chances are you're in trouble."

"I understand," Anika said. "But I have to go."

"I'll make the arrangements," Vy said. Then added, "And get you some track pants. There's a convenience store at the end of the block, if you give me your measurements, I can have Chernov get you some replacement clothes."

Anika shook her head. "Let me borrow his jacket, if I can do it. I don't want to be a bother."

"No bother," Chernov said.

"You don't want to run into any cops," Vy said.

But Anika pressed on. "No, I need to do something. I can't just sit here while everyone does all this for me."

Vy nodded, opened a drawer, and tossed Anika a thick roll of cash held together with a rubber band.

"Don't trust Chernov's sense of style?" she asked.

For the first time in several days, Anika laughed.

It was just a small chuckle. And it hurt: her ribs shot pain up her sides.

But it felt good.

# 15

Down toward the docks Anika found a thrift shop she'd eyed a few times before while on the way to The Greenhouse. There were no cameras in the ceiling that might recognize her as she pulled the hood off Chernov's oversized coat to reveal her face. Tired-looking mothers and burnt-out young men with tattoos wandered the racks, and the store smelled of antiseptic.

And there were some good finds: jeans with thermal lining, a thick, gray wool turtleneck, an oversized fisherman's jacket that came down past her knees that contained a multitude of useful pockets.

She paid and changed into these, folding Chernov's jacket away into a shopping bag, then continued through the store until she had three or four days' clothes.

At a small convenience store she packed everything into a backpack, and then purchased two disposable phones.

The clerk, a teenager with tiger tattoos on her forearms that fluoresced, sighed. "I can't take cash for those," she announced, reciting it tonelessly, obviously having memorized it. "You need to let me photocopy some form of ID, or pay with a credit card."

Anika slid the clerk more than she'd make in a week. "I was attacked," she explained. "They took my wallet and everything in it and my phone. I had to go to the bank to get them canceled, and get some money for myself for the week."

The clerk eyed the money, and a pink tongue briefly licked an upper lip. She looked at the bruises on Anika's neck and her scuffed knuckles. "Then why two of them, eh?"

"Work." Anika held up one phone. "Personal." She held up the other.

"Yeah. Okay."

The money disappeared with the pass of a hand.

Outside, Anika ripped the phone open, activated it, and checked her voice mail. Two disposable phones, maybe she'd buy some more before leaving for Greenland.

This was how criminals stayed untraceable, right?

There was a message on it from Anton, one of the two agents from Resolute, with a brief comment about him having some new information. "Call me back," he said cheerfully on the recording.

It had been left before Commander Claude had handcuffed her.

Anton betrayed no surprise at the sound of her voice when he picked up. "Anika Duncan, you're in great trouble. I was not expecting you to ever call after I heard about what happened."

"You work very late," she said. "I was wondering if you would answer."

"Your commanding officer was almost killed. Two MPs were killed. All of this as follow-up to the attack on your airship. I am drinking lots of coffee, and there is much adrenaline. And paperwork."

"Michel is okay?" Anika asked, shocked, and relieved.

"Not okay. He was airlifted out to burn ward. Critical, but alive."

"Thank God." Anika rubbed her forehead. "When I saw him on the ground, I was sure he was dead."

"Anika, what are you doing here? Why are you running?"

"People keep trying to kill me, Anton. First it was the *Kosatka,* then someone attacked me on the road back from Arctic Bay." She summarized everything that had happened for him, but left out where she was calling from, and anything about Vy. "I don't trust anyone."

"You are not investigator." Anton's voice was tight and stressed. She noticed he was dropping articles from his speech, like "an" or "the" at random. English was not his first language, and as he got stressed, it was getting harder for him to focus. "You think you can solve this alone? Like Nancy Drew? Come into protective custody, we can help. You are wanted for questioning, you are *not* prime suspect."

He said that last thing with such a heartfelt plea. "I believe you," she said. "But what happens once I'm locked up and you're investigating? I become a target, again, Anton. I don't want to be a target." She rubbed her neck.

The cold air made her shiver. She'd been standing out in the wind too long. The hot air of The Greenhouse sounded more and more appealing.

Anton was quiet for a long time, until he finally said, "If you think there are answers in Greenland, you are wrong."

That spooked her. "Greenland? Why do you think I would go to Greenland?"

"The last person to clear *Kosatka* was stationed in Nuuk."

Shit. They were following her line of thinking.

"Braffit. That's who the commander told me it was," she said, crushed. "Have you talked to him?"

"Brauthwaite. Peter Brauthwaite," corrected Anton. "There are people monitoring this phone call right here getting mad at me now. But trust me, I am telling you this to let you know you are not a suspect. I want to help you."

"What did Peter Brauthwaite say? Who paid him to do this?" Why was all this happening?

"Here is why I think you are not a suspect," Anton said. "This man walked out of his office the moment news that you were shot down began to spread. He booked a flight from Nuuk to Thule. . . ."

Anika interrupted. "He was going to the Pole?"

"Yes. He disappeared there. So please, prove me right, and come in and we can help each other. Anika, now is the only time I may be able to help you. Interpol, CIA, MI6—everyone is involved now."

"Why?"

"Those radiation readings you think you saw?

Two weeks ago, in Siberia, a nuclear warhead was stolen. So now, if you can get me that backed-up data, I think we might be able to put these two cases together instead of pursuing them separately."

"Stolen? A nuclear warhead was *stolen*?"

"Everything is moving to high alert. And these people who stole the nuclear device, they know your name now. You understand? I know you are worried about security in the UNPG, but I will bring you right into my own office, Anika. Under protection of a close handful that I trust with my own life."

She knew he was earnest. But she couldn't figure how to undo what had been done.

And she couldn't stop wondering what these people were planning to do with a nuclear device in the Arctic Circle.

It had to be destined for somewhere. She doubted it had been dumped overboard. Was this going to be another Karachi? Terrorists there had gotten a Pakistani army nuclear bomb and set it off in the capital. The UN was still overseeing reconstruction of the country as a result of the fallout.

At least, she thought, everything that had happened to her and Tom wasn't over dumping waste. For some, morbid, deviant reason, it felt slightly better that someone had tried to kill over something far more menacing.

"I don't have the data," Anika said. "I gave it to Claude." She turned the phone off and threw it into the trash can on the corner of the street and headed back for The Greenhouse. She pulled the parka's hood up around her face tight, shoved her hands in the pockets, and headed off down the street.

She had to get Vy to cancel plans to get her to Greenland. And apologize.

And beg her to help get to Thule.

The last time she'd seen Thule was on her first flight out to Baffin. She'd been getting ready for a proof-of-concept heavy-lift airship flight out of Chengdu. The task was to drop a two-megawatt, fully contained solar power substation into the middle of a Chinese Army camp on the base of a mountain somewhere in South China. The army was looking at outsourcing the delivery of solar substations that allowed a garrison to camp somewhere without needing to be resupplied.

The Chinese Army was obsessed, along with most of the rest of the world's armies, with divorcing itself from fossil fuels for transportation.

With oil reserves the world over at uncertain levels, geologists claiming a limited supply anywhere outside of the booming Arctic, and oil at increasingly higher prices, the world's armed forces had been doubling down on non-oil technology for as long as Anika could remember.

When the call had come in that her UNPG application was accepted, Anika had taken the first bullet train to Beijing from Chengdu and skipped out on her contract.

From Beijing she'd flown north.

Over Russia, and then out over the sea. And eventually, the large jet began to descend, toward the gray ocean and occasional plates of stubborn pack ice.

Anika remembered when she saw Thule: a ragged

bowl of, according to the chatty pilot, the last thirty thousand square miles of floating ice in the world.

A city clung to the remains of the polar ice cap. Initially a sargasso of decommissioned floating drill rigs, tankers, and supercarriers, the metal infection had spread out across the ice when retired ice island experts began blowing snow out on the cap to thicken it, inserting metal poles to help further cool the ice, and moving out onto it.

Thule was initially an over-polar trade port. And then it became a town. And then a city. All in thirty years.

Out in the international waters, peopled with immigrants from all over the entire world, it had somehow, despite everyone's best efforts, turned itself into a country. A petri dish of a country, unrecognized by the UN, and yet, like Somaliland, issuing its own currency, electing its own officials, and carrying on its own trade.

Thule was exactly the sort of place you ran to when you were in trouble.

It was also where Anika realized she'd packed wrong for the Arctic. Global warming or not, it still didn't mean the North Pole was anything even vaguely tropical. She'd purchased her first winter coat at Thule's airport.

Anika turned the corner to The Greenhouse, and stopped. Two policemen stood outside talking to Chernov, who stood with his arms folded.

There were three cars parked outside, meaning someone was inside. Talking to Vy.

Anika let out the deep breath she'd been holding. More shit.

She was going to turn back around the way she'd come, but someone grabbed her by the elbow. "I'm from Violet," a gravelly voice whispered cheerfully. "No, don't look over at me, keep walking, there are other eyes looking for you. We don't want to raise their attention."

Anika kept walking forward, and the man to her right fell into step with her. She felt he was somewhat shorter than her, maybe five feet six?

"I'm going to slip my hand around the small of your back, now, okay?"

"Sure." He did so, pulling her close into his hip.

"Now we're just a couple out for a walk," he said. "Stare at the police."

"What?"

"That's what people do. Slow down."

They slowed and stared at the police, who ignored them. After a moment they sped back up, and the man steered her back down the other side of the block.

Out of sight from The Greenhouse now, he stopped her by a set of steps. He was a wiry man, with crow's-feet wrinkles around his brown eyes. And from the rounded face and features, Anika'd bet he was at least part Inuit.

"I'm Jim Kusugak," he said, confirming her guess as he shook her hand briefly. "I'm an associate of Violet's. The police are all over The Greenhouse looking for you. Violet's keeping them busy."

She wanted to trust him. But then she thought about everything that had happened up to this point. "How did she know to send you out here to help me?"

Jim grinned. "Violet has friends everywhere here. She was given a few minutes notice before the police arrived. Enough time for her to call me about her . . . problem."

"Me?"

"Yes." Jim reached into a pocket in the duffel bag he had slung by his side and pulled out a very thick envelope. "Violet can't help you make it to Greenland right now. The authorities have always been willing to work with her, as most of her business is legitimate. But now they're apparently shocked—shocked—to find out about the shady sides of her businesses in Baffin. So it's time to retreat, and retrench."

Anika sighed. She was causing trouble for everyone she got involved with.

Jim handed her the envelope. "So you have a choice. This is enough cash to disappear with. Could get you to Greenland."

It was tempting. She couldn't imagine Vy wanted to see more of her after Anika'd dragged her down with her. This would avoid complications, more people hurt. "Or?"

"Meet Violet at her safe house, and plan your next step with more help."

Anika sat down on the steps. How well did she know Vy? Well enough not to assume Baffin's drug lord wasn't going to cut her throat and leave her for dead as revenge for bringing the police down on her favorite place of business?

She doubted it. Or Jim would have done that already.

No, Vy was reaching out. Offering to get even further deeply involved.

But could she do that?

It wasn't like Vy was an innocent. She was a goddamned drug lord. She might be bubbly and blond and cute, but . . .

But . . .

Vy would be a powerful person to have at Anika's side.

That was the cold calculation.

The other was that, Anika found herself looking back at The Greenhouse and thinking that she really didn't want to just run away without at least talking to Vy one last time. To at least apologize.

"I'll go to the safe house," she told Jim. "Where is it?"

Jim Kusugak held out a hand. "You won't like this," he grinned. "We have a hundred-mile kayak trip out into the Lancaster Sound ahead of us."

"Kayaking?"

"Kayaking." He pointed at the cold sea out past the harbor. Miles and miles of cold, wet nothingness.

He was right. Anika didn't like it.

# 16

Jim Kusugak dragged the two-person kayak down to a small concrete ramp hidden away behind a rickety wooden pier. A few fishing boats lay scattered around the top of the ramp.

Anika had expected an Inuit kayak when Jim explained the trip to her: something made of sealskin and bone, or wood. She'd seen a few local handmade kayaks.

This kayak was yellow plastic with red racing stripes and what looked like exhaust vents coming out of the back. She'd be just inches above the frigid water.

"Is that really going to hold the both of us?" she asked, thoughts of nuclear warheads and torture set aside as she considered the dangers of riding so close to the ocean. It was time to focus on the little steps just in front of her.

Jim tossed the duffel bag onto the ground. "There're two neoprene tuiliqs in there. You wear the red one, toss me the green one."

"A what?"

"Looks like a wet suit and a kilt made out of rubber. Put it on. Put your shopping in the duffel when you're done."

Inside the duffel were two pieces of clothing just as he'd described. Sort of like kayak survival suits. He pulled the green one on over his clothes, adjusting the cap around his face, and Anika struggled into the red one.

Jim walked over and inspected it. It was very much a wet suit that started as a hood and then ran down into a long-sleeved shirt. But once down to the waist, the shirt flared out into a skirt with a tough zipper that ran around it, along with a Velcro overlap.

"Looks good." He pointed at the kayak. "Hop in the front."

Anika clambered in. There was a comfortable seat in the front hole. Except for a tiny piece of the bow, the kayak was mostly on the concrete.

Jim grabbed the skirt of the tuiliq and zipped it onto a matching zipper running around the seat, sealing her into the front section of the kayak. Then he fastened the Velcro lip on as well. She was a part of the kayak, and waterproofed.

It was an oddly intimate melding of person and tool, she thought, turning around to test how much movement she had.

"I've never been kayaking," she said. "Isn't there a boat or something we could use for this?"

Jim shoved the kayak halfway into the water, causing her to flail a bit. "No one's going to stop a pair of sport kayakers from leaving the harbor." He tossed the duffel bag into the space between them inside the kayak and hopped into his seat.

"Where are we going?"

He looked around. "Out to sea. To meet a friend."

She wiggled, making the whole kayak roll back and forth with her. "And what if we roll over?"

"It's a sea kayak, it's very stable." Jim zipped himself in, then used the paddle strapped to the top of the kayak to shove it off the ground. "Just relax. Tourists usually pay good money for this sort of thing. Although for them I use a more traditional-styled kayak."

"I was surprised by all the modern plastic, too," she admitted. "I guess it is like when people ask me if I had lions in my backyard growing up in Nigeria. Or worse, wore grass skirts."

She heard a laugh from behind her. "Where did you go to see lions, then?"

"The zoo. Just like everyone else." Then she amended that. "Well, I flew a bush plane on a circle-around tour of one of Kenya's wildlife parks for a few months once, but I hated dealing with all the tourists. And the planes were not well maintained. I crashed in a cheetah preserve."

"Shit. Cheetahs? How did you get out of that?"

"I forced everyone to stay in the plane and I called a helicopter. One man from Brussels panicked—he ran away."

"I can only imagine what happened to him."

"Park rangers picked him up, half crazy from dehydration, that night. After that, anyone visiting the park had to pay to carry a GPS beacon to make search and rescue easier."

Jim picked up the one paddle and began moving them out past the pier with strong, smooth strokes. The kayak gained speed, the bow tapping and slicing through the small waves.

Someone passed by in a long aluminum boat with a loud engine on the back. They waved, and she could feel Jim pause and raise the paddle to wave back.

"It took me a month to make the traditional kayak," Jim said, as the paddles bit back into the water along with a steady side to side motion as he leaned into the movement. "I don't go out very far with it, stay close to shore. Not very sure about my workmanship. I mean, yes, I guess my ancestors made them for many generations. My dad died young and my mother wasn't involved in stuff like that. I had to look up instructions and order the bone ribs from a specialty shop to make the 'authentic' kayak. This one I initially purchased for the Kulusuk Race. It's more handmade than the skin one: I used computer-aided modeling to design it, and sent that off to a fabbing factory that extruded the whole thing for me."

"What's the Kulusuk Race?"

"In Aberdeen, Scotland, there's an old kayak on display in a museum along with the hunting tools and iquilik made from skins that were taken from an Inuit kayaker. He was found in the North Sea in the sixteen-hundreds, and taken back to Aberdeen, but died shortly after."

"That sounds like a lonely death."

"So a handful of Inuit kayakers decided to set up a modern race in memory of their distant, lonely ancestor who died in Aberdeen. They started a sea canoe race from Kulusuk, Greenland, to Scotland.

Nine hundred miles by kayak. Extreme sports. Diehard kayakers come from all over the world."

Anika looked around at the water. Jim had told the truth. The large kayak felt solid underneath them, even with the slight rocking from his paddling. "You actually paddled all the way to Scotland?"

Jim snorted. "I got hit by a squall just after leaving Reykjavik. They fished me out of the water in one of the chase boats and treated me and five others for hypothermia. We spent the rest of the race drinking broth and watching from the decks."

"And that was in this kayak?" She couldn't imagine heading off into the deep ocean in this thing.

"Yes, but I'm working on plans for a bigger kayak for this year's Kulusuk Race. This one is disqualified, now: I've made some modifications."

"What modifications?"

"I'll show you once we're out of sight of Arctic Bay," Jim said, jutting his chin at one of the patrol boats off in the distance. "And well clear of the local water police."

He paddled them on. It was a good mile and a half before they rounded the rock and Arctic Bay disappeared.

Then Jim snapped the paddle back onto the kayak's small deck, and reached around behind him. Anika twisted around just in time to see him yank on a cord, and the suddenly alien, and loud, roar of a two-stroke engine filled the air.

The plastic of the kayak thrummed.

"I ripped an old Sea-Doo's water jet engine out, drilled some holes, and installed it on the kayak," Jim explained, shouting.

The kayak leapt forward up onto the plane of the ocean's surface, skimming over it. Jim had his paddles back in hand, tapping the water to keep the kayak upright, or occasionally leaning and carving through the water in one direction or another.

Baffin Island's northeastern tip was a thick horn that came off the island's main section and thrust upward in a slow curve. Arctic Bay was deep inside the long inlet created by the space between the horn and the mainland.

As they skimmed northward, the waves grew. Jim slowed down, as the bow of the kayak kept diving into the water. Anika would get, disconcertingly, slammed into the ocean as they descended the back of a passing swell. Water would rise to her armpits, flowing around the tuiliq, and then the kayak would pop out.

Now that he slowed, they motored up and down the swells, the engine in the back of the kayak chuffing quietly along.

Up in the sky, the long streaming fingers of the green, shifting into blue, Northern Lights, reached down toward the horizon, then dissolved into curtains of slowly dancing light.

Closer to the land on the other side of the inlet, the eastern side of Baffin's horn, the swells faded away again. But Jim didn't speed them back up.

Anika spotted why. A small catamaran floated at anchor, tucked in behind a rocky peninsula that calmed the water even further.

There were satellite dishes off the back, and solar panels unfurled from stands, like giant, silver sunflowers. SPITFIRE was printed across the left hull in black letters.

"The boat belongs to a man named Prudence Jones," Jim explained. "He's an intelligence operative who works in the area."

Anika spun around, twisting the tuiliq with her, to look at Jim. Was this another trap? "A spy? You're handing me over to a spy? How is that helpful?"

Jim smiled. "The reason Violet sent you out here is that Jones can get you safely to her retreat. And, because Jones keeps his ear to the ground, he's someone you should meet in your situation."

Anika sighed and looked back at the boat. "I guess."

"Listen," Jim said, his voice suddenly steely. "Violet is a good person. A lot of people, they freeze First Nations people out of the jobs, forget them, or just think of them as people who sell interesting art and talk about their history. Not Violet. I like her, so do a lot of other people here on Baffin. She's putting a lot on the line because she likes you, and we don't want to see her burned because of it."

"I *know* she's good." Anika turned back around. "I should have taken the cash."

Jim shook his head. "Jones is one of Violet's most important working relationships. I'm just asking you to be . . . careful. She's already lost The Greenhouse for now. For what it's worth, I think, having heard what Chernov told me about your problems, that you should meet Jones."

"Okay. But who does Jones work for?" Anika asked.

Jim smiled and cut the engine off, and they coasted up to the leftmost scooped-back pontoon of the catamaran.

"Jones!" Jim shouted as they bumped up against the fiberglass stairs. He unzipped his skirt from the kayak. "Jones!"

A tall black man with dreadlocks opened the sliding door of the cabin and stepped out into the cockpit to look down at them. He smiled. "Jim *fucking* Kusugak," he shouted. "Is good to see you, man."

"Violet left you a message?" Jim said.

Prudence Jones walked over to the back of the pontoon and held out a hand to Anika. "Anika Duncan, right?"

Prudence Jones, thought Anika as she unzipped herself out of the tuiliq, had to have come from the Caribbean somewhere. The accent was . . . well, not quite Jamaican as she thought Jamaican should sound. It sounded very much like some of the English Nigerian patois she'd heard on the streets in Lagos.

Prudence had a very light accent, though. He'd been away, and far from home, for a long time, she guessed. "Yes," she said, and held up a hand.

"Call me Roo," the tall spy said as he grabbed the offered hand and yanked her right up on out of the kayak onto the steps. "Got some iced beer in the fridge, Jim. You coming aboard?"

"No," Jim said. He pulled her backpack out and threw it up onto the cockpit deck, then zipped a cover over the exposed hole Anika had sat in. He started paddling backward. "I have to go and post bail for Violet and set up the escape trip."

Roo sucked his teeth, making a frustrated sound. One familiar enough to Anika that she felt like Roo was a distant cousin she was visiting.

Then what Jim said sunk in. "You didn't tell me she was in jail!"

Jim nodded. "They were going to be taking her in, they said. Best to keep you in the dark and get you out of Arctic Bay. Don't worry. I'll have her out by the morning."

He fired up the engine, and the kayak surged into motion. Minutes later it was a distant dot.

"So you're a spy?" Anika said.

"And you a fugitive, yeah . . ." Roo pointed at the cabin's door. "Beer?"

The cabin, which sat straddling the large pontoons, was spacious. A U-shaped settee and polished wood table dominated the area as they stepped down a few stairs and went in. Varnished floors sparkled, and the large oval windows let in lots of light.

Roo stepped down a small set of stairs into the right-hand hull, his head now just above the main cabin's floor. There was a small kitchen laid out along the side of the right hull: three-burner stove, a freezer, and a small fridge. Anika leaned over a wooden rail to see more shelves on her side: spice racks, dishes, and boxes of pasta cluttered them.

She was able to look down toward the back of the right hand hull, and saw a small office with four screens mounted on swinging arms. To the front was a bathroom.

Roo handed her a bottle of Red Stripe. "It's a cliché," he said. "But also a taste of home."

He showed her where she'd be sleeping. The left hull, to the rear, had a twin-sized bunk in the very back. The bathroom was to the very front, and in between was more storage: shelves full of dried goods, cans, a locker of heavy weather gear.

Back up in the main cabin, Anika frowned. "Where do you sleep?" she asked.

Roo pointed to the wall the settee backed up against. "I have a very comfortable room up in there. The door opens on the office you was peeking at by the galley."

"Oh."

"And, after this beer, we need to get moving."

"Where are we going?"

"Pleasure Island. You been?"

"No. I've heard of it. That's where Vy's hideout is? That's eight hundred miles of sailing."

Roo grinned. "The cockpit's enclosed, so you be helping keep watch. But I don't want you on deck. Don't want you washed over, or for anyone to see you."

"Why the hurry?" She swigged the rest of the Red Stripe, and he took the empty bottle.

"This UNPG cutter that lurks around Somerset Island. Trying to avoid a boarding." He waved a hand.

"And if we get boarded?" Anika asked.

Roo's smiled wavered. "Then we have to get creative, yeah?"

# 17

The anchor took all of a few minutes to haul up by hand. Roo leaned over the front of the boat, grunting, his back flexing and arms rippling as he pulled the rope up, hand over hand. His tightly wound dreadlocks swayed about as he moved.

For a few minutes, the *Spitfire* drifted aimlessly without the anchor, but then Roo bounded back to the cockpit and yanked on ropes.

Another minute of vigorous winching later the catamaran's two sails were filled with wind. They'd both been wrapped up on thin spindles, and had easily deployed.

The boat now slipped through the water with Roo at the helm.

Around the horn of Baffin Island the wind kicked up and the catamaran sped up, climbing the swells and sliding down them with her twin hulls cutting cleanly and quickly through the water.

From the cockpit Anika could just see over the top

of the cabin. Occasionally they'd slap a wave roughly enough that a massive blast of ocean spray would slap the cockpit windows.

"Nice and dry up in here," Roo declared. "And *Spitfire* makes good time."

He stood in front of a large, white leather command chair that let him look out over the catamaran. An array of small LCD screens were bolted onto the fiberglass surfaces around him, just underneath the plane of various winches on the cabin top. Cold air, and some water, leaked through holes that led sheets through.

After an hour, her brief education in sailing began.

The large wheel: that controlled the rudder, of course. Although, in this case, the catamaran had two rudders, one on each pontoon. Either way, turn the wheel and the *Spitfire* turned.

There was also an autopilot for the catamaran that could take control of the wheel for her. Roo showed her how to set it. It would keep them pointed in the right direction using the compass, GPS, and some other internal sensors.

Anika had the radar figured out in a few seconds.

One winch controlled how far out the boom went for the main sail, the one over her head. She could see that one by looking up through the plexiglas skylights over her head.

The jib—that was the triangular sail up at the very front—was controlled by the winch just ahead of the main's winch. Both of the sails could be reeled in and out by other winches, and there was also one that caused the jib to roll itself up.

There was a lot to a boat she knew she didn't understand. Maintenance. How wind and sails worked. But looking at the *Spitfire*'s setup, she could see how Roo sailed it around the Arctic by himself.

"You got the radar," he said, but showed it to her again just to make sure. "And here you have the collision avoidance alarms. That's how I single-hand the long hauls. Catch my sleep right on this floor."

During one jarring thump coming down off a wave, she winced and Roo noticed it. "You all right?"

"Someone attacked me, and now my ribs are bruised. A medical student looked me over and said I need rest and painkillers. Vy gave me some oxycodone."

He studied her face for a moment, and then her neck, and nodded. "I can help with that."

He was gone for a moment, leaving her alone with the waves that rose high enough to block the horizon out, but then gently lifted *Spitfire* up on their backs, before they let her down again.

When he came back, she took the pills and the bottle of water offered, then turned the chair back over to him.

"I've seen the weather from up in the sky," she said. "What's it like down here?"

"You get a taste soon."

The oxy rolled over her and wrapped her up in a cocoon of relief. "What do you do, exactly, Roo? As a spy? And who do you work for?"

And why did Vy think it was a good idea to pair us up, she wondered.

"Is mostly deskwork, you know?" Roo said. "No

James Bond types running around these days. Agencies: they like their gadgets, their networks."

But she looked at the wiry musculature that had yanked up the fifty-or-so-pound anchor so easily by hand. Roo wasn't just a desk jockey.

"And a desk worker. What does he do, out here in the sea?"

Roo scratched his nose. "This Coast Guard cutter we trying to avoid. Back in the old days, we would skulk around trying to move past it. Today, I have a peer-to-peer system, right? I hire a bunch of people online to keep an eye on the cutter. They ain't doing nothing illegal. Most of the time, no one realizes anything is strange, because if you clever, maybe you start a site for fans of the Coast Guard, and wherever they see a cutter, they report which one and where it is. Whether it's cutters, or a crowd of people online all being given pieces of a satellite photo and being asked to look for a certain shape that's really a piece of some army we're looking for, I'm pulling the strings from back here."

"So where is it?"

"The Coast Guard cutter?" He pulled a satphone out of his front jeans pocket and thumbed around on its screen a bit. "According to the Coast Guard cutter fan club, she's moving south down the western side of Somerset Island. Three hours ago."

He smiled at her. Terrorists had been buying satellite footage for years to help build pictures of their targets, he said as they continued to sail farther from Baffin. While police arrested vacationing tourists for taking shots of national monuments, bombers used Google Earth and online photo-sharing sites.

So now small nation states, like those in the Caribbean that couldn't afford full intelligence agencies, hired freelancers and used the tools on the ground.

"You don't mind not having a full-time job, then?"

"Look, working in an office somewhere, unless your job really requires you to interface with that environment for a customer, like a waiter, or a factory worker, then why should you remain in a single place? It's a fool's job to stay put if you don't have to, right? Is more efficient to hire out, and for all the Caribbean islands to pool their agents. We island nations trying to guide a course through the tempest of the world without getting run over by the big ones."

They hit a point in the conversation where Anika realized she would have to reciprocate, to give something of herself up to Roo. But she didn't feel like it.

After everything she'd been through, she felt she deserved to be selfish for a bit. She had days ahead to try to decide who Roo really was, and what she might reveal to him.

She looked around. "This is a beautiful boat. I've never been on one that someone lives aboard."

"I won it."

"Like, in a bet?"

"A lawsuit. Purchased it with my share. Anegada versus the United States of America, Europe, China, Japan, and South Korea et al."

"Who was Anegada?"

"What, not who. It used to be home," Roo said, looking out at the sea. "Before the sea levels rose. We sued, and I decided I'd put my share of the settlement into something that would float."

And like that, the conversation died.

In a way, Anika was relieved.

She took a shower. An acrobatic procedure. At first she'd been a bit alarmed at the small, claustrophobic fiberglass confines of the shower. But now, with the entire hull pitching about, she was relieved she could jam a foot up against a wall, her back against the other side, and keep herself locked in place.

It was not a relaxing, luxurious shower, but she enjoyed the feeling of accomplishment and the mild sense of routine it gave her.

If the weather got any rougher, she decided it would be better just to wipe herself down quick rather than risk another shower.

She crawled into the bed. Within minutes she found herself dozing off. This was really no worse than sleeping through turbulence, she thought.

"Anika!" Roo banged on the cabin door, and she sat up.

"Yes?"

"Your watch," Roo said. "You been asleep for half the day, and I need to turn in a bit. Time for you to stand watch."

She stared at him, shaking her head and trying to get up to speed. "You *really* want me to sail your ship?"

"We at sea for a week, yes, I need you to sail."

"I don't know the first thing . . ."

He cut her off. "Just stand there, keep an eye on the radar. Look around. See any ships: wake me up quick. Look, it's not as hard as flying a blimp, right?"

So he knew who she was, she thought. Then she nodded. "Airship. Not a blimp. But wake you up. Okay."

He escorted her up to the enclosed cockpit, and she hugged herself as the cold wind blew in through the eyeholes the sheets ran through.

"Four hours," Roo said.

"And what about that Coast Guard cutter?"

"An hour ago it was still headed south." Roo left, sliding the salon door behind him.

And then it was just her alone with her thoughts and the open sea again. The tap of saltwater spray against the cockpit windows.

It was a rhythm she felt comfortable with. Watches in the air, or watches on a deck, the life remained the same: four-hour intervals, broken down between leisure, watch, and sleep.

She chose sleep for the first two days, aided by more oxycodone.

In the cockpit, she played with the sails a bit. Nothing drastic, just trying to understand how they worked. She understood the theory. They were like plane wings. Another curved surface that wind rushed past, and where the negative pressure was created, it pulled the ship forward.

Unless you were going downwind, she knew. Then you were just letting the wind push you.

On her morning watch of the second day, she'd changed course to dodge a large container ship on the horizon. Why bother Roo? she reasoned.

But as the ship grew larger, bearing toward the

*Spitfire*'s right-hand side (starboard, Roo had explained), a shrieking alarm had gone off, and Roo had come running up.

He wore shorts and nothing else, his eyes wide. He looked at the container ship. "Fucking Christ, fucking hell."

"I changed course. We're fine," she said.

For a moment he squinted at the ship, then relaxed and nodded. "If it gets close, the proximity alarm goes." He reached over to the radar and hit a button, and the alarm cut off.

"I'm sorry." She was looking at his torso. Three bullet wounds on his shoulder, one in his stomach. All scar tissue now.

Not a desk jockey.

He sat down and they watched the freighter pass together. And now Anika found her pulse racing. Seeing the large steel hull glide past made her think of the *Kosatka* ripping past her in the water, shoving the debris aside.

"Tack," he ordered.

"What?"

She'd started to understand the sails, that tightening them in closer would let her point farther into the wind, but now he showed her a great deal more about how to handle the boat, teaching her until he was satisfied. "Keep further away next time."

"I could shut off the alarm."

"It's tied to my thumbprint, and no, this is my home. Still rather wake up and see a close one myself. But yeah, you seem to be getting the hang of things." He rubbed his eyes. "You hungry?"

"Yes."

. . .

The winds died and the ocean turned to glass. They ate on the front of the boat, letting the autopilot guide them along. "There are no satellites overhead, or airships, for a while," Roo told her. "You should come out on deck and enjoy the weather!"

The space between the two hulls, forward of the cabin, was a large piece of fabric laced onto the hulls, like a trampoline. He set down a few sandwiches on plates and tossed her a soda.

"I'm sorry I was short, earlier. Not things I like talking about. After Anegada, it was too hard for me to stay in the British Virgin Islands," he told her. "I used the leftover money and went to Britain. The BVI is a part of the empire still. Studied. And ran out of money. Didn't know what to do, until I ended up being recruited. Spent time with MI6: they needed more dark-skinned agents. Learned Arabic and ended up in North Africa. But I left."

She pointed at his shoulder. "You were shot."

"That's another story. No, I just . . . left once I could. Everything we were doing, the great game. I couldn't play. The small countries, they were pawns in a greater battle. Multinational corporations, media empires, larger nations, all fighting their proxy battles, eating through these places. I just wanted to come home and protect it."

"So you're in the Arctic."

"Of late," Roo grinned. "See, until me and a number of cohorts came in, the Caribbean nations weren't thinking expansion. They would beg a European or a U.S. factory to open a branch down there. Beg a hotel to develop, so more tourists could be housed.

But that money, the tourist brings, just leaves and goes back to the mother hotel corporation. That factory's profits, they don't stay."

He took a sip of water. "When the Arctic began to melt and open, we persuaded some people in government to think a little . . . sideways. Oil corporation needs a nation to permit drilling somewhere in the Arctic? Well, it's international waters. Come apply for a permit in sunny Antigua, and we'll let you set up a satellite offshore company that feeds the profits where you need it. For a percent. So now we get a taste of the north while giving a flag of convenience."

"Cynical."

"Always," Roo said, very seriously.

"Thanks for letting me, and teaching me, to pilot," she said. "I know, with the automatic gear, all you really need is for me to be a better collision alarm than the automatic one."

"It's good to have something to do, to focus on, simple, when you recovering off a shock."

Anika nodded. "You know about the airship."

"Violet didn't tell me much, other than your name. That's enough. I wouldn't be a good intelligence man if I didn't do at least a quick search. But the deeper I dig, the stranger your problem becomes."

Now Anika sat up. "What do you mean?"

"You're a UNPG pilot. Shot out of the sky. Survive. The men who shot you were captured by the U.S. Navy. Now you're on the run, Vy's helping you. The heat is pushing hard on her. More interesting to me: the men who tried to kill you have disappeared."

"What?"

"Poof. Like they never existed." He threw the remains of his meal over the side. "So, if you willing, I can draw up a nondisclosure agreement regarding anything you can tell me. Because at this point, anything I can figure out about what is happening around you might be the sort of thing that could, depending on what you know and are willing to talk about, let me turn a tidy profit in terms of anticipating certain people's movements and actions. But even more important, I might be able to help you by connecting the dots, right? That's why Violet put us together. I know a lot about what's happening around here."

Anika nodded. "Let me think about it."

"Of course. But don't take too long."

He leaned back and looked up at the sky. "Time to be getting back inside."

The collision alarm snapped Anika out of a groggy sleep in her cabin a day later. Fear hammered through her and cleared her head.

She grabbed her jacket, gloves, and shoes and dressed in seconds as she also hopped out the door and toward the salon. "Pack your shit up quick," Roo yelled through the door at her. "And keep low. Don't come up."

"What is it?"

"Coast Guard. And this ain't the ship from Somerset I was tracking."

Anika got back to her room and stuffed everything in there into her backpack. She looked the room over twice to make sure she wasn't forgetting anything.

Roo jumped down. "Got it? Come on." He led her up the hull, through the bathroom at the tip of the bow. At the back of the small toilet, he banged on the wall.

It opened slightly, and he pulled the panel open.

Slimy, wet organic ocean smell spilled out. "What's that?"

"It's the anchor locker." He pushed her toward it. "Come on, we don't have much time."

She crawled up on the toilet and into the crawl space. The stench of barnacles and seaweed caused her to gag a bit, but she held it.

Wet seaweed clinging to the anchor line squelched as she pushed herself into the mass of soaked rope that had been festering in the locker since Roo had pulled it up. She had to curl up into a tiny ball to fit, and could barely breathe. And already it felt like the fiberglass walls were pushing at her sides, closing in on her.

Roo gave her a gray blanket. "Put this over yourself, and then pull those ropes over your head, get them all piled up on top of you good, in case they look in from on top," Roo pointed up. There was a hatch right there that led to the deck.

"Won't that be the first place they look?" Anika asked.

"Sure," he said cheerily. "As well as the bilges, engine room, and so on. We just hope they won't be expecting this side panel by the toilet and don't poke around too much. The obvious place is a better chance. Let the dirty anchor rope do the work, it's why I don't clean them."

"Has it worked before?" Anika asked, burrowing into the slime and rope, pulling it over herself and the blanket.

"I don't smuggle people, I was doing a favor for a friend, see? I'd have put you in the water tank with scuba gear, or something clever if this was something I did regularly. I'm improvising, okay?"

He clicked the panel shut, leaving her shoved against the rope, a piece of anchor jammed against her cheek, and the horrible stench. Just her, alone in the dark. A small cramp began to form in her bunched-up legs, and she had to force herself to take slow, deep, calming breaths that then gagged her with the smell of dead sea life that was all around her.

A few minutes later, the *Spitfire* changed direction, facing the waves and slowing.

Then the loud gurgle of engines approached, and loud voices shouted commands, and then finally, boots hit the deck and spread out.

They were being searched.

Anika tensed as footsteps passed nearby. She could hear them on deck, voices muffled by the distance and anchor gear lying on top of her. The hatch above her opened, and she tensed. Small pieces of light pierced the few spots she'd failed to cover with the ropes, but the blanket did the job. Someone kicked around with a foot, then evidently satisfied, shut the hatch, plunging her back into the dark.

Anika allowed herself to move slightly, take a deeper breath. This might work.

Eventually the voices moved inside the boat. The bathroom was searched, and then to her dismay, a surprisingly gentle voice asked, "So that would be that anchor locker, just through there, wouldn't it?"

Roo replied quietly, "Yes. But . . ."

A loud smack cut him off as someone hit the panel.

It very quietly, but certainly audibly, clicked open. There was no way the gray blanket and ropes were hiding her from the side Roo had stuffed her in.

Anika turned her head to face a serious-looking man holding a small submachine gun up at shoulder height. "Please step slowly down, ma'am, and come toward me with your hands up. Leave that bag there."

Anika nodded, and almost grateful to be out of the stench, stepped onto the bathroom floor.

Roo looked at her apologetically.

# 18

Three armed crewmen led her down the scoop of the port hull into a bright red semirigid inflatable dinghy half the length of the *Spitfire*.

Without ever meeting her eyes, they asked her to turn around, and one of the men zip-tied her hands behind her back. Roo jumped down a second or two later, was restrained, and then they were taken over to the patrol ship.

It was a hundred-and-forty-foot-long Damen Stan hull. She recognized the old compressed, mid-hulled bridge in the center and low profile. The UNPG had a few of these in the Northwest Passage as well.

There was a ramp that led down to the water smack in the middle of the ship's transom. The solid slab of metal that usually dropped down to fill in the stern's gap was currently raised in the air; it looked like a giant garage door on the back of the ship. They shot up the flooded boat ramp in their dinghy, were attached to a winch to get pulled the rest of the way up onto the deck, and then the transom of the patrol ship slid back down into place.

A helicopter arrived and swooped around to circle the patrol boat as two crewmen took Anika forward and down a set of steep stairs. She was locked into what was clearly a conference room, but everything had been pulled out so that it was now just a giant holding cell. There was room for ten or so people, and there were three bunks along the back end.

She was tired, reeking of dead barnacles and seaweed from the anchor rope, and terrified.

The fact that the clean-cut, uniformed Coast Guard who zip-tied her had refused to look directly at her—that burrowed down into her subconscious. She'd once flown a charter from the edge of a DESERTEC station in the Sahara to the Democratic Republic of Congo with four prisoners. They'd been zip-tied, dark sacks over their heads. Four grim, Nigerian soldiers working for the Intelligence Department had sat with guns on their laps, guarding them. She'd had to agree to turn off her GPS and let them guide her in with small pocket systems.

She'd been told not to look at the prisoners. After landing in a strip over the border and dropping them off at the squat, recently built buildings at the edge of the airstrip, she'd been told, "This didn't happen, no one was here."

A guard flew back with her to make sure she didn't turn on any location systems.

In the DRC, anything that happened to those prisoners was legal. In a more prosperous, careful Nigeria, the middle class wouldn't put up with such things as torture. But in the DRC, European and Nigerian and U.S. and Canadian forces could yank terrorists into a world that was all but invisible.

Current world powers like Brazil, India, and Nigeria were once on the blunt end of that stick, indignant as Western European and American forces hopped in and out of their borders like they didn't exist to find people they wanted. But now those same countries had their own sophisticated intelligence forces carry on much the same missions in the dark. The price of growing national power, some said.

Outside, she could distantly hear the helicopter land, and the rotors spin slowly down.

The door creaked open, and a thin, older white man who looked like he should be well past retirement walked in. She noticed the fluid walk, the hard strength underneath the soft, wrinkled skin. The almost Zen-like eyes.

As the door shut, and locked, behind him, he held out a hand. "Ms. Anika Duncan, correct?"

He wore an expensive suit, already wet in places and crusted with some salt. His thinning hair was whipped loose and crazy by rotor wash.

Anika twisted to show him her bound hands and so that she could shake his. "Yes."

"I'm Gabriel."

"No last name?"

"Not for you."

The sound of the ship's .50-caliber deck gun shook the deck. Anika looked up instinctively. "What's going on?"

"I think they're sinking the catamaran before we move on."

"That's his whole life," she said. "Couldn't they have just assigned a few crew to pilot it back?"

Gabriel carried a small suitcase. He set it on one of the bunks and sat down himself. He waved a hand at one of the others, expecting Anika to sit.

But she remained standing. It felt good to tower over him. He waved at her to turn around. He pulled out a pair of snips and cut her hands free as he talked. "Prudence Jones is a spy for hire, Ms. Duncan. He is not a patriot, nor a recognized agent of any country. He is, at best, a mercenary, and a cheap one at that. Who knows what he's involved in? He knows the consequences of his sorts of actions."

"So for helping me, you sink his home?" She rubbed her hands. It felt good to move her arms around in front of her.

"We do not show him the same courtesy as we would another agent, no. It's not good to trust someone who doesn't belong anywhere. They are adrift, without borders, without moral compass." He snapped open his briefcase. "A man is nothing without a country."

Anika realized she'd been holding her breath. There were, thankfully, no knives or medieval cutting instruments inside the case. Because that was what she had been expecting.

There was what looked like a shower cap, with wires leading from it. There were leads and a small readout. It all connected to the case, which had a screen built into the inside of the open top.

Gabriel pointed for her to sit. This time, she could tell it was not a request. People would be called in if she didn't.

He handed her the cap, and she pulled it on over her hair as best she could. He placed electrodes on her wrists, ankles, and then he pointed at spots on her chest and ribs.

Anika reached under her shirt to place them, and after checking the readouts on the screen, he nodded, satisfied.

"Lie detector?" she asked.

He didn't answer. He turned from the screen to look directly at her. "If you knew a nuclear bomb was about to explode somewhere soon, killing innocent people, do you think it would be justifiable to torture someone you knew had the information that could stop it from happening?"

She couldn't help it: fear crawled across her skin and her mouth dried. Gabriel looked intense, like a snake about to strike her. She'd never thought about the idea of Canadian special agents much, but here it was. They were the same, she guessed. Dangerous men, all convinced they were playing the world's most dangerous game.

And maybe they were.

All of them, though, were sincere, possessed, and willing to do whatever it would take to get what they thought they needed, she presumed.

Including flying her out of country to do "what needed to be done."

"You would have to know for sure, that the person you had *was* someone who knew that," she finally said. "Or you would do something horrible to someone innocent."

"Or the person could be innocent and give you the wrong information out of a desire to please, fear, or to mislead or confuse the situation. Yes." Gabriel looked back at his screen for a moment. "I started out as an observer to the U.S. military during the height of their activities in the Middle East. Historically, see, the trick is not using anything that will leave a physical mark. These turn public opinion against the torturers. It can also be used as a recruiting tool against your cause, whatever that may be. The Americans lost tremendous public credibility at the turn of the century, just as the Soviets did in the middle of the last century."

Anika glanced at the electrodes, suddenly nervous.

Gabriel wasn't paying attention. "That is why the Americans liked sleep deprivation, or waterboarding, so much. No marks. But even then, the idea that torturing a person and leaving them apparently whole is a viable method comes from a naïve belief that the watchers aren't being watched. One leak, one person with misgivings, or one person with a social media account and no common sense, and suddenly there is video of the process. And the laity can suddenly model what is happening in their own minds. They can understand that the human body is not designed to be forced into one position for interminable hours. And then, that has the same damage as a physical mark. So where does that leave us, Ms. Duncan?"

He was staring right at her. She had this vague sense of sadness behind his eyes. Like he was looking forward to retirement, because the world had changed, and his job didn't make sense anymore. "I don't know, Gabriel."

He sighed. "It leaves us considering that one of the best forms of interrogation is Stockholm syndrome, wherein a captive transfers their allegiance to their captors. Counterintuitively, and historically, friendliness has gotten more actionable information than torture."

At that, Anika finally relaxed a bit.

"But the problem is, Ms. Duncan, our situation doesn't leave us much *time*." Now Anika was back to drowning in the room's odd tension as she tried to figure this man out. He was playing with her, she thought, even though his voice sounded conversational and tired, with a tinge of sadness. "Lives hang in the balance now, and time is short. So, are you friendly?"

She wet her lips. "I'm friendly. I have nothing to hide. I haven't *done* anything."

Gabriel relaxed and smiled. "Well," he said. "That's good. And fortunately for you, lie detection technology has come a long way since I was wet behind the ears. That thing on your head images your brain, it maps how long you hesitate, and studies whether you're accessing real memories, or creating new ones."

"You're looking into my mind." It somehow didn't feel any less invasive that it was a cap. She still imagined tendrils reaching into her mind, stealing her thoughts.

"If you create new memories," the interrogator continued. "If you're using the areas of your mind associated with your imagination, we can determine that you might well be lying."

"And does it work?" Anika asked. "Or is it like those others? Where it works better than half the time, but a lot of people still get false results? Enough to ruin many lives?"

Gabriel smiled. "It works well enough, Ms. Duncan. So what are you willing to tell me about why you're on a boat with a spy-for-hire who's known to work for a drug lord?"

Anika looked at the screen on the inside of the briefcase, then at Gabriel. "Someone on a ship called the *Kosatka* shot my airship out of the sky with an RPG after a radiation alarm triggered and we moved in for a closer look. I've been trying to figure out why, and what they were hiding."

Gabriel hardly looked at her for the detailed question and answer session. He kept his attention on the screen, which he had positioned so that Anika could follow it and realize that he had been honest about its capabilities to ferret out the truth. That was part of his interrogation process.

The gadget was, she decided, accurate enough. Occasionally Gabriel paused the conversation after prompts, tied to colors and alerts mapped over an eerily detailed representation of her actual brain, flashed yellow or red. These were areas of her brain that involved imagination.

At that point, Gabriel would back the conversation up, and narrow in to yes-or-no questions, creating a flowchart of responses that allowed him to look at her neural reactions to determine if she was lying.

Knowing what was in her own mind, Anika realized that this was happening as she tried to ascribe motives, or reasons to what was happening.

She stuck to just the facts after that. The attack. The explosion. Her killer. Deciding to run away.

The questions stopped; eventually it was just Gabriel sitting, waiting for her to wrap up her story.

And then Anika had nothing left.

Gabriel, after a half-minute détente, folded his hands together. "The man who tried to kill you wasn't a government agent, but that's how these things work nowadays. He was a contractor from Florida. Hard to trace back who paid him, though we have some very good forensic accountants working on it."

"So you don't know who the killer was. You don't seem to know what the radiation was, but the UNPG agents I talked to think it's a nuclear bomb. So what *do* you know?"

"This isn't a two-way street, Ms. Duncan. Consider yourself lucky. We know you're honest to a fault. I spoke to Anton, one of your UNPG agents. He worked very hard to convince me you're a straight arrow caught up in a messy situation. Why don't we leave this all at that? Walk away. Consider yourself lucky to be alive."

Anika ripped the electrodes off and threw the hair cap at him. "Fuck you and fuck your 'lucky,' " she told him icily. "Tom was a good man, and he leaves his family alone and scared. Violet lost her business, and you know she was mostly legal. Roo—his boat, and equipment. Those MPs who searched my home lost their *lives*. There is no going back for me. Back to what? Being a pilot for the UNPG? That's not on the table. This is lucky?"

Gabriel took the electrodes and popped them off the wires and put them in a small bag. The cap he carefully dusted off and put inside the briefcase. "No one owes you anything," he said as he did this. "Innocent bystanders die all the time. In the great scheme of history, empires fall, and you're a statistic sitting next to the debris. You'll tell your children about how you lived through this pivotal event one day."

He snapped the case closed. Anika cocked her head and looked at him. Patronizing, decrepit, creepy little man. She stood up and blocked his way to the door.

Maybe, she thought immediately, that had been the wrong move. But she wasn't backing down now.

"That's a bad idea, Anika," he said softly.

"We're all going to die, not just the bystanders," she said. "We're all just statistics, in the long run. That is true. But in this modern world, I am not some anonymous creature, like a serf in the middle ages. I bow to no man. This is a flat world, Mr. Gabriel. One of information, and democracy, and access. I am your equal. And I am not moving."

His nostrils flared. "What is it you want?"

"Quid pro quo. There is a nuclear weapon floating around the Arctic Circle. You don't know for sure why, but what do you *suspect*?"

For a moment he stood still. Then he looked tiredly over at her. "Use your God-given imagination, Ms.

Duncan. I can think of fifteen worst-case scenarios where Canada's enemies could creatively destroy everyone's interests out here. You remember Karachi?"

"What were those globes the ship was transporting?"

And there, for a moment, she'd scored . . . something. She wasn't sure what. But he flinched. Just as hard as if she'd slapped him. His thin lips tightened, his lined face hardened. "That . . . is none of your business."

He hadn't asked any questions about them, during the interrogation, she realized.

Anika frowned. He hadn't been surprised when she'd mentioned them either.

"It's time for me to leave," Gabriel said. In the distance, she could hear the sound of the helicopter starting up.

"And what happens to *me* now?"

"You will remain out of the way." Gabriel pushed past her. "You will thank me later, when this is all over and settled."

Anika opened her mouth. It sounded like Gabriel knew far more than he was letting on, and it looked like he believed he was doing her a genuine favor.

In her experience, all the people who did harm believed they were doing it because they had to. His conviction only chilled her further.

But there was nothing she could do as he stepped out, the door clanging shut behind him.

# 19

Anika banged on the door until a young Coast Guard crewman opened it. Her guard. He had a pistol holstered at his hip, and he looked nervous. His name patch said OSTERMAN.

"What do you need?" he asked.

"Where are you taking me?" Anika asked.

"I can't say, ma'am."

She leaned against the door, and he took a step back, hand going to the holster. Anika sighed and stepped back, showing that she wasn't going to try anything stupid. "Can I have a phone, to call my lawyer?" They'd taken everything from her: extra prepaid phone, the wad of cash Vy had given her, her IDs.

Osterman looked around, as if seeking support from an officer. But there were none in the corridor outside the room. "No. You can't," he said.

"How is that legal?" Anika demanded.

Osterman looked miserable. "I can't comment, ma'am."

He took a step forward, one hand still on the holster, and raised the other to close the door again.

"I need to use the bathroom," Anika said. "Surely that isn't something you can't comment on either."

He nodded. "Okay. I'll take you."

This type of patrol ship usually had eighteen or so sailors and two officers crewing it. The ship had maybe six days of range, which meant it harbored somewhere fairly close by. The ship was based on the same Damen Stan hulls that the UNPG used for its small patrol vessels, so it wasn't too unfamiliar to Anika.

It meant she also could guess that wherever she was going, it would most likely be a day or two away.

Her personal guard walked her through the crew bunks, and several relaxing members of the crew watched curiously as she was led past them to the bathrooms at the end of the corridor.

She used some paper towels, the industrial-smelling soap in a dispenser, and water from the basin to wash the stench of the anchor rope off her as best she could. Near the end, her guard banged on the door. "What's taking so long?"

"Cleaning up," she yelled back. "I was hiding in an anchor locker for almost an hour."

She opened the door, and he looked suspiciously around and sniffed. She smelled strongly of cheap soap, but had gotten the worst of the dead ocean smell off her.

"Do you have anything to drink or eat?" she asked.

He escorted her back to the sparse room. "I'll call for something."

That something was a ham sandwich, a granola bar, and Coke. Anika sat them down on her chosen bunk and ate them as she was locked in again.

She had a day or two left before she was locked up wherever Gabriel had decided to put her, where she would be out of everyone's way.

And what did he mean by that? That he knew what was happening. And it was something big?

He didn't mean her harm, she understood that. He did feel he was doing the right thing. And yet, she was still in the dark. She didn't trust him. And then there was that nuclear device out there.

Remember Karachi? he'd asked. She'd grown up watching the before and after images of crowded Pakistani markets and streets on Lagos cable channels turned into flattened wasteland. She'd had nightmares about the stains: human shapes etched in black silhouettes on the ground. The famous photo of a woman with a veil half-melted onto her face, waiting for medical help outside a UN tent. A second century had tasted the hell of a nuclear event. Who could imagine more?

And then there was this question of vengeance that stirred her mind up every time she returned to it. She couldn't let it go. The anguish in Jenny's voice. The smack of the car against Karl's bike, the feel of a killer's muscles against hers.

What did it take for evil to prevail? Simply for good people to step aside and let it happen.

She thought of her father's stories about what Nigeria was like when he grew up. The violence between the religions, the military cracking down too hard while trying to keep order, burning cars in the streets of the small towns far from the stable urbanity of Lagos.

Even when she grew up, when that was all long past, sometimes she saw the scars when out in the countryside: the skeletons of vehicles in the undergrowth by the side of the roads, or still-abandoned houses with blackened, peeling walls.

These things had always been around, an unconscious series of tombstones marking conflicts that only existed in an academic sense for her. And yet, as her father had told her stories, they'd solidified and called out to her more and more vividly.

A brick ruin that was once a grocery store owned by a Muslim man. That empty lot: once a schoolhouse. That new bridge: built over a bombed-out old one.

Her father worshiped stability and had a love of rights, an indignation about suffering. Anika now found herself surprised to find how thoroughly he had infected her with it, despite the things she had seen once she'd left Nigeria.

All those years of manning the machine gun in the cabin of the airship, working as a corporate mercenary, and the cynicism that she lived around, had slid off her. Sure, she found herself an outsider, slow to make friends. But that hadn't made her any less outraged by what had just happened to what friends she had.

And, she realized, thinking about Commander Michel Claude, friends she might have had without realizing it.

She couldn't sit still. And suddenly thought about the kids from the *Kosatka,* who'd disappeared. Maybe Gabriel was a good liar. Maybe those kids were alive, maybe they weren't. But that wasn't going to be her. No one was going to disappear Anika.

She knew the layout of the ship, how the crews worked. She was going to get out.

If there was a nuclear device floating around out there, then she was going to help track it down and stop it.

She wasn't going to allow chaos to descend into her world and turn it upside down. Not if she could do something to stop it.

She waited until the earliest hours of the morning. There were two watches worth of crew trying to get sleep in their darkened bunks, now. The bustle of the day and clanging of boots on metal floors had faded, which meant only seven or so crew were awake and on watch.

Osterman, still stuck with guarding her and yawning, followed her past the crew quarters back to the adapted conference room. She'd been getting him used to a docile routine.

But instead of meekly going inside this time, Anika whipped around and pulled him in with her.

He didn't have time to shout because she had her belt around his throat, choking him. He instinctively grabbed for it and pulled it off, which is exactly what she'd hoped for.

She pulled his gun out of the holster and placed it against the back of his head. "Shhhh."

He froze.

She backed up and shut the door. "Now, get down on the floor, and place your hands behind your back."

He did. He looked very, very scared. But holding it together. She wanted to pat him and tell him it would be okay, that it was her that would probably end up shot.

Instead, she checked his pockets until she found what she was looking for: more zip ties.

She looped two together to tie his hands and feet behind his back and to one of the bunks. Then she used a torn piece of sheet to gag him. "Can you breathe through your nose okay?" she asked.

He nodded, looking suddenly hopeful.

"Do you know where the man is, that they captured with me? Prudence Jones?"

He nodded. She pulled the balled up strip of cloth part of the way out of his mouth.

"Upstairs in the mess," he said, voice garbled by the partial unstuffing.

Anika stuffed his mouth again. "I'm very sorry about this," she told him.

Someone knocked on the door.

She whipped around and trotted up to it, the gun in front of her at the ready. Damn it. She'd barely had time to put her plan into action and it was already falling apart.

Who was this going to be?

The door eased open, and Anika jammed her newly acquired gun against a familiar set of dreadlocks. "Roo?"

He looked at the hog-tied crew member on the floor as she yanked him inside and shut the door. "You looking to escape as well?" he asked, looking over at the tied-up crewman.

"They won't tell me where they are taking me. I don't like that."

"Yeah, I hear you. Usually when I get picked up, I can give my credentials and after a few phone calls, things get all cleared up. This time, they just handcuffed me to a bunk upstairs and put a guard on me." He held up a gun of his own. "My guard's relaxing inside a large fridge right now."

The fact that he hadn't killed his guard to escape clarified a lot about Roo in that second. Vy was right. Roo was someone she could trust.

She lowered her voice so that the tied-up guard couldn't hear them. "That rigid-hull inflatable dinghy, the big one? It's designed to be launched from the moving boat. It has a top speed of thirty knots, which is roughly the same as this ship's speed," Anika said. Nanisivik had a number of them at the UNPG station, and she'd trained on them like any other UNPG member. "Can we get somewhere safe with it? You know the area better than I do."

Roo sucked his teeth loudly and shook his head, his locks slapping his neck and shoulders. He kept his voice low as well. "Depends on how much fuel the dinghy carries. And if we can really outrun this beast once we get away. We been headed west for the last day. Add in two good days of sailing on *Spitfire*." His face quirked. He'd just lost his home, she realized. "I'll know for sure when I get a look at a GPS. But I think so. We can get somewhere north on Victoria Island, then pay for a ride to Cambridge Bay. They have a fairly busy airport; that'll give us some options for getting to Pleasure Island and meeting up with Vy, just like we'd planned. I still believe your best way to get to Thule is with Vy's help. Plus, I promised Vy I'd get you there. Don't want to make this the first time I failed to come through."

"And we can't get to Pleasure Island by dinghy?" Anika asked.

Roo shook his head. "No. Too far. Is dangerous enough out here in that thing, and if a storm kicks up who knows what happens to us. But we dead for sure even if we had enough fuel."

"Okay, Victoria Island then," Anika agreed. And from there she'd get to Thule and start hunting. "When we get on deck, I won't fire at the crew. The gun is only for show. I will not be shooting at someone who is innocent, who is trying to do their job. Understand?"

Roo nodded. "Is a running escape, yeah."

They ghosted up the stairs, then out onto the deck, guns out, tense. But they met no one. "They are all up in the pilothouse, staying warm and dry," Anika said, glancing upward in the direction of the lighted windows. Roo leaned over the side of the dinghy to look in while she kept an eye out for anyone coming out onto the deck.

"Do we have enough fuel in the dinghy to get where we need to go?" Anika asked.

Roo leaned over and shook one of the two large red plastic gas cans loosely tied down in the back of the dinghy. "They're full. Yeah. I'm willing to bet."

"Then let's do it."

"You said you've trained on a ship like this? How do we raise the transom?" Roo asked, moving back over behind her.

Anika pointed at the manual controls on the deck. "One gets in the dinghy, another opens the transom then jumps in quick."

"You ever do it?"

"No. I've been on a UNPG patrol boat, but I have never used those controls."

Roo shrugged. "I spent more time on boats, I'll go look."

Out in the rush of wind and cold, they moved quickly across the deck. Anika crawled into the large dinghy and kept low.

"Last chance to back out," Roo said.

"Do you think we're really going to a normal jail? Where we could call our lawyers? And talk to our families?"

Roo shook his head. "No, whoever waiting for us at dock, it ain't police. Trust me. They had the pull to send a ship after us and access to live satellite data to backtrack all ships from Baffin. Including my little one. That scares me."

"Then we go," Anika said with a bit more determination than she felt, glancing worriedly back up at the lit-up pilothouse.

"Then we go," Roo said, and scuttled over to a set of deck controls. He studied them for a moment and then pushed a lever all the way up.

The large metal slab at the end of the ramp clunked upward as motors whined into life, and Roo ran and back leapt into the dinghy.

They both looked up at the pilothouse. The five men inside moved to the rear windows to look out over the deck. Then there was an explosion of movement.

With a final clunk and shudder, the slab came to a stop. Anika was already belted into a seat in front of the windshield and control center. Roo pulled out the hook holding them at the top of the ramp and they started sliding down.

One of the crew burst out of the back of the pilothouse deck with a submachine gun. He was pulling it up to aim.

Roo hit the seat next to her and braced. "Now *this* is some crazy James Bond shit," he shouted as they hit the churning froth behind the patrol ship, bucking and spinning, spray slapping the windshield. Anika gasped and sucked in diesel fumes from the patrol ship's exhaust.

Roo started the motors up and jammed the throttle forward, turning them off to the right.

Gunfire barked out; shots slapped the water in front of them, and then right near the wooden transom of the dinghy. Anika heard wood splinter.

They roared off perpendicular to the patrol boat, engine screaming. Anika could see the compass whirl around, and then settle in. They were headed north.

"Shit," Roo said, just barely audible over the noise of the engine.

"What?"

He pointed back. A bullet had clipped the transom and ripped open one of the fuel tanks and then left a hole in the fiberglass hull.

"We're lucky we didn't blow up," Anika said, swallowing.

"Losing gas though," Roo pointed out.

He was right. Seawater sloshed in through the bullet hole, mixed with gas pouring out of the hole, and then both were draining out of the back of the boat through one of two one-way valves in the transom to allow water to channel out of the boat. They wouldn't sink, the pontoons around the rigid hull they stood in would stop that.

But they were certainly losing gas.

The Coast Guard ship turned, rolling wildly, to chase them.

Anika crab-walked back, bracing herself against the painful bucking of the dinghy as it hit random waves. Gassy water sloshed around her ankles as she looked around for something to plug the hole.

Nothing.

The plastic tank was hooked up to the engine by black rubber hoses. Anika unstrapped the gas tank and pushed it up onto its side so that the bullet hole was up higher than the level of the remaining gas inside, maybe a third, and then strapped it back in place.

She struggled back forward.

Roo glanced back and nodded in approval at her handiwork.

"What does that do to our escape plan?" she asked.

"We're still working on the first part here," he grunted. He waved back at the Coast Guard vessel, which broke the crest of a large wave in a burst of spray as it gunned its engines.

# 20

Roo never let up on the throttles. Even when the light boat would hit the crest of a wave wrong and leap up, the tip high in the air and threatening to flip them, he kept it all out.

The Canadian Coast Guard ship remained on their tail and Roo struggled to read the GPS as they bounced around.

"Melville Island's closer by," Roo finally announced. "Since we lost most of that half tank of gas, we need to change our plan. We getting close to the east side of it and to Byam Martin. We head north instead of south to Victoria like we planned."

"And?"

"We can bust free from this patrol ship in fifty miles, yeah? There're a bunch of islands and tight channels off Bathurst. There are some places we can get help around here. If we shake that ship."

The swells faded. The boat was battering itself over the top of a heavy chop, engines screaming and props cavitating as they burst into the air every few seconds and hit water again.

After a half mile, even that smoothed out.

They had a half-mile lead on the patrol boat, and hitting the smooth water first gave them an even greater lead. And . . . the patrol boat was slowing.

The swells started up again, though, as Roo carved eastward. As the morning brightened and the grim ocean-pounding race continued, Anika began to just stare bleakly at the ocean directly ahead, anticipating each pounding leap into the air.

It took three hours to reach the coast of Bathurst.

Roo plunged them in between islands, inlets, rocks, and ice. The farther north into these clusters of islands the more ice hung to the edges of the islands, and choked into the channels between them. They were well north of the Northwest Passage here.

Here clumps of ice floated free, the size of small houses or boats. And Roo flew between them, weaving in and out, while a mile behind, the patrol boat finally came to a slow idle.

"Those hulls aren't built for the level of ice that builds up around the islands north of the Passage," Roo said, slowing down as well. "South of it is very much ice free, other than the occasional glacier chunks that fall off an island. So these small patrol ships are cheap to build. He's going to have to call this off."

They had a two-mile lead on the ship as they hooked around the north end of Alexander Island a couple hours later and saw it slowly turning back.

At that point Roo wasn't worrying about the patrol boat, but trying to get the weather loaded up on the small GPS unit to see what they were facing next.

. . .

It was a bad situation to be wearing nothing but clothes usually fit for walking about Baffin Island while in an open boat at sea north of the Passage. In the just-slightly-above freezing temperature of the summer, and the salt-spray soak she'd gotten during their full speed sprint, she knew hypothermia was a real risk.

Roo, his face caked with salt, and looking tired and older, was shivering as he piloted them along at quarter throttle.

Anika stood up.

"What are you doing?" Roo asked.

"Locker."

She walked to the back bench of the boat and forced it open. She found what she was looking for: a first-aid kit. And underneath, three tightly folded thermal blankets.

Roo nodded gratefully as she wrapped one around his shoulders, and then one around herself. "We will keep the other one in the locker, dry," she said.

Still shivering, Roo huddled into his blanket. "If we can get to Cameron Island, we'll be okay."

"What's there?"

"Bent Horn refinery. There are derricks all over the place out here, but Bent Horn is the closest hub. The refinery is the heart of it, but it's a corporate town, three thousand people. We'd be able to refit and restart and not attract too much attention if we lucky."

"Why do you say 'if we can get there'? Is it the weather?"

"Lotta ice between here and there."

. . .

The weather quieted into a still, chilly silence. The water turned to glass. The blankets did their trick, warming them up, and Anika relaxed.

"Were they after just me?" Anika asked. "Or you as well?" She'd gotten him into a lot of trouble. Hopefully they, whoever 'they' were, thought that Roo was just someone she was using, and not a true accomplice.

"Just you," Roo said. "I think a lot of people are convinced that you know something about a heavy situation in the Arctic."

"The nuke?" There it was again.

"Yes, that had come up." Roo looked to his side at her. "You know anything about it? Vy says you a pilot. A clean one. You all mixed up in this?"

"I am pretty sure I spotted it on a freighter during my last flight, and I wasn't supposed to." She wrapped the blanket even tighter, and then summarized the entire nightmare: getting shot down, Tom's death. The bomb.

And now Coast Guard ships trying to pick her up and take her God only knew where.

"A man tried to kill me on the road, too. Before I went to the commander. I strangled him to death." She looked over at him. "I think . . . it's the most horrible thing I've ever done to another human. It took so long. But it was him or me. I didn't have a choice."

Roo nodded. He didn't say anything for a long time as they idled past table-sized chunks of floating ice.

"The worst thing I ever did to another human was marry her," he said.

"Jesus! Roo!" She half laughed. But when she looked over at him, she saw his clenched jaw and realized he hadn't been making a joke.

The sound of the water slapping gently against the hull faded as he whispered, "It was a big contract, to get inside a corporation. I used one of the largest shareholders, a widow, who was on vacation in Saba. Spent a year becoming a part of this person's world, family, influences. A lot of people, they come down to the islands looking for excitement, to cut loose. But she wouldn't let go, and I couldn't stop going down this path. It had momentum, like a cart down a hill."

"So you married her . . ."

"The company spent tens of millions buying politicians off, allowing them to force spice prices down with government subsidies and support. They were going to devastate the island economies as a side effect, and we had to figure out how to get in so we could stay a step ahead. I made half a million for the mission. Cheaper than the islands trying to outbuy the company's pet American, Canadian, and European politicians." He shrugged. "But when it ended, it was like I cut her puppet strings—her world shattered, she slumped away."

They motored on, mulling over the tempest of their personal landscapes for a while. It was better than focusing on the cold.

"The nuclear weapon thing," Roo said. "Before, you were a pilot. You paid attention to basic politics, your command structure, your job. But you've stepped onto a different field now.

"Back in the day of the colonialists, they called it the Great Game. Nation-backed spies crossing the world to pay this group or that, get this person to fight that person, while they stayed in the shadows. Nation's shadows playing for territory, economics, and more. Nowadays, anyone can play. Non-state actors, corporations, activist groups. Everything's in play. You down the rabbit hole that lies under the real world, unseen by the good people focusing on they daily bread."

"I know it exists," Anika said. "But a nuke?"

"The Arctic Circle is the big spoils." Roo turned them a bit to pass around a small chunk of ice. "A lot of the Great Game is focused here now. Canada claims most of the Arctic islands here north of it. The U.S. claims ocean out past Alaska."

"And Northern Europe and Russia, yes. Then China, India, and Brazil pushed hard for the Circle to be international waters, so it's all up in the air. I do work for the UNPG."

"Yeah. And the basin is full of gas and natural resources, all easier and easier to get at now that the ice all but gone. Greenland is a natural resources superpower, a few hundred thousand Inuit made rich by nationalized returns of their claims. Canada exploiting these islands hard. And where oil is plenty, intrigue comes with it. Basic history. Middle East, Nigeria, South America . . . when it's outside their borders, the other big nations play hard for control of it." He tapped the console. "Plastic has to be made. It covers the modern world. Motors need to be lubricated. Most nations still move from point to point with oil."

"And the nuke?" Anika still couldn't figure out how it played into all this.

"Well, someone has one. Which means someone probably wants to use it. And a lot of people want to know why. And many of them want to stop it. That's what the Caribbean network is hearing. Most likely, whoever backing this is someone who wants oil prices to rise. That could be anyone: Middle East, Nigeria, South America, solar power manufacturers, green fanatics."

"Greens?"

"Five major bomb detonations on oil rigs in the Circle in six years, using little boats just like this one with GPS autopilots and a few cameras for navigation. Any more, they get a lot of funding from Saudi princes; every event raises the price of oil."

Anika thought about that. The real people who had tried to kill her could be someone who was trying to edge out a better trade on the oil futures market.

Where the hell was this mission of revenge taking her? And was there even going to be someone she could hunt down for what had happened?

Down the rabbit hole, Roo had said.

He wasn't half kidding.

# 21

The Bent Horn refinery dominated the southern tip of Cameron Island. Stacks belched fire and smoke, pipes clustered and ran from bell-shaped building to building, and the docks harbored massive oil tankers with extra-thick ice-breaking prows. It was an industrial, post-apocalyptic sprawl of brutal architecture made more forbidding by the gray low hills of the island and the Arctic tundra, lit by the perpetual gray day and the sudden lightning-like orange bursts of fire from the stack tops.

To the back of the refinery, rusting derricks slumped over—remnants of the original drilling operation on the island from the 1970s, abandoned just before the turn of the century.

Company dorms, brightly colored but square-block apartment buildings, loomed around the edge of the refinery. Beyond it, another hundred or so buildings crept up the side of a hill, the nascent form of a town springing up around the economic activity of the refinery as year-round workers pulled in family and then all the other needs of a large group of humanity: bars, eateries, stores, recreation, infrastructure.

Roo guided them around the shadows of barges and tugs toward the docks. No one paid much attention to them, as several other dinghies moved around the harbor to get people to and from anchored ships that couldn't fit. There was no reason for anyone to assume they came out of the ocean, as Roo had initially come around the coast to the harbor.

By the time they tied up, the wind had started to howl and rain pelted the artificial harbor. They hurried toward a bright green dormitory building.

Anika browsed a company store attached to the dorm, soaking in the warmth and calm, while Roo disappeared. "Going to find an ATM for some cash from one of my backup accounts, and seeing if we can get transport to Pleasure Island," he told her tersely.

He came back an hour later reequipped with a phone he'd purchased off someone, two large Arctic peacoats, hats, gloves, and a thick wad of cash.

Anika stole a few bills from him to buy three chocolate bars she'd been eyeing and a large hot chocolate. They sat at a small plastic table in the corner of the store. It was quiet, in between shifts, though a handful of men in overalls sat in the other corner downing coffee and bitching about one of their managers.

"There's a helicopter pilot taking supplies out to a couple of mist boats near that area," Roo said. "One of the crew is a journalist with money who has fresh stuff flown in once a month. If we agree to help unload, and we pay for his refueling there, he'll get us to Pleasure Island."

Rain sleeted against the window, howling away outside, as she sipped and let the warmth spread through her.

"I think," Roo said, "we're okay. For tonight. We should stay inside as much as we can, come out in between shifts."

He'd found a room. It was filled with gear: heavy boots, warm clothing. Posters of naked airbrushed women holding impossible poses and hungry expressions hung from the wall, tacked into place. A perfectly clean, empty, white fridge.

They were in a quiet cocoon of temporary safety. A stillness after a storm of danger and activity that felt far away.

Roo sat down on the couch and unlaced his shoes. He paused, thinking about something. He stopped. "So . . . you're Vy's girl, right?"

Anika sat on the bed. She would have taken the couch, it was a friendly thing to do. But Roo had done it first, and she was all but drooling at the thought of sinking in between the covers and getting warm and rested. "I don't know. It's complicated. We got interrupted, and we barely know each other."

"So you like girls?"

Anika sighed. In Africa, she'd been a monk outside the city. Conversations like this caused her to tense up. Suddenly Roo wasn't a compatriot, but a possible problem. "Yes. I like women," she said. It was a flat statement.

"You ever try it with a man?" Roo asked.

Anika sighed. "Have you?"

Roo continued unlacing his shoes. "No. But if you never . . ."

"Roo, would you like to take a hot throbbing cock between your lips?"

"No."

"Neither would I. I didn't wake up one day and decide I hated men and liked women. I see a woman, I like what I see. I want to be with that. Not the other. It's been that way for as long as I can remember."

"Okay." He lay down on the couch and propped his feet up on the end.

If he hadn't grabbed the couch first, she'd have considered it a bad pass at her. But he was aware that Vy and she had something.

If it was curiosity, she felt that was *somewhat* forgivable. She'd downgrade it to merely annoying. She owed Roo her life. He could ask annoying questions.

But to be honest, right now, she just really wanted to disappear into this bed and not hold some deep, intimate discussion about the nature of sexual orientation. She was too fucking tired for it.

"Do your parents know?" he asked.

"Roo, do you really want to talk about this right here? Now?" She pulled the covers back, and threw the topmost blanket at him.

Nestled inside, she stripped down to an undershirt and leaned back against the pillows. The bed smelled of someone else: sweat, oil, grime, dirt. But it didn't matter. It was warm and soft.

Right then, the howling wind of the Arctic, the cold ocean, the people trying to kill her: they were all things outside this little warren of a room.

"Back in the islands, it ain't the mainland. Not very accepted, you know? Most people don't come out, and I never felt like I could just ask questions. Other than Violet, no one ever spoke to me as a friend where I could just . . . ask."

Her eyes were closed, sleep creeping up on her. "No, my parents don't know. My father, he is a very traditional Lagos man. He was raised fire-and-brimstone style. He used to watch these Nollywood movies made by the megachurches about the dangers of witches and the devil and so on."

"Megachurches make Nollywood movies? Serious?"

"Some, yeah. A lot of money in there. Big productions. They even send missionaries to Western Europe and the U.S. to knock on doors." She yawned deeply and thoroughly.

"And what about your mother?" Roo asked.

Anika snorted. "She probably wouldn't care. But I haven't talked to her since I was a child."

Roo sat up. "You split with her?"

"She split with us. She was a Nollywood actress. Not a lot of white women from England around Lagos aspired to be Nollywood stars back then; she stood out. She was in high demand. She mistook that for something else, and then left to try her luck in America. Then Vancouver."

"And you haven't talked to her since then?"

"No."

"That's sad," Roo said.

"She has never, ever tried to contact me," Anika said. After all, it was just as easy the other way. "Now leave me to sleep, Roo. Please."

"Okay," he said. "Just one thing."

"Yes."

"Be good to Violet. She been through a lot. She's a good friend."

Okay, Roo, she thought. But I didn't ask her to do all this. She chose to.

"Tomorrow we have to think about changing your appearance," Roo said through a large yawn.

"Okay," Anika murmured.

Wait! What?

But she had already slipped under into grateful sleep, though with a frown still on her face.

The next morning Roo woke her up and put two plastic bags down on a foldout table in the corner of the room. One had milk and an assortment of tiny boxed cereals, as well as some plastic bowls.

As they ate a quick breakfast, Roo laid out the contents of the other plastic bag: clippers, hair straighteners, dyes, combs, twist ties.

"We need to change you look," Roo said, crumpling his bowl up and putting it in a bag. "People looking for you. My advice: stand out, grab a bold look."

"Bold?"

He smiled. "Most of the eyes on you will be computers using public-classified cameras. Change you hair, change you style." He tugged on his dreadlocks.

"I wouldn't know how. . . ."

"I do," he said. "That and some glasses. Yes. And I have some combat makeup."

"Combat makeup?"

"To confuse facial analysis software."

Anika looked down at the remains of her cereal. "I thought getting locks took years."

"Real natty dreads, yeah." Roo stood up and swept everything back into a plastic bag. "But I can back-comb you hair into locks. I did it for my sister once." He held out a hand.

Anika took it and followed him into the bathroom.

"I always wanted to look like Dakore Egbuson," she said with a big smile.

"Who?" Roo started lining the lip of the tub with all the items in his bag.

"When I was eight or nine, she was one of the Queens of Nollywood. She was so beautiful. And she had locks. I wanted to have hair like that, but my father said no."

But he did let her hang the poster in her room. Dakore's brown eyes looked down at her every night, her warm brown figure in a curvy white cocktail dress.

"Little Anika's first celebrity crush?" Roo asked from the edge of the bathtub. Anika smiled, remembering closing her eyes and imagining the tips of Dakore's locks brushing against her shoulders, remembering the feel of her own fingers creeping down to her thighs, the back of her hands sliding against the sheets.

"Something like that," Anika said, sitting down on the floor in front of him.

Roo began to section off her hair. She couldn't see what he was doing from her position on the floor, but over the next hour, she could feel it.

After creating sections, he began twisting, rolling,

and combing toward her scalp on each section, using twists to hold the lengths in place. Each lock also got waxed.

He worked quickly, efficiently, and with practiced hands.

Which made sense, she realized. He would have experience with his own locks.

When she stood and looked in the mirror, she had to smile. The locks came down right to the tops of her ears, longer than she thought she had the hair for.

After all this time pinning it back for the UNPG, she had to admit she liked it.

Roo held up four bottles of hair color. "Henna-based, it won't fuck up you hair like the regular stuff. Got it from the hair place."

Anika looked at the bottles, and then tapped the left-most one. "Purple," she said.

Her professional UNPG look was long gone now. And it was about to get worse, she knew, because Roo had pulled out a small kit. "Face paint," he said. "Facial recognition cameras can be fooled, if you willing to get a little . . . dramatic. We don't know who here is hunting for you, and what resources they have, but better safe than sorry, yeah?"

Anika looked down at the makeup kit. "Okay," she said hesitantly.

"To fool the cameras, we need to put a pattern on your face, a solid cover that distorts your cheekbones, nose, and eyes. Almost like what you see on a picture of a harlequin. Like you getting into carnival." Roo held up the makeup, and then his phone. On it were several line drawings of faces with swooshing patterns crossing the eyes and cheeks. "Pick a color and a pattern you like."

Anika sighed deeply and took the makeup and his phone, then turned to the mirror.

Using a green that complemented her new locks, she slowly covered the top left half of her face, then drew the solid patch of color down under her right eye.

"How does this look?" she finally asked, turning to face Roo.

He held up his phone and took a picture, then tapped around the screen. "I have a facial recognition program here, looks for pictures I take and tags them for me." He smiled. "And you fooling it. We ready. Maybe even cutting it a bit close to late. We have to hurry."

Chandra Gupta, a leather-faced helicopter pilot with piercing green eyes and a thick mustache, directed them to the back of the helicopter. "You're late," he told Roo. "I should have left without you." Anika kept waiting for Chandra to ask about her, standing there with loudly colored hair and a wildly made-up face, but the old helicopter pilot didn't even bat an eye.

There were no seats in the back, they perched on crates of medical supplies and boxes of fresh produce.

Chandra was an old Indian Air Force pilot. Once he was finished complaining to Roo about messing with his schedule, he kept on chatting to them as he got the helicopter ready to fly, flipping through a checklist.

He'd served in combat over Kashmir and Pakistan. "It's better here," he told them while flipping switches. "It's just cold here. There, it was cold and really fucking high altitude. That flying, it was murderous, and in the hills, some separatist with a rocket launcher sitting on a rock at the same height or higher than you is just waiting for you to turn the corner. Miserable times. Miserable times."

The helicopter rose from its pad, rising above the towers and stacks of Bent Horn, then tilting and swinging out over the sea.

Turbulence shook them around a bit, and Roo swore as a crate hit him in the back.

But then it smoothed, and the miles whipped by underneath.

"See that!" Chandra shouted over the cabin noise back at them. He jabbed a finger off in the distance as they banked. Three large U.S. Navy ships were pushing through the heavy seas at top speed. A carrier and two support ships. A destroyer or cruiser may have been on the distant horizon, Anika couldn't quite make it out. Even this far away, she could see bow spray as the ships slammed against the large waves. It would have been dangerous down there in their stolen Coast Guard boat.

"Yeah?" she shouted forward.

"They are headed to join the U.S. Polar Fleet. They are beefing it up."

"Why?"

Chandra shrugged. "Supposedly it is a joint fleet maneuver with the Europeans. I think they're just trying to show everyone they still have the military edge, even in the Arctic."

Roo looked out the window. He didn't seem to believe Chandra's theory, but he didn't add anything to the conversation.

But he was very interested in the ships. He kept staring out of the window until they were past the wakes they left behind and banking into a new direction once more.

# 22

Chandra called them mist boats. They had been oil tankers at one point and then obviously rebuilt. Large helipads dominated their massive prows.

But that wasn't the largest structural adjustment: each tanker had five massive funnels grafted onto the decks. These reached up like radio towers or small skyscrapers, using the decks of the tankers as firm ground.

Mist poured out of the tips of the funnels, slowly rising up into the heavily clouded sky.

Chandra flew them in low, low enough that Anika could see the churning whitecaps at the tip of each wave below them whipped into the air by the driving winds buffeting the copter.

There were three mist boats at anchor. Chandra gained altitude and flared the copter out in a motion that made Anika's stomach lurch, and then they dropped onto the helipad of the lead mist boat.

The tanker rode the swells. Disconcerting, because it felt, to Anika, as if she were standing on the street of a large city that rose and fell with the waves. Something this large, with the deck and metal as far as she could see, with funnels stretching overhead like downtown buildings, and all of it dominating her field of vision, all this simply shouldn't move underfoot.

A cheerful looking blond in a red windbreaker opened Chandra's door with an accompanying gust of cold air and peered in. "Rough landing, Chandra!" He looked like he would be much more comfortable surfing off the California coast or backpacking through Oregon.

He looked back, saw Anika and Roo, and ran a hand self-consciously through his wind-harried hair. "Hey guys, I didn't realize Chandra was ferrying anyone out."

"I am not." Their pilot pushed the blond aside and got out. "They're on their way to Pleasure Island." He heaved the side door out of the way.

"It's awesome to see some new faces, even if for a few hours." The blond stuck out a hand and helped Anika out, but left Roo on his own. "My name's Martin Frobish. Everyone just calls me Bish."

Bish had a handcart with him. He and Chandra started pulling the boxes out of the helicopter. After a second Roo and Anika got in the line and helped.

Then together they all manhandled the unruly cart along the nine hundred feet of deck.

They pushed it through watertight steel doors into the warm fluorescent lights and gray paint of the corridors. Bish led them to the large kitchen where Lars, a burly Scandinavian who looked every bit a descendant of the Vikings, ripped open the boxes with eagerness.

He held up a fresh clump of lettuce with something approaching reverence. "Finally, a fucking salad," he growled.

Chandra pulled Bish aside as the Scandinivian began chopping lettuce and puttering around the boxes, grabbing fresh produce with a grin. "I need to barter for the extra fuel to get to Pleasure Island, and I'll be landing back on my way."

"Talk to Everson, he'll fuel you up," Bish said softly. Then even softer. "And I'll buy your fuel for a trip back south on your return."

"What is happening with you?" Chandra asked.

Bish chuckled and stole a slice of tomato while Lars had his back turned. "Any of you been following the news this morning?"

"No," Anika said. After getting Anika disguised they'd abandoned the room to head straight over to the helicopter.

Lars had his head in the fridge. He slammed the door shut, shaking the wall. "We have been fucked." He had a pair of beers in his hand, he threw one at Bish, who snagged it out of the air with ease and popped the top.

Both men, Anika realized, had been drinking heavily before she'd arrived. Lars had bloodshot eyes.

A heavy thunk, and a steady shaking rumbled through the floor.

"Shit, they're opening the hold doors." Bish's head snapped around, facing the direction of the decks.

Lars dropped his beer on the floor. "Get the backup cameras. I want everything on!"

Bish grabbed Chandra's shoulders. "I'll need to join you guys on the trip out. Lars, too. But first, you'll want to see what's going down here, man."

Lars thudded out of the kitchen, and Bish followed close behind. "Six months ago the *Hinum* was a thousand-foot-long floating offshore factory owned by a Chinese corporation, further up the Arctic Circle, all in strictly multinational waters. They were closer to the oil and were using it to make plastic toys. I guess it helped the margins to be right by the source, and then they could be shipped right to Alaska, or Northern Europe."

"It was anchored near Thule," Lars said, leading them down a set of stairs and through a quiet and empty common area.

"I've seen the floating factories," Anika said. As it got harder and harder to find nations without protective labor laws, corporations got more creative.

"The company went bankrupt," Bish said, ducking another low bulkhead. "The creditors were fighting over who owned the factory and who could get it towed to Chittagong and have it scrapped. Meanwhile, there's this whole multinational workforce quartered on the ship. I'm getting e-mails and pictures from a friend who's in the middle of writing a story about the floating factory. I mean, no regulations, labor laws, or oversight. Sounds like hell? But since they're all trapped aboard, after a few really crazy protests and a few overzealous overseers go missing overboard, they'd built a life here."

"They had greenhouses." Lars led them into a small room with a single bare bunk and a gray blanket. Work boots lay scattered under the bunk, heavy coats on the hook behind the door. The desk had four cases stacked on it. Lars opened one of them to reveal padded foam and a two fist-sized cameras. He moved with practiced, precise haste as he opened another case and pulled out a tripod. "You wouldn't believe the things they grew on the decks."

"They had everything set up," Bish said. "Hospitals, greenhouses on deck for fresh veggies, even a small pen with chickens for fresh eggs. These workers from Thailand, Vietnam, Russia, China, they'd built a whole world on this ship. Lars and I wanted to film it before it was all ripped out and scrapped. We flew out, and my story got even fucking better."

Lars opened another case and pulled out a shoulder-stabilized camera rig.

Bish shut the cases for Lars, but he was waving his hands around as he got more animated. An inner intensity tumbled out with his words. "So these guys revolted when one of the creditors finally got a tug boat out here to commandeer the factory. They tooled up to build weapons and held everyone off, and they declared that the ship was owned by them. Turned it into a worker-owned and -run business. Everyone had a share. They started production up again."

"They lasted two months." Lars pointed them out of the cabin, and everyone backed out. "Then Gaia purchased the company's debt."

"So get this: Lars has cameras all over the place streaming back to our box at home, and I'm interviewing everyone I can get my hands on, when fucking paratroopers literally drop out of the fucking sky." Bish paused for dramatic effect.

"For hire?" Anika asked.

"Edgewater, yah." Lars was leading them down the corridor again, trotting along. The rumbling grew louder now as they got closer to the decks. "Everyone is thinking: hey, Gaia purchases the debt. They are the biggest green company in the world. They are nice people, yeah? Turns out, not so nice after all."

"It's a whole standoff," Bish said as they started climbing stairs again. "Gaia's founders, Paige Greer and Ivan Cohen, make an offer: we could all accept a like/kind exchange of Gaia shares and a free ferry ticket anywhere in the Circle, or . . . get arrested. There we are, weapons aimed at us, gunships circling the ship. I was scared shitless."

"They took the deal," Roo said from behind Anika. "I remember all those workers showed up on the docks at Thule."

"Then it got hairy when they found out I had recorded it all. I was like, you have to let me get out of here. They wanted the footage before they'd release me. I told them I had rights. They said I was in international waters, and I'd been filming on their property. I had no rights."

"So they bargain with us," Lars said, panting and out of breath. They'd gone up three flights, and now he walked over to a large observation window. "They promise us the story of the century if we agree to never release the footage of Gaia-paid goons pointing guns at factory workers. We met with lawyers for two days. We agreed to stay on board for six months. It was just us, Gaia had these ships switched over to their automated systems with an occasional weekly fly-in by engineers to check on the systems. After the manufacturing stuff was done, all the workers left."

He set the tripod down in front of the window, and they all walked up to it.

Bish looked out over the decks. "But after all that, they still fucked us."

"Fucked us hard." Lars set up one camera to look down at the decks. Anika looked out. The deck's floodlights revealed the source of the loud rumbling: several massive steel hatches slowly rolled themselves open. Fifteen-foot cracks of dark had appeared. They were going to be looking down into the holds soon, if the hatches kept trundling back. "You should show them a close-up," Lars told Bish. "It doesn't matter anymore. Might as well break the story to *someone*."

Bish smiled sadly. "I was supposed to break the news about how Gaia, Inc., was going to save the world. But that news broke this morning while you guys were getting out here. At least I get some exclusive documentary footage."

He shrugged, then turned back for the stairs and waved them along.

"Where are we going?" Anika asked.

"Down to the holds. Trust me, I'm about to blow your minds," Bish said, grinning.

# 23

The mist boats were going to be Gaia's big silver bullet," Bish said, leading Roo and Anika down the stairs. "Cohen and Greer had been holding press conferences about how bad shit was getting out there. Glaciers disappearing, storms ripping through the Atlantic coast, Caribbean. Typhoons getting worse. The Arctic melting."

Bish led them through a long corridor away from the bridge superstructure, deep inside the hull.

"Gaia doesn't *have* a formal position about whether the warming trends were human caused or not," Roo said.

"That's just PR to protect them from conservatives and religious Midwesterners in the U.S. during their start-up phase. Greer and Cohen figured that if they could build what we needed and let businesses solve the issue, they could route around that shit. But the political will for Western nations to get big serious faded, man."

"Westerners get all the benefits," Anika said. More land in Canada, Russia, and Northern Europe. Greenland opened up. Iceland became even more comfortable. New England and Britain are suffering cold snaps now that the Gulf Stream is being forced lower by the billions of tons of Arctic fresh water dumped into the North Atlantic, but they were the minority.

The Midwest and Siberia did just fine.

Anika looked at Roo. "All those people in the equators without water, suffering heavy weather and drought and less arable land? It's not happening in their backyard, it's not their problem. That is what the politicians say."

Bish stopped in front of a door. "So the mist boats help clouds form and bounce sunlight back into space. But Gaia is blocked by governments who maintain that it's an attempt at radical geoengineering, and that we can't model the unanticipated side effects."

Roo folded his arms. "They banned them in the Caribbean. It rained saltwater. It's not good for the plants, yeah?"

"So then the question is," Bish said, opening the doors behind him slowly, "if you're the leaders of a multitrillion-dollar corporation, how do you reverse a global trend, when many people don't want you to even try? When many who believe there is a problem have thrown up their hands at the enormity of it? When many believe there is no problem?"

The doors clanged open, showing only the utter darkness of the ship's holds ahead.

"You have to become . . . slightly mad." Bish moved toward a control panel. "There are futurists and space nuts who talk about 'terraforming' another planet: making an uninhabitable planet habitable for humans. Like Mars. Drop some comets on it, add atmosphere. Put a giant mirror in orbit to heat it up a bit. Big idea stuff. So Ivan Cohen and Paige Greer decided that they would motherfucking terraform Earth to stop it from turning into Venus. So when they took over this factory ship, they started making something new, and filling holds all over the Arctic with these things."

He tapped a code on the panel, and the lights came on.

For a long moment Anika couldn't grasp what she was looking at—until she focused her eyes on the smallest unit in front of her.

She walked forward, and out of a solid wall of shiny metal globules, plucked out a transparent ball the size of her fist.

"I've seen one of these before," she whispered.

"For six months Gaia has been churning these things out," Bish said. He looked morose. "I was supposed to get an exclusive, in exchange for silence, but this morning the story broke. Someone working in a factory finally leaked video of the things. Now everyone's figuring out what they're for."

Roo, the information gatherer, held a sphere up, looking into the shiny insides. There was a mirror inside, gimbaled and motorized so it could adjust itself to face any direction it wanted. "What *do* they do?"

Bish looked at the two of them as if they were stupid. "It's a lot more effective than a fucking mist cloud, right? And it's a hell of a lot cheaper than trying to build a giant mirror in space to deflect some of the sun's heat. Millions of these things, floating around. Mini-blimps. They're programmable, little chips inside that cost no more than a penny. You can direct the motored mirrors to face any direction, so in a cloud of them you can use heat to let them rise up or fall, so they can use wind and weather patterns to move around as a unit. They're shiftable into one giant clump of a mirror, able to focus heat or deflect it where needed. Gaia created their silver bullet, man."

He held his hands out and walked into the silvered, jostling mass of floating balls. The tinkling sound of hundreds of floating spheres moved with him as he was enveloped by them.

Overhead, the hatch ground to a halt.

The sound of rattling, hundreds of tiny balls slapping against the walls and each other, filled the hold.

"They initially planned to release them a hold at a time," shouted Bish from inside the now slowly rising mass of spheres escaping the bonds of the hold. "So they could inject them into the upper atmosphere over the Arctic slowly so as not to alarm satellites and radar systems."

"Or get caught," Roo muttered.

"Now they'll be releasing them as fast as they can," Bish said.

The spheres were thinning out as they rose into the air. Anika could see through gaps to the sky and the edges of the hatch far over her head. Thousands bumped along the sides of the massive funnels, and then they merged into the streams of mist.

Anika was standing beside a moment in history, she thought. This was amazing. Stunning. This company had been laboring in secret to build something vast right here in the Arctic Circle.

Something that would change the world.

For a moment, her head craned back looking at this exodus of tiny machines into the sky, she wasn't wondering about radiation, revenge, or the cold. She just stared at the metal, glinting cloud in wonder as it rose to reach the dark clouds far overhead.

Roo grabbed her arm. He didn't look awed. He looked scared. "We have to get off this ship right *fast,*" he hissed.

"What are you talking about?"

"Those navy ships? They reacting to *this*. We don't want to be on none of these ships. No telling how they thinking to react."

Bish walked across the empty hold floor, sending several straggling spheres that couldn't quite rise into the air wobbling her way. "You think they'd fire on us?"

"I can't believe they'd do that," Anika said.

"I don't know." Bish rubbed his forehead. "But why risk it? Take us with you to Pleasure Island. I don't have anything left here. I've lost six months, we have the sphere launch video now. It's all I need if I'm not getting an exclusive."

"What about crew? Is there anyone else on board?" Anika asked.

"Like I said, automated and on autopilot," Bish said.

Roo had his new phone already up to his ear. "Chandra? Spin up, we leaving *now*."

# 24

Rotor wash whipped Anika's hair about as she climbed the steps back onto the helicopter pad. Lars joined a second later, staggering up with five cases in his hands and a duffel bag over a shoulder. His jacket flapped wildly as he leaned into the gust.

Anika helped him get the cases in, and once they were all inside, Chandra grabbed Roo and yelled, "Are you sure all of those things are out of the air?"

Bish leaned forward. "Should be, there's no reason for them to wait anymore."

"Anyone else on board?" Chandra asked.

"It's on autopilot, just us."

Chandra looked out around the entire helicopter, hunting to see if more of the spheres were around, then, satisfied, lifted off the helipad and pitched them toward the open sea.

"Stay as low as you dare," Roo reminded him.

Chandra nodded. He was still glancing around,

looking for threats. Anika looked out the windows as well. They were skimming along just over the tips of the waves, spray even slapping the windward side of the helicopter.

It looked like the helicopter's skids could kiss the waves at any second. Anika really had to admire the piloting. This was old school, fly by wire, brain and muscle and twitch reflexes all working together.

Chandra was something else.

"You really think they will do something to the mist boats?" Lars asked Roo and Bish. He reached into his duffel bag and pulled out another beer.

"Four years ago the U.S. Army got ready to launch a test orbital mirror," Roo shouted. "They were thinking it would allow them to focus solar energy down on a solar engine. They could power an army, no need for oil, with a beam of concentrated solar light anywhere in the world. China got all threatened, said that beam could be directed anywhere. Flash vaporize an army, see? They said it weaponizing space, and was a treaty violation. Said they would attack it with anything they had. Everyone backed down. So now Gaia's weaponizing the upper atmosphere. There'll be consequences. . . ."

Chandra slammed the helicopter sideways, throwing around everyone inside it. Anika slapped into the side of the door, feeling it shake as her shoulder smashed against the handle.

Lars and Bish smacked into her ribs, dizzying her with the familiar pain.

And with her face smashed against the glass, Anika saw the long, dark shape of a cruise missile gliding mysteriously toward them just over the wave caps. It dodged, violently arcing around them with a quick burst of several adjusting jets.

They were not its target.

Anika sat up to look out the other side of the helicopter just in time to see the cruise missile silently fly into the side of the ship, a mile behind them. A split second later a fireball gushed out of the side, then broke out of the holds, sending the massive steel hatches spinning up into the air.

Secondary explosions visibly rippled the hull, vomiting debris and surviving clouds of spheres that rose above the conflagration in slow motion.

As they stared the funnels toppled over, striking the heaving seas and breaking apart.

More explosions ripped through and, slowly, the mist boat began to settle deeper into the water.

"Jesus," Bish muttered.

Lars didn't say anything; he had one of his cameras held tight in his hand and was filming. A trickle of blood ran down his temple, but he didn't seem to notice.

The cabin reeked of spilled beer.

Anika flinched as the other two mist boats in the distance exploded.

"Were the other two ships fully automated?" Roo asked.

"There was a maintenance crew," Bish said. "They cycled between the Arctic mist boats. They might have been aboard . . . I don't know."

Chandra circled around looking for survivors as the ships burned and slowly sank.

"Roo . . ." Anika pointed out another gliding missile in the distance, curving through a roiling column of smoke. Another metallic shark, hunting for something.

Light abruptly split the sky as tens of thousands of mirrors scattered in the air turned their attention to one single point in space. But the missile easily danced away. The beam of light boiled water on the surface of the ocean for a moment, then faded away, leaving nothing but a wisp of steam to show it ever existed.

"Jesus." Roo shook his head. "That's just one hold's worth of those floating things. It's not quick enough to fry a missile, but whoever controls it was trying."

Finding no more targets, the cruise missile splashed down into the ocean and sank. The floating mirrors rose above the clouds, and they were left alone circling the destruction.

Oil coated the frothy sea, as did tens of thousands of now-dead spheres. They had to keep upwind; Chandra couldn't risk any low-floating spheres hitting his blades or getting sucked into the motor.

But no bright red suits waved for help, and no emergency boats had been launched. No rafts. Nothing.

For fifteen minutes they whirled around the mess, until Chandra shouted, "We'll run out of fuel before Paradise Island if we don't leave now!"

"Let's go," Roo told him, barely audible.

Chandra banked away, and slowly the burning ships disappeared behind the waves and horizon.

Lars turned his camera off and packed it back away. They all sat quietly, lost in their own thoughts, sobered by the sight.

# 25

Pleasure Island was the fourth in an arc of oil platforms on the edge of the western side of the Northwest Passage.

Brock and Borden islands perched on the western edge of the Sverdrup Basin. There was more wealth out in the basin's oil field than in any area in Western Canada. And all of it had been left alone by the twentieth century due to an inability to cope with the choking Arctic ice.

With the oil now accessible, rigs popping up every couple weeks, people poured in from around the world to work in the industry. And all the people in that cloud of an ecosystem that served the drilling, the manufacturing, the shipping, and activity of the Sverdrup Basin needed somewhere to cut loose.

Baffin was too far. Prudhoe Bay was too far.

So Pleasure Island accreted around the remains of a shut down offshore platform: the rights to set up its bars, casinos, and other venues leased from Trans-Oceanic, the owner of the platform.

The rig had started out looking like a small industrial city sitting on top of the usual assortment of tubular metal legs that stuck out of the water. That original city had been built up on, so that it now looked dangerously top-heavy, brimming with extensions to the sides and buildings that drooped off the rim.

They landed on a floating airstrip anchored off the back of the rig, Chandra swearing for the last four minutes of the flight, terrified that they were going to run out of fuel and have to ditch. But the helicopter coughed its way on its last fumes to the helicopter pad on the barge and Chandra leaned over his controls and kissed his instruments when they landed softly.

Roo sat with him in the cockpit, transferring money around via phone through emergency, secret, and according to him, quite shielded accounts he had access to thanks to his part-time Caribbean spy contacts, and then he shook Chandra's hand and wished him luck.

Chandra looked somewhat relieved to be seeing the last of them, Anika thought.

Seven other helicopters were tied down around them on the pad, including one ancient and quite massive sixty-passenger Russian Mi-26 with its sagging eight-bladed rotors.

They silently walked along under the helicopter blades, and then past the sheltered docks filled with bouncing boats of all shapes and sizes. People filtered up the docks with them.

From the airstrip's barge, a large gangplank led them to scaffolding stairs built along the side of the rig. They walked on up, the cold Arctic wind tugging at them.

Anika paused a moment as they crested the final steps. The center of the artificial island, a whole city block, was packed with drunk people. Neon flashed from every crevice of every walkway. Bulbs had been hung up, glittering from rails and pipes.

They'd turned an oil rig into Las Vegas, Anika thought. Everything blinked, or had been repainted garishly. Every nook and cranny along the outer edge of the platform had been turned into a bar, or strip club, or dance club, or store. Everywhere she turned, something was being sold.

On the third floor of what had once been an observation tower, three women yanked their tops down and threw beads out into the masses below.

As the beads struck the ground they snapped open into little squares, advertising one of the platform's clubs with a hologram.

Roo led them through an epileptic's worst nightmare of throbbing music from ten different sources, flashing lights, gaudy colors, and nearly naked men and women dancing in doorways with come-hither glances despite the cold air.

After the shock of the attack on the mist boats, it was a complete assault on the senses.

"It's noon, right?" Bish asked her, somewhat stunned.

Anika looked around. "I think so."

A burly woman with ripped forearms stumbled to

her knees and retched as someone shouted, "Gina, Gina, Gina," at her.

Roo stopped as they reached a large entryway on the other side of the rig.

Anika looked up at the giant neon sign overhead. Two large thighs spread out on either side of the door. And the letters, in glowing pink.

"Pussy Galore's," Anika read out loud. "Roo?"

He didn't say anything. He walked in ahead of her, his face still tight and serious. Two large, hairy men who looked like they would be at home riding Harleys stepped in front of him. Despite the cold, they wore nothing but leather thongs and leather face masks, zippers up the back, and dog collars. No leashes though, Anika noticed. She guessed she could see where that would get in the way of a bouncer's duties.

"Hello, Moneypenny," Roo said to the two men. "We're here for Violet."

"You." The man pointed at Anika. "And you." His voice was muffled behind the mask as he then pointed at Roo.

"The other two aren't on the list," said the other bouncer, his voice also muffled.

"Guys," Roo said. "You can't run a strip club if you don't let customers in."

The two burly men did not budge. "No customers right now. Just expected guests."

Roo started to argue, but Bish tapped his shoulder. "It's okay, man. We need to find pipe to upload what just happened and decide what to do next. And drink. I lived with the guys on those boats for months. I'm ready to stir up some serious shit. Thank you for flying us out."

Lars nodded. He still looked dazed and hadn't spoken since the explosions. But he shook Anika's hand, and Roo's, and then followed Bish back off into the crowd. A crowd which didn't seem to give a damn that something was happening beyond the confines of the neon of Pleasure Island.

It would affect them soon, though, Anika thought. If Gaia was effective in its attempt to "terraform" Earth, the gold rush to the Arctic Circle would slow down as the oil and other resources were buried back under ice.

The economies of the Arctic Tigers would slow down. Denmark, Finland, Norway, Greenland, Iceland, Russia, Canada, Alaska, would fall back into pre-warming levels of expansion.

No shipping would crisscross the Arctic.

Thule would whither away.

There would be no reason for the bustle of humanity to be up here.

And those were the local effects. Global oil production was mostly focused on making plastics, not burning it. If plastics rose in price, bioplastics would go up as well. There wouldn't just be oil shocks, but manufacturing shocks, and then down the line, food shocks as bioplastics tried to fill in the gap. Companies would fail, fortunes would be destroyed, economies would falter.

The entire world would feel the ripple from this.

# 26

The gloomy inside of Pussy Galore's faced the ocean with giant balconies of enclosed glass. On a bright day, they'd let the sun in. But today gray light cloaked the dark sea.

Anika stared at the seventy-year-old posters of bikinied women with retro hairstyles. A tiny silver gun rested in a display case. A scale model of an Aston Martin hung from a corner of the ceiling near a pole.

Roo noticed her looking around. "Someone with a 3-D fab machine printed a lot of these out for them. But the posters are originals from the movies."

A short middle-aged women with a fitness trainer's body broke away from a huddle of fifteen other women, most of them topless, at a large round table near the balconies and the brass poles. "Hey Roo," she said. "Caught us at a bad time. We're shut down right now."

She wore a too-tight shirt that said MILF-QUEEN, cropped to leave her very noticeable, very cut abs exposed.

"Hey Kerrie. What's up? And why the posse?" Roo jerked his head at the table.

"Miss Estonia here was caught giving a client a blow job in the VIP room," Kerrie muttered. A tired-looking Eastern European girl was sitting a table over, drinking out of a tumbler. She'd tossed a blond wig on the table's surface by the drink. "We're casting a vote."

"A vote?" Anika looked over. Sure enough, someone was passing around a cheap wooden box with a slit cut out of the top, and they were all dropping pieces of paper in.

"Galore's is a worker-owned co-op," Kerrie said. "On policy violations, we have to decide what to do with the offender. In the case of Adriana over there, it's her second time pulling this shit. We're entertainers, not hookers. We want a safe environment, and she's jeopardizing it. I called the referendum: time to vote the bitch off the island."

Anika thought about Bish's story of the factory workers' revolt. "There are a lot of communists out here," she observed.

Kerrie pointed at her. "What the fuck? This isn't some socialist strip club. That's from each according to their ability, to each their needs. None of that shit here. It's a worker-owned small business. We all have shares. Don't let serf-acquiring corporations bullshit you into their feudalistic mind-sets. The harder we work, the more fucking money we make because we're each part owners of the company, and part of the profit-making mechanism. We're not working *our* asses off to profit some distant fucking middle manager or stockholder. We're the owners, the management, *and* the talent. And we're all about the earnings, got it?"

Anika held her hands up. "Sorry."

"Sorry my ass. People living in a democratic world go all floozy for corporations run like the most asshat evil empires ever seen. Get all wet when some corporate ruler shits all over the environment, cuts costs by laying people off, but handed over a nice quarter according to the nerds in accounting. The sort of shit they'd scream about if it were dressed up as politics, they just shrug when it happens under a corporate byline. Fuck that, we got democracy, baby, and it's profitable. Roo, you're in room fifteen. That cool?"

Roo was grinning at the whole dressing down. "Yeah." He nodded at Anika. "You good by yourself? I've got calls to make and favors to call in."

"You can dock your boat underneath if you need," Kerrie said.

Roo took a deep breath. "It . . . didn't make it. We flew."

Kerrie raised her eyebrows. "Okay. I'll take care of . . ."

"Anika." Anika held out a hand, and Kerrie took it and smiled.

"Nice to meet you, Anika. You must be someone very special if Violet's letting you into her little hideaway here."

Anika felt her cheeks flush a bit, and she looked away. "Vy's been . . . very helpful in a difficult situation. When will she get here?"

"Tomorrow morning. Let me take you to Vy's room. And we'll find you some clean clothes."

"Thank you." Anika glanced down at the MILF-QUEEN shirt.

Kerrie held a hand up to her chest. "These are work clothes, sweetie, we'll get you something respectable."

Again, Anika felt the heat rise to her face. "I'm sorry. . . ."

Kerrie smiled and grabbed her elbow and led her down a corridor to an elevator. "It's okay," Kerrie reassured her. "Don't worry. You're among friends."

The club, Anika realized, hung over the edge of the platform, and dropped several floors down toward the water, using one of the pylons as a main support. Vy's room was three floors underneath the main dancing floor.

Anika wasn't sure if she should be offended that she was being put in Vy's own room. Did Vy have some expectations?

Well, she would cross that bridge when Vy arrived tomorrow, she decided. Not now.

The room was surprisingly modest, though the padded carpet felt comfortable underfoot after she'd kicked her shoes off. Similar to a hotel suite, there was a small antechamber with a couch, coffee table, computer equipment on a desk and executive chair, and an entertainment cabinet built into the wall. The door out led into a larger room with a king-sized bed and eight overstuffed pillows.

A vase of fresh flowers was centered on a dresser. There were pictures set up on it that Anika didn't get close enough to look at, and the walls were oddly bare. An empty walk-in closet led into a bathroom with a large built-in tub and a glass-enclosed shower.

Kerrie got her some oversized, fluffy bath towels and a robe, and then disappeared to find clothes.

Alone, Anika locked the bathroom door, then stripped. She looked at the bruises turning purple on her arms, her chest, her ribs, her thighs, and in the mirror, her left eye.

Who was this looking back at her? Purple-haired, dreadlocked, a quarter of her face turned green, some of that smudged off from hitting the side of the helicopter.

The new Anika. The vengeful Anika. Anika on a mission.

She leaned forward and scrubbed the green from her skin. And in the mirror, there she was again. Anika.

The shower, it turned out, had serious water pressure. The showerhead kicked and spat a nearly solid stream of water.

Anika grinned.

She disappeared under a haze of heat, just focusing on the slap of water against her body ripping away an outer layer of skin.

For fifteen minutes, time stopped.

Roo knocked, and Anika let him in. Kerrie hadn't returned, but Anika had the bathrobe tied on and a towel wrapped around her hair.

He had a laptop, and balanced on it, a large platter with two plates. "Is mostly bar food up there," he apologized. "But good bar food."

Anika's mouth watered as he set the food on the coffee table. She didn't wait for permission to start scarfing.

"Sorry to come down," Roo said. "But I wanted to show you something."

He opened the laptop with greasy fingers, burger in one hand, and rotated it toward her.

The picture on the screen was fuzzy, but Anika recognized the man's face anyway. She wasn't going to forget anytime soon. "I recognize him. The Canadian Coast Guard ship. Gabriel."

Roo nodded. "Garret Dubuque is his real name, but he had gone by Gabriel in the community for a serious while back then. And the thing about him is, the man been retired a decade."

Anika looked up from the picture. "What do you mean by retired?"

"That man don't work for no one anymore. Certainly no Canadians. Everyone I talk to say he's out."

"Roo, that is impossible," Anika protested. "He flew out to that ship. He had us picked up. They imprisoned us for him!"

"He ain't no state actor. He must have pulled favors and paid people off to make that happen. I also bet no one knows we were picked up. We were never officially on that ship. We never officially got away from it. No one knew."

Anika put down the remains of her burger, her appetite lost. "Jesus. Roo. Jesus. What would have happened after we docked? What is happening to us?"

"These globes trickling up to the air. U.S., China, Russia, India, Europe, Turkey, all working together to try and find and stop these things." Roo shook his head in a sort of puzzled wonder. "Gaia launch vehicles getting destroyed. But still these globes are being launched from new places no one knew Gaia owned every few hours, and the globes are gathering in the Arctic air here, over international waters. I'm reading that everyone's on red alert. Politicians trying to decide whether to launch World War Three up against a company. Today a 'Friends of the World' ship rammed a Chinese destroyer trying to board a mist boat, and the Chinese opened fire. Sunk it. And no one knows what to think."

"And then there's the nuke," Anika said. "It was on a Gaia-chartered ship, I assume, as they had those globes inside it. What are they planning with it?"

"Can't be nothing good," Roo said. "Nothing good at all."

They finished dinner in thoughtful silence.

# 27

Kerrie knocked on the door, and Anika opened it to find that she was standing there with an armful of clothes.

"Thank you." Anika briefly peeked at the black jeans and plain black tee, oversized wool sweater, socks, and Windbreaker.

"No problem, hon. Sleep well."

Anika retreated with the clothes back into the bedroom. She put them on top of the dresser and paused to look at the photos. They were in cheap fake-wooden frames, painted black. There was a picture of Vy as a teenager, grinning wildly, on a beach with an American skyline behind her. Chicago? Vy on a boat, beautiful bright blue water sparkling behind her.

Behind those two was a picture of a large gate, snow packed along the bottom. A line of footsteps in the snow led away from a small access door beside the gate. Barbed wire rolled along the top of the gate's metal spikes, and a grim-looking man in a thick fur hat, rifle slung on his shoulder, stood on the other side of the gate looking blankly toward the camera.

The pixelated quality meant it had probably been snatched from an old camera phone and printed.

Anika looked at the fourth photo and came across Vy kissing a cute girl with green eyes, limp hair, and glossy lips.

Who was this?

She stared at it for a long time, and then finally reached up and faced it down on the dresser, gently.

No. This wasn't her stuff to meddle with, Anika thought. She was a guest. She set the photo back up.

That was the right thing to do, wasn't it?

Right or not, Anika changed her mind, and faced the photo back down.

Not while she was staying the night, alone.

She turned away, slid the bathrobe off, and crawled into the large bed. She arranged the overstuffed pillows in a circle around herself, as if she were making a nest.

Propped up, the large comforter pulled up to her neck, Anika found a remote to the wall-mounted screen. News programs were now, she saw, covering the "Crisis in the Arctic."

She'd been hunkered down, away from her phone or any connections. Focused on her own problems. She felt like she was coming up for media air and looking around, now.

This morning the news had broken about the spheres, just as Bish said. Grainy green-hued footage of crates of spheres being packed away as they rolled off assembly lines had leaked to the world at large.

Now came zooming maps of the world, with existing launch points highlighted. And the Arctic Circle bloomed with little red dots.

Navy ships steamed northward at high speed in shaky videos taken by passing ships. And then Anika watched mist boats vomiting spheres, and teams of international peacekeeping forces storming them to put a stop to it.

And then . . . video of the mist boats blowing up. Anika recognized the jerky movement and perspective right away, and realized this was *Bish*'s doing. He'd gotten his video uploaded. Somewhere, she was willing to bet, video of the holds opening and releasing spheres was floating around as well.

Now Lars's video from the helicopter, jerked around, trying to focus on the destruction.

"This was not an American attack," a fully uniformed admiral told an interviewer as the screen split. "Our policy for this crisis has been to capture store-holds of Gaia's devices and prevent further launches."

Again Anika focused on Lars's video, and her eyes widened. There she was, for the briefest second, glimpsed out of the corner of the video, leaning against the door and wincing. Green makeup and purple hair and all.

Her own mother wouldn't have recognized her.

Then Lars was back to the burning ships.

Anika changed to a different news show.

"No one knows what a large mirror could do," an expert was interviewed as saying. "You can't just start moving massive amounts of heat around the atmosphere willy-nilly and not expect catastrophic results! What Gaia is doing is dangerous to us all. We can't have maverick geo-engineering projects."

Another guest yelled, "Companies have been moving heat around 'willy-nilly' for centuries, and when people complained they were told we couldn't say anything negative about industry or growth. That's a complete double standard. Dumping heat and carbon is *why* we're in trouble now. That was the geo-engineering project."

Anika turned it all off.

She wondered where Vy was, and what she was doing. Then she hoped that Bish had found a place to stay, and wasn't wandering Pleasure Island alone after all he'd been through.

Halfway through the night she thought she felt someone slide into the bed behind her, breasts pushing softly against her back.

But as she half-flailed awake, picked up empty comforters and shoved pillows aside, she realized it was a half-awake fantasy. The cold truth was that she was alone and sore and very, very tired.

She slumped back asleep.

Someone shook her gently awake. Anika bolted upright, and the person jumped back away from her.

It was Kerrie. Dressed in a top hat and a full black tuxedo with tails. "Sorry sweetie, you weren't answering the door. Roo was worried."

Anika sat up and rubbed her eyes with one hand while holding the comforter over her chest with the other. "Thanks."

"No problem."

Kerrie walked out of the room, the tails gently slapping the backs of her knees.

Once she was dressed she hunted around for a comb that would work halfway decently on her hair, then realized she had dreadlocks now and wouldn't be combing them.

Roo waited outside in the corridor. "I was worried for you," he said. "And they ready with breakfast."

"You're safe to come in, Roo. I won't bite you."

"Alright."

They strolled down the corridor. "Why is this Vy's retreat?" Anika asked. "What is her connection to this place?"

"Back in the day Violet used to work here. After Siberia. Gave her a fresh start, right? Two years ago the old owner made a move to evict all of them, so Violet ran a deal to buy him out. A favor to her past."

"Siberia?" Anika asked.

Roo looked over. "That'll be her story to tell, not mine."

They took the small elevator up. Roo leaned over. "Just ask her about the tattoos."

"Okay," Anika replied, while wondering what tattoos Vy had. She'd never noticed any. At least, not on any of Vy's skin exposed in the club.

She looked at Roo with a stab of sudden suspicion. He saw it, and laughed. "No, Anika. I know some of Violet's past, that's all. Is good business to know such things."

Fair enough.

But Anika was realizing she really didn't know much about Vy, did she? Why was she putting so much at risk? Why turn her life upside down just to help Anika?

Did Vy expect some sort of debt to be paid? Was that why she'd been put in Vy's room?

And, Anika wondered, was that even a bad thing in and of itself?

Breakfast was ready, buffet style, in the commercial kitchen gleaming with stainless steel tables and equipment. The club wasn't open yet. "Waiting for Violet," Kerrie told her as she slid bacon onto her plate with a spatula. "A courtesy."

The women were all dressed differently, and Anika enjoyed the spectacle. From bikinis to suits to jeans and a loose shirt, it looked like a parade in the kitchen.

Kerrie noticed her looking around as they filed out into the top floor dance area booths to eat. "Men don't like particular women so much as archetypes. Objectification is a tool in this business. They're coming in here looking for specific looks to fill fantasies."

"And what's your look?" Anika asked.

Kerrie reached into a pocket and pulled out square, black-rimmed glasses. She pulled her hair back into a bun and clipped it in place. "Hot teacher or secretary."

They sat down, and as everyone filed out from the kitchen, Kerrie kept the commentary going. "That's Alicia. Tattoos and dark eyes and all black clothes, piercings, she gave you her clothes there. She works the programmers and engineers. Truth is, she's a soccer nut and gym-rat and pretty bubbly. Tempo, over there, she's our blonde. All dyed, she complains about the upkeep. Toya is our ample-breasted and curvy dancer, very Marilyn Monroe-ish, but also works as our resident redhead and bush-queen, as the ginger-lovers want to see the red down there to reassure themselves it's real. All archetypes."

Anika nodded and watched the fifteen dancers all group around different tables, trying to guess which identity they were playing to. She didn't see Adriana anywhere.

The vote must have been against her staying.

"When is Vy getting here?" she asked.

"Another hour."

Anika's stomach knotted slightly.

To keep herself busy she borrowed a phone to look up information about Gaia while sitting off by herself at one of the booths in the corner of the floor.

There wasn't much she could find that wasn't already common knowledge. Gaia was another garage-launched green company from just after the turn of the century. Back when that wasn't big business.

When Ivan Cohen and Paige Greer teamed up, they began a ten-year spree of gobbling up anyone playing with alternative energy and batteries. At first, everyone assumed they were battery geeks obsessed with making gadgets last longer between recharging.

But then Gaia began using its capital and money leverage to roll out the bigger projects: wind farms or small nuclear reactors for small towns.

They began trying to acquire power companies, carbon sequestration companies, water filtration technology, anything that assumed global warming would get worse and these technologies would be needed.

And now they were. And Cohen and Greer were the ones to go to if you wanted to kick oil dependency. Or turn ocean water into fresh for your coastal cities.

Corporate headquarters was now a former Russian aircraft carrier called *The Green Monster* after the public's not-so-affectionate nickname for Gaia, Inc. Gaia's home page showed video of it anchored off New York City. The mobile headquarters had left after a G-35 summit where Cohen and Greer had tried to force a controversial—and doomed in the public and politicians' eyes—measure to ban internal combustion engines and coal-fired plants throughout the G-35. U.S. officials had walked out. The country had a two-hundred-year supply of coal; it would not be doing any such thing.

Where was *The Green Monster* headed next?

Anika bit her lips. It was already here in the Circle. It was supposed to dock at Thule three days ago.

Now that, she thought, was interesting.

The door cracked open, making her wince and blink as she looked up from the phone's screen. Vy stood at the door. Anika smiled at her, and almost stood. But then froze when she realized Vy wasn't smiling back.

As Anika's eyes adjusted she saw the seven men wearing gray suits who stood grimly behind Vy. Out of place here on Pleasure Island, where most people were hard workers. Functional clothing reigned in these parts, not thousand-dollar brands.

They'd walked right past the masked bouncers outside, too. What did *that* mean? That Vy had allowed them past, or that the bouncers, realizing these men were more dangerous, had let them through rather than start a firefight? Then, as the doors opened further, Anika saw that two suited men stood outside with the bouncers, guns aimed at them.

Anika shivered, but not from the blast of cold air that had swept through from the doors.

A thin, leathery-faced Gabriel stepped out from behind Vy and her escorts. He looked around Pussy Galore's, a twinge of disgust quirking his lips.

"You were hard to track. Fooling facial scanners. Quite clever. So I had to intercept Violet's ship and get her to . . . help us reintroduce each other." He shook his head slightly, as if disappointed. "You should have stayed put."

The ladies of Pussy Galore's melted out of the room without a word, slipping into the kitchen or back down the corridor toward their rooms, leaving Anika very much alone.

# 28

The suits spread out, two of them turning to cover the door they'd just walked in. They had their hands in their jackets—resting on guns, no doubt.

Anika stood up, mouth open in shock. "Vy? What have you done?"

Vy smiled sadly. "I'm sorry, Anika, it's complicated right now."

*Who was Vy?* Anika had wondered. She still didn't know, but she was certainly not necessarily a friend. She'd sold Anika out. Handed her back over to Gabriel.

Anika looked around the room, but Gabriel shook his head and pulled a handgun out from a shoulder holster. "Don't try to run, Anika. I would have to shoot you. Which is not what I want. Understand me?"

"Yes." Anika glared at Vy, who didn't seem affected by this at all. "Who are you?"

Vy looked down. "Gabriel won't hurt you. He just needs to take you somewhere where you won't get hurt."

"He is a liar, I would not trust a word of his," Anika said. "We know for a fact he no longer works for the Canadians. He's not an official of any sort."

Vy raised an eyebrow, but did not look all that surprised. "Working more than one side, Gabriel?"

Gabriel squinted. "Don't try to muddle your way into all this. Let's just get this done."

Vy raised her hand. "Now, please . . ." she said, almost in a bored tone of voice.

The two bouncers, hairy chests and zipped masks and all, stepped inside from their posts outside. They had disabled the two men who were watching them. And they were now carrying very large assault rifles. "Hands up gentlemen."

Hands, however, did not go up. The men in suits split, the ones on the edges of the group diving for cover and pulling guns out from under their jackets. Not for even a second did they consider disarming.

The two club guards opened fire after a second of hesitation, surprised at the reaction.

The three nearest suits fired at the same instant as the guards. Blood exploded out the backs of the gray material with the loud crack of the rifles, and at the same time, the pop of handguns dropped the two guards. Blood sprayed from their bare chests as they stumbled back against the doors and fell.

Vy and Gabriel hit the floor.

One of the suits worked his way around behind a booth, gun out, to make sure Anika wouldn't run.

She turned and glared at him. He kept his distance, though, cautious.

In the silence that had settled over the dance floor, the very distinct sound of a shotgun round being chambered echoed.

Gabriel, now getting to his knees, frowned.

None of his men carried shotguns.

Tempo, the blonde, shoved the kitchen doors open, forcing one of the suits out in front of her at the end of the shotgun. Behind her came Alicia, armed with a submachine gun.

She turned right, focusing on another suit standing beside the door. Anika noticed that she had a half-crouch walk and the submachine gun pulled tightly to her shoulder.

These performers had been trained to handle their respective weapons.

"Throw down your fucking weapons," Alicia shouted. "There are more of us, we're well fucking armed."

The two men held their weapons out, handle-first, and started to get to the floor.

But the three men using the booths for cover opened fire.

Tempo jerked, hit, and the shotgun went off. Point blank. Blood and flesh sprayed across the floor. The second round of the shotgun hit the ceiling as she fell.

Shards of glass from the mirrored tile shattered and fell, and Alicia fired a burst into the man by her and dove at Gabriel, who held Vy down with a gun to her head.

Smooth hands grabbed Anika and shoved a gun

against her temple. "We're just going to sit here for a moment, and if you move, you'll die," her captor said.

Anika was not going to sit passively. She elbowed the man behind her and grabbed his gun hand, shoving it up into the air.

Right by her head, the shot sounded impossibly loud, instead of the pops she'd heard when they first started firing.

Bits of ceiling fell down and shattered on the floor around them.

Anika managed to twist her other arm up, and now held on to the man's gun hand desperately with both hands.

He grabbed her head with his free hand and smacked it into the booth's table. Her vision narrowed, but she hung on to the gun. Her sore muscles and bruised ribs protested as they scrabbled around the cushions of the booth. The gun fired twice again into the air.

He managed to get her up against the back of the booth and shoved his forearm underneath her throat to choke her.

Then a loud smack staggered him. He let go of her and slumped over.

Kerrie stood over him with a baseball bat, blood smearing the end of it. She grabbed the gun.

Anika shoved the man off her, and he slid down under the booth's table.

She took a deep breath and looked around. Alicia sat on the floor, submachine gun hanging by a strap on her shoulder, crying as she held Tempo on her lap.

A couple of the suits crawled in their own pools of

blood, lost in a haze of personal pain, trying to get . . . somewhere.

Two of the performers sat on chairs holding dish towels to wounds.

And Vy had Gabriel standing up. She held his own gun to his head. Her hand shook slightly as she also scanned the room, and then spotted Anika.

She looked relieved.

# 29

The club was locked down and quiet for the day, the neon signs over the doors turned off. Gabriel had been tied up to a pipe in a storeroom in the kitchen.

Vy spent most of the hour after the gunfight on her phone. Within minutes she'd called in a dark-haired Italian doctor, who'd been escorted quickly through the door—which was barred shut again.

He confirmed Tempo was dead, stabilized one of the suits, then confirmed the rest of them dead. Both bouncers were dead. Several of the performers had cuts from glass and debris.

A silent cleanup began, everyone pitching in to sweep up glass and mop up blood. Someone started crying halfway through.

No one would look at Anika. And she could hardly bring herself to look up from the area she'd decided to clean up either.

So much blood.

. . .

Vy touched her shoulder. "Anika?"

Anika was sitting on the carpet just outside the elevator on the lower floor, her back against the wall. She'd meant to get back to the room for a time-out, to try and process everything, but she'd only made it a few steps out of the elevator before needing to sit. She looked up. "Hi, Vy."

"How are you doing?" Vy cocked her head as she reached out a hand. "The new hair is different. I almost didn't recognize you when we came in."

"I thought you had handed me over to Gabriel back there." Anika pulled herself up. "He captured us. He sank Roo's boat."

"I know. I couldn't send a message ahead. He boarded the boat we were taking here. Took us by surprise. Chernov's dead."

"Chernov?"

Vy looked over, her body language heavy and tired. "My bodyguard, assistant, you met him back at the club?"

"I'm sorry."

"No, I'm sorry," Vy said. "I should have taken this all more seriously than I did."

"It's okay. They have me staying in your room. . . ."

"That was a mistake," Vy said gently. "They should have given you your own room."

Anika swallowed. "Tempo, and the others. Why did they do that for me?"

"Fight back?" Vy put a hand on her shoulder. "They're tough people in a tough place. They don't take well to being pushed around. It wasn't for you, it's how we all handle security. They all know crowd control. Most of them take personal defense classes, most of them practice target shooting. Some of them . . . have had rough experiences. We all have. I know you have, too."

"This is a lot of bad shit, Vy."

Vy pulled her closer into a tight hug. "Don't worry about where things stand, okay? We need to go talk to Roo, right now, and figure out what we're all going to do next."

"Why are you helping me?" Anika whispered into her shoulder.

"You're not the only person who knew Tom. You two came in to The Greenhouse a couple times, when he was showing you around. Tom and I went back a ways. I asked him about you the second time you two came in. I saw you flirting with one of the bartenders."

"Tom knew little about me then," Anika said.

"He knew enough. You were quiet, kept your head down. Worked hard. Family was important to you. And Tom swore you had his back, no matter what. I don't give friendship easily, but after hearing him and other people from your base talk, I liked you. Tom trusted you completely. Even with his life."

"And look where that got him," Anika said. She kept holding on, though. The hug was real. It was contact. It felt better than a down bed and a hot shower and a pillow and oxycodone all rolled into one.

"What would you think about yourself if you knew you had let a nuclear device through your hands?" Vy asked. Anika let go, and Vy looked at her and nodded. "I thought so. Tom was a friend. You're a friend. I'm helping. We've got this whole 'different worlds' thing going, but right now, you should stop asking why. Unless you want to hang all this up and go back."

"I'm not going back," Anika said.

"Me either." Vy took her arm. "Someone has a motherfucking nuclear device. And chances are, they're going to use it. If we can figure out how to stop them, we should. Basic fucking morality, right? Now let's go talk to our pet secret agent."

"Roo?"

"Yes. The other secret agent is hardly a pet. We'll deal with him soon."

"We have here," Roo said, turning his laptop to face them, "a chance to make some serious serious money off Gabriel. Or, get us all some real favors."

"I have money," Vy said.

"Favors it is then, girl." He swiveled the laptop back around and started typing furiously. "Everyone's combing for information about that nuclear weapon. We have a solid lead. Anything we can get out of this-here mysterious Mr. Gabriel, that'll be worth a lot. And it's for sure he knows something. So the question: how do we make that man talk?"

Vy cleared her throat. Her voice was suddenly chilly. "It's been a long time since I've had to do anything like that, Prudence."

"Then maybe he tells us everything he knows because he a nice guy, right?" Roo folded his arms.

Vy looked downward. "If we have to."

Anika had been following the exchange. She was

pretty sure they were talking about torture. She didn't like where this was going and stepped in. "Did he come with luggage, or a briefcase?"

Roo looked at her. "Yeah, a briefcase."

"Then maybe it won't come to whatever it is you're thinking," she said, while wondering, once again, who Vy really was. What had she been through that she'd been forced to do something like that?

Upstairs in the kitchen, Anika cracked the familiar briefcase open. Vy and Roo moved Gabriel to a chair and tied him to it while Anika looked at the cluster of leads, trying to remember what attached to what.

Chest leads, both sides of the ribs, ankles. Cap on the hair.

She turned the machine on, looking at the various screens slowly drawing the brain map. She'd been distracted and scared when it had been used on her. But she'd paid enough attention.

"Would you like to skip all this and just tell us what you know about the nuclear device?" Anika asked their captive.

Gabriel looked at her, lips pressed firmly together, betraying no emotion at all. The lead wires trailed down the front of his body to the machine, rustling slightly on his shirt as he moved.

"Okay," Anika said. She had a feeling that would be his response. "Is your name really Gabriel?"

She saw Roo smile briefly out of the corner of her eye.

Gabriel cleared his throat and spoke softly, as if

each word were something he was compelled to say. "Anika, this will not be that easy. I am not going to say yes or no to anything you ask me. At all. Do you understand?"

"Gabriel . . ." Anika said.

"I have my convictions," he said. "Do you have yours?"

"Damn it, Gabriel, there's a nuclear weapon free out here."

He leaned forward, straining against the rope binding him to the chair. "It's not going to be simple, Anika. Or easy." He looked around at Vy and Roo. "They understand."

Anika leaned back and looked over at Roo, who shook his head. Anika looked over at Vy. "Vy?"

Vy had a hand in her pocket. "Fuck it," she said.

Then she drew out a pair of brass knuckles and threw a punch against the side of Gabriel's head. Skin split, blood flew, and Gabriel rocked back in the chair.

# 30

Roo dragged Anika out of the kitchen. He was, as she remembered, surprisingly strong. She tried to twist free, and he moved with her, fluidly, easily, and redirected her movement so that she spun all the way back around and kept walking out with him.

"This is *not* good," Anika shouted. There were a handful of performers outside still. They all looked up. "We shouldn't be doing this. Not Vy."

Inside the kitchen, a loud smack dribbled out through the doors. Anika flinched.

"There was a girl, once, running weed up and down the Alaska corridor. She made good money, right?" Roo said, holding Anika back by the shoulders. "But one day, off the Bering Coast, she was picked up by Russian Coast Guard. And she disappeared into the prison systems. You understand?"

"Yes."

"I got her out a year later," Roo said. "By then . . . she'd learned some things. Like when she started out in Baffin, a short, blond woman dealer would have to be tougher, more brutal, than a man, or people wouldn't listen closely. It took a while for things to settle."

"No." Anika tried to push past Roo, but he held her. "Roo!" She shouted that loud enough everyone openly stared.

"Anika, let her do it."

Anika held her hands up. "No. We won't leave her to do it alone. So let me go, and quit trying to be protective. You are my friend, let go of me."

Roo did, and Anika marched back into the kitchen. She ran into Vy with her shoulder, shoving her aside, and looked down at Gabriel.

He looked up, face bruised and bloodied. A tear rolled off his cheek. "It's okay, Anika." Blood dripped from his lips. "It's okay. It's repayment. I deserve this. We all know it. I've done worse. You've seen some of the things I've done. I've cost enough lives, I knew this would come some day. But I cannot give you what you want. And I'm sorry."

She thought about the sadness in him. And the disgust and regret in his voice when he'd talked to her about torture back on the Canadian Patrol Boat.

He was not an immoral man.

And also, not a masochist. He was suffering.

"Gabriel, please. Please answer a question. Just one. We've stopped. It's me." A thick rivulet of blood dripped down the side of his left eye as she looked right at him and leaned forward, half hugging him. He rested his head, wires and all, on her shoulder. "When that nuclear bomb explodes, will it hurt people?"

She could feel him pause. It was the muscle language. He was refusing to answer, one way or another, but she could feel him gather himself to resist more torture.

"A moral man can condemn innocents to death in war," she said softly, letting him go. "The religious, the righteous, those getting ready for war, they agree to sacrifice innocents caught between them. The lives are filed under 'collateral damage.' That is the price," Anika said. "I'm not so innocent either, Gabriel. And I know that even they, when forced to stare into what they're about to do, flinch slightly."

"Anika?" Vy asked. "What are you talking about?"

"He's trained for resistance," Roo said, squatting in front of Gabriel. "No one survives torture forever. He's hanging in there, long enough so that whatever he's hiding, it will be over soon. But he doesn't like it."

"He's conflicted about his mission," Anika said. "Regret, guilt. That's why he almost welcomes this."

"He's conflicted, but determined," Roo said. "We could beat something out of him, with the help of that machine, but how long will that take?"

They all looked down at the beaten man, who remained slumped, looking down at the floor.

"Fuck," Vy spat. "Just . . . fuck."

"The nuclear weapon was on what we presume was a Gaia-chartered ship," Anika said. "And Gaia headquarters is docked in Thule. The man running away from the UNPG is in Thule. Everything, it seems, leads to Thule. Doesn't it, Mr. Garret Dubuque?"

Gabriel didn't answer.

Anika leaned over and slid the brass knuckles off Vy's fingers, and gently pushed them onto hers.

"All I want is a yes or no answer, Gabriel, for the machine. You don't have to tell us where the bomb actually is. But I wonder if you might point us in the right direction? Because there are a lot of people who live their lives in Thule. Innocent people. You yourself asked me a question—about what I would do, if I could get information that could save lives. Now I know."

He shook his head.

She hit him. They both flinched. Her own body shuddered in empathy, and she wanted to throw up. But he was a killer. He knew where this bomb was.

This could save lives.

He wouldn't break. But he could let her know if Thule was the right direction.

She hit him again—in the ribs, the brass knuckles digging hard into the palms of her hand—thinking of the people who could die. Thinking of Tom.

Tom. That made it easier to punch again, this time hearing something crack. To hit the face and see the blood and spit and not even care.

Think of the man who tried to kill her.

Think of being tied up, helpless on the ship, wondering what would happen to her.

And yet. If this was vengeance, the blood didn't feel very good. Even the blood of a dangerous man like Gabriel. Something in the back of her brain screamed stop, that he was tied-up, defenseless, no longer a threat.

But that was her lizard brain. A poor moralist. Gabriel was no longer a threat directly. Like a caged lion, he had been neutered. But the greater machine of plans he was a part of, something the back of her brain struggled to literalize, that was still a threat.

Gabriel's body twitched with sobs. "You wouldn't be able to find it. It'll be hidden. Shielded."

He was convincing himself, she knew. Convincing himself that he could make the pain stop, but that he wouldn't be betraying whatever it was he was a part of.

"But it's in Thule, right?" Anika asked, out of breath.

Gabriel nodded. Ashamed. For being weak, for giving this up. "But that's as much as I'll tell you," he grunted. "Any more, any more, and it would be better for me to die. Maybe . . . maybe you can get some people to leave Thule. Evacuate."

He looked up at her with pleading eyes.

"Vy?" Anika pulled the knuckles off and let them drop to the floor, relieved. She was ready to cry herself. "Can we get to Thule quickly?"

"We're owed favors," Roo said. "I'll get on it."

"Vy, call your doctor back," Anika said. And she kneeled in front of Gabriel.

He looked at her through blood and puffed skin, coughed, and leaned further forward. "It's okay," he said.

Anika shook her head. "No, it isn't. I don't know what the fuck you're involved with, Gabriel. But it was far from fucking okay. It'll never be okay. I won't be okay."

He started laughing, a wet choking sound that ended with a cry of pain. The ribs. "Please stay away from Thule, Anika. Send them a warning, tell them to leave. But don't go. I'm sorry you've lost friends.

But no good will come of going to Thule. I promise you."

"Good-bye, Gabriel." You weird, strange, little old man, she thought.

And then: I'm so sorry. She'd have nightmares about what she'd just done for the rest of her life.

Outside the kitchen doors, Roo was on his phone. He gave her a thumbs-up. "We have transportation into Thule," he said. "Courtesy of the Dutch Navy. They'll also pick up Gabriel. Various people are very interested in him now. For one, we're all really interested to know who he's working for."

Anika could imagine. "How long?"

"They land in fifteen minutes. Grab what stuff you need and let's run. And yes, I am definitely flying out with you. I've been officially attached to you by the Caribbean Intelligence Agencies." Roo left to find a bag for the laptop he'd somehow acquired and some spare phones.

Anika looked over at Vy. "You don't have to come any further. You've done too much."

But Vy shook her head. "With all the trouble you've already gotten into, you'll need someone who knows Thule. And who can watch your back. Besides, this has gotten somewhat personal. They killed Chernov. I owe them."

Deep down, she'd been hoping Vy would come. "Thanks." She let out a breath she'd been holding in.

"It's going to get ugly, I think." Vy crossed her arms.

"I know," Anika said. "I've seen ugly. But I'm not backing down, either."

Vy nodded.

And Roo returned. He threw a duffel bag that

clanked loudly down on the floor. He unzipped it to reveal semiautomatic weapons, pistols, several grenades, and an assortment of very large knives.

"Pick your weapons of choice. Seeing what happened the last few times we ventured out, I think from now on, we stay heavily armed." He looked at Anika. "Get ready to get back outside, you'll need to fool the cameras again, just to be safe."

Anika picked up a pistol, checked it over, and then found an ammunition clip in a separate part of Roo's arsenal. She tucked it into the back of the waistband of her newly acquired jeans.

"What about you, you getting made up?"

Roo nodded. "War paint for the digital world."

# 31

They flew out of Pleasure Island aboard a Dutch Navy helicopter. Unlike the last pilot, this one flew high over the water, leaving Anika feeling more comfortable.

She preferred it when the water looked like a solid surface far below.

The bench seats behind the pilot and copilot had room for six people. Roo, Anika, and Vy had been joined by an officer, who patiently waited for them to put on large headphones with mics.

Noise cancellation washed over them.

"Hello, I am Albus Van Petersen," their host told them in precise English. He hadn't even blinked at their camera-confusing makeup. "I am pleased to be meeting you. I'm an intelligence officer attached to the Standing NATO Naval Response Force Three. I serve aboard the HDMS *De Ruyter*. I have been assigned to make sure you understand the position in which you are about to place yourselves."

He pulled out a pad with a long, legal-looking document on it.

"What's that?" Vy asked.

"Right now the Response Force is blockading Thule. A coordinated, multinational response has demanded that Gaia, Inc., immediately cease releasing its products into the upper atmosphere." Albus pointed out the window. They were flying over more naval ships steaming north, wakes stretching behind them like long arrows of disturbed ocean. "Ships and troop transports from the G-35 nations are contributing more forces to the blockade of Thule. Gaia, Inc., has had its assets seized in most G-35s, but we have found that a considerable amount of assets, particularly factories, have been moved over the last decade to non–G-35 nations. We've moved past demands and into all-out military action."

"And if Gaia doesn't stop releasing those devices?" Roo asked.

"If non–G-35s refuse to shut the factories down, there *will* be airstrikes, which will, of course, cause all sorts of blowback. Sovereignty will be violated, nations upset. And it looks likely the standoff with Thule will turn into conflict at any moment. I think the non–G-35s are basing their decisions on what happens in the next forty-eight hours over Thule. I am guessing that will be a full invasion, the way things are moving." Albus thrust the pad all the way forward between them all. "That's why you need to sign this document. All of you. It states that we are not responsible for whatever happens to you as a result of us transporting you into the middle of all this."

"The Dutch Armed Forces want us to sign a waiver to cover their ass?" Vy asked, amazement tingeing her voice.

"Yes."

Roo took the pad. "Yeah, man, why not?"

As they signed the pad and passed it around, Anika looked over at Albus. "You think the G-35 nations are really are going to attack Gaia headquarters?"

Albus shrugged. "I don't know for sure. But look outside the window. I think many of the rules are changing." He pointed.

Anika craned her neck to look up in the direction Albus pointed.

The sky flashed silver, as if God himself had sprayed a mirror finish on the clouds that normally sheeted the highest part of the sky. She could see that there were still clumps of air in between five different masses of silvered clouds as the spheres were still coagulating over whatever position Gaia was commanding them to slowly move into.

"There must be billions of them," Anika said.

"And more launching every hour," Albus said. "Once those five formations join up, they become as powerful as if Gaia had launched a giant mirror into orbit. In fact, more so. A mirror could be shot out of orbit. The spheres cannot be destroyed—an explosion would damage some spheres; the rest would scatter from the concussion. We're trying to compute how powerful the mirror will be, but until we see it in action it is hard to say. Right now it's mainly using heat energy to move itself around, we're not seeing it in full action."

Anika thought about the flash of light that boiled the water back at the mist boats. It wasn't just navigating—that cloud had destructive power. But she had another pressing concern: "How will we land at the harbor if Thule is being blockaded? Won't they refuse to let us land?"

"It's Thule," Albus said, sounding puzzled. "Even if you declare war on them, if you pay for the harbor fee and entrance visa, they'll happily trade with you."

Someone, somewhere, once realized that the Arctic Circle needed its very own Hong Kong, its very own Singapore. A replication of relatively unfettered laissez-faire mercantilism run amok. A free-trade harbor. Low-tax haven. A place for the edges of Arctic society to experiment and innovate.

It began with offshore oil ships used for storage, rafted together, serving as the hub for cross-polar oil shipping. Several oil multinationals joined their resources and gave birth to a new entity responsible for maintaining the flotilla and storing the oil. It also buffered them against liability in the event of a spill.

And then things went their own direction. The flotilla began serving as a free harbor for not only oil, but *any* shipping. Floating factories were towed into place so that midsized and pico-sized factories could manufacture on the spot the objects that were being shipped, using raw materials shipping in from other directions.

The flotilla grew. The harbor ossified. Tall buildings grew out of the decks of the ships. Floating derricks the size of skyscrapers were purchased. Anika could see this seed that began Thule as they flew in, a twenty-square-mile area of glittering, floating metal. The harbor side of Thule consisted mainly of barges lashed to other barges to create a miniature Venice at sea here on the edge of the ice. Towering apartment blocks really were encased derricks, their feet stretching out far below to stabilize them.

Thule Corporation leased space to the various entities that grew into being under its larger umbrella, made few rules, and profited. As the old flotilla harbor grew, its board of directors realized that gaining more usable "land" would allow unprecedented profits.

So they decided to save the polar ice cap and move aboard.

Who was going to complain? After all, the rest of the world was resigned to just letting it slowly . . . melt away.

That part of Thule stretched out past the industrial metal grime of the harbor and its swinging walkways and long piers. Fresh, pristine ice architecture radiated away from the blotch of the harbor. The size of this salvaged ice-island was famously compared to roughly that of Rhode Island. Underneath the igloos and ice apartments, burrowed in and insulated, Thule's explosive growth continued on, reaching icy fingers out until it reached the North Pole Arctic Preserve.

Massive snow machines, just like the ones usually seen at ski resorts but scaled up an extra magnitude, spat snow out from the tops of buildings and artificial hills, constantly laying down inches of new snowpack to compensate for the continuous ablation of warmer water.

Fields of solar panels glinted in the harsh, cold air. Massive wind turbines poked their superstructures out from between buildings; several even had buildings on their bases. Offshore, away from the ice pack, even larger wind farms floated, tethered in place by anchors, blades spinning slowly and patiently. Oil might have fueled the rush to the North, but Thule's constituents had a radical commitment to power independence that was visible right from the air.

They circled the harbor, passing through a hail of small midge-like insects that rattled against the outside of the helicopter. The pilot landed at the margin of the airport on the edge of a disk of asphalt raised over the snowpack.

Welcome to the tip-top of the world, Anika thought as the blades began slowing, the pitched whine drawing down. It was a relief to get out and stretch after several hours in the bumpy helicopter.

And then she thought: I'm carrying a pistol in my waistband into an international airport. She leaned over. "Roo, we're all armed and this is an international airport."

"It's Thule," Roo said. "The wild, wild North. You have to use it to do something stupid before they jump at you, and it's just as likely everyone else is armed."

A customs official, looking just like any other cold-weather citizen in a heavy parka and hood with faux-fur lining, waited for them outside as the kicked-up snow blew away.

He held up a phone and took a picture of each of them as they stepped out of the helicopter. "Welcome to Thule," he said, shaking Roo's gloved hand. "The picture is a public-record file of your arrival. The Dutch Navy already paid your entrance fee, so you're welcome to travel where you wish. The fee paid for two weeks of temporary Thule citizenship. As a citizen of Thule you have the following right:

"The right to travel anywhere in Thule you wish, or to leave Thule whenever you wish. Hindrance of free movement of any other person is prohibited.

"All other rights and laws are determined by the demesne you are physically in." The various entities that made up Thule were called demesnes, each allowed to create its own legal and political system. Last count, Anika recalled there being some forty mini-countries within Thule, each an experiment in whatever its founders considered the most optimal way to thrive. "Violation of any law that doesn't involve physical bodily harm to the victim results in demesne expulsion. Violating a standing demesne restraining order results in revocation of Thule citizenship and banishment. Do you accept and understand your rights?"

They all nodded.

"One last thing," the customs official said. "All of Thule is in full little brother protocol mode due to the blockade by the G-35 nations. Just so you're aware."

"And what is that?" Vy asked.

"One hundred percent two-way surveillance," Roo cut in, smiling. "All public camera feeds and monitoring services are open to the outside world to peruse. All outgoing phone calls, even the meetings by the leaders of the demesnes, are broadcast out. Nothing is secret, anything that happens next will be seen live by the entire world."

"Right," the customs official said. "Radical public transparency, or sousveillance, if you will. All of our drones are broadcasting what they see. We have mites in the air and in the water, and they're broadcasting the location and shape of whatever they're sticking to by networking to each other and passing the data back however they can to Thule's servers. Anything we know about military action around Thule, the world is witness to."

Albus Petersen smiled thinly and turned back to scrape one of the midges off the helicopter. He held it up between his fingers, and Anika could see that it glinted where it wasn't covered in some sort of goo. "Well, you have just made my return trip that much more complicated," he said, thoughtfully. "These are everywhere?"

"You will find a declaration and the codes to access what information we're gathering on our public pages," the official said.

Albus sighed. "I have to figure out what they are going to want me to do for the return trip." He nodded at everyone. "Good luck."

He got back in and shut the door and started talking to the pilot. A heated conference between them began on the other side of the window.

"You're here to find the missing nuke?" the official asked, almost casually, pointedly ignoring the commotion between Albus and his pilot.

The engine began to whine behind them. The rotors slowly began to turn.

Anika turned to stare at him. He smiled back. "Little brother protocol. You came in on a military copter with intelligence agencies covering your entry fee and request to land. And when intelligence officials gave the leaders of our demesnes information, they shared it with everyone. Pytheas's dictator is waiting to meet you. I guess you're expected. In other countries they might get annoyed by outsiders coming in to muck around, but we welcome any and all help in resolving this fucking mess. You'll find we do things a bit differently in Thule."

Yeah, thought Anika.

Very differently.

The words "Pytheas's dictator" sunk in, but she ignored them as the helicopter's blades kicked snow and cold air at them in a miniature gale. They hurried away from the landing pad and into the warmth of the Thule airport's swooping glass and steel embrace.

# 32

A six-foot-tall woman with startling blue eyes and pale hair waited for them inside the warm and bright airport terminal. She wore large, white fox furs and grinned with diamond-crusted teeth—which sort-of ruined her otherworldly, almost elfin look, Anika thought. She had a jet-black cane held in one hand, with what looked like an impossibly large diamond on the top.

The flow of people moving to leave Thule passed around her: a stream flowing around a white rock. If Thule was as open as the customs agent indicated, and Anika imagined it was, then everyone knew there was trouble, and the packed mob crushing every inch of the airport terminal was part of a rush to get out of here before things got worse—human rats leaping from a sinking ship.

"Wynter: the dictator of Pytheas," Roo said to Anika. "And that's 'Winter' spelled with a 'y.' I used to know her as Beverly Smithwyck, back when she was a vice president of a mobile factory business. What worries me is . . . why she's here personally."

"Why?" Anika asked. But now Wynter was close enough to overhear them, and she got no answer.

Anika moved to shake the woman's hand, but Wynter made no such move. "You are all posing a rather annoying dilemma for me," she said. "Come."

Four men in cream suits waited outside by a chrome-accented all-white limousine with triangular snow treads instead of wheels.

Once everyone climbed in, Wynter tapped the glass partition with her cane, and the limo rattled into motion.

"My problem is that you're asking me to give up people who've used the submarine docks to enter Thule," Wynter said, her teeth sparkling in the rope lighting of the limo's interior. "My people are going to cry bloody murder. The demesne I run has utter privacy as rule of law. Violet, you understand. You've used the docks before."

"There's a nuclear bomb somewhere in Thule, doesn't that trump everything?" Anika interrupted.

Wynter craned her head to the side and stared at Anika. "Those who give up liberty for security deserve neither," she said. "What else will the Pytheas demesne hand over in order to find this nuclear device? Shall I have you all search house by house? Will my demesne even exist after this?"

"It won't exist if a nuke goes off," Anika pointed out, amazed.

Wynter shook her head. "But we cease to exist if we drastically change the nature of what makes us . . . us. If I do this, the demesne falls apart as I'm accused of turning against the core principles that founded the demesne. My citizenry believes they should not be tracked. Looking at the makeup on your faces; Anika I must ask, surely you understand the inherent value of privacy?"

"And the bomb?" Vy asked.

"There's always some threat that asks us to sacrifice freedoms to combat it. The only truly safe environ is a one-hundred-percent-controlled one. Not a free one." Wynter leaned back against her seat and sighed. "It is a great, modern dilemma."

"I thought you were the dictator of Pytheas, right?" Anika asked. "How are you the dictator if you can't even do this small thing to help us?"

"I'm a *benevolent* dictator," Wynter smiled. "Anyone can lease land from Thule, and that covers maintenance of the snowpack and some minor infrastructure. Everything else is up to the demesne, and anyone can leave: right of movement is the one thing you sign up for. So if what I offer as dictator of Pytheas pales compared to other demesnes, I can't compete. The effectiveness of my policies determines my demesne's viability. And that is why I have a dilemma: people *will* walk away if I do what you're asking. A lot of people."

They continued on in silence, through a streetscape of wide plowed sidewalks and buildings that sat on pylons. Anika was missing having sunglasses; she could use a heads-up display right about now. They'd be popping up little tags telling her what the street was, what demesne they were in, and help her feel a lot less lost.

The leather seats crinkled as Roo leaned forward. "Your citizens understand that business and travel are evaporating if this bomb goes off, right?"

"My subjects voluntarily live under a dictatorship," Wynter said. "They've ceded the worrying about that to me. They don't like hearing about this. All they want to know is that Wynter's got it under control."

"But you don't," said Vy. "No one in the whole Circle's got this under control."

"That's *why* it's a called a dilemma, Violet," Wynter snapped. "There are people in Pytheas actually begging me to kick down every door I can and backtrack your UNPG man's movements so we can ask about the bomb, privacy be damned. I also have the responsibility of fifty thousand loyal subjects' lives, and they absolutely will not understand or appreciate my selling them out, regardless of how much *more* annoyed they'd be if a bomb actually does go off. I also have to wonder if the bomb threat is real, which is why I'm here to meet your new friend, Roo, before I decide to do anything."

Anika stared into the clear blue eyes, and realized that they were artificially colored. She could see faint green rings around the edges. "What do you want from me?"

Wynter wrapped her hands around the top of her cane. "So far we have a lot of paper trail bullshit. It could be the same intelligence agencies working for the blockade messing with our heads. I don't want to make a mistake over a ghost, you understand? I want to look right at you and ask: What *did* you really see, Anika, up there in your little UNPG blimp?"

Anika leaned forward. "The scatter camera got a solid hit. Something radioactive was on board *Kosatka*. Something they worked hard to protect by shooting me down. I wouldn't be here, on Thule, if I thought it was just some barrels of waste they were dumping."

They stared at each other, then Wynter grimaced. "I doubt it's dumping, either, from what I'm seeing." She uncovered the tip of her cane, and a small projector buried in the tip lit up the dark mirror that separated them from the driver.

The picture the cane transmitted was of an older white man with graying hair. He stood near a concrete pier, inside a large ice cavern. The sub harbor, Anika presumed. Somewhere under the ice, under the Pytheas demesne.

"You have public cameras, after all that about privacy?" Roo smirked.

"I'm the *dictator* of this demesne, might I remind you? The rules don't apply to me, and I like to know who comes and goes in my territory. That information has never been shared, other than my using it to keep things quiet and orderly. But . . . being a good dictator means knowing when to toss the rules out. I hope. What you have here is one Mr. Peter Braithwaite," Wynter muttered. "Meeting him is someone I don't recognize. May I add, if anyone finds out I handed these men over to you, I will take it very, fucking, personally."

"Heard." Roo sucked his teeth. He looked back at the frozen scene projected against the window and tapped one of the figures. "We know who this one is."

Wynter raised an eyebrow.

Anika was staring, because she knew that figure, too: it was Gabriel. He stood just on the edge of the image, reaching out to shake Braithwaite's hand.

"This was taken the morning you were shot down," Wynter said. "Those are the sub docks. A lot of this demesne's more interesting characters come through there. That's why I like to keep an eye on it." Braithwaite's image faded away. The next frozen image was a closer still of Gabriel.

Five men surrounded a fifteen-foot-long wooden case, moving it into place aboard the back of a flatbed truck with the help of several small jack stands and ramps. It looked like it was going to stick out of the end a bit, but just barely fit anyway.

There it was, Anika thought, her mouth drying. That was the thing that had caused all this trouble.

"His name is Gabriel. Where did he go after this was taken?" Anika asked. That could lead them to where the bomb was hidden.

"This is all I can show you." Wynter tapped the cane, and the image faded away.

"Damn it," Anika said. "This almost killed me. It killed my copilot. It's hurt people I value."

"I can't give it to you because I don't have it. I have a secret camera on some of the docks. There are some voluntarily public cameras on the edges of Pytheas, looking out at other demesnes, but we're pretty dark."

"So Gabriel's people could be anywhere in your demesne, or could have left for anywhere in Thule," Anika said. "The nuclear device could be anywhere."

"If they've left my demesne, I doubt they can hide for long. There's an ad hoc group of concerned citizens parsing the few public camera archives looking for the vehicle they used to see if it left Pytheas and where it was going. You can look them up, search for 'concerned citizens Thule and nuclear' and they'll pop up. So far it hasn't been found. But thirty vehicles large enough to conceal the device were rented and moved in and out of Pytheas during the time frame we're looking at. I'm reasonably sure they're not currently in Pytheas, but they used the vehicles to cover their movements."

"They knew you were privacy-obsessed; they used that as a cover." Roo looked out the window. "We're not even close to Pytheas, Wynter, we're ten miles the other direction. What are you doing out of your demesne?"

They'd slowed down and the buildings had petered out. Four large structures dominated the area, though; they looked like giant igloos, but multiplied in size many times so that they would have engulfed an aircraft hanger. A few people walked around them and streamed out onto the road, headed toward a large wrought-iron gate.

"You're right. This is the North Polar Conservation Demesne, or the North Pole Arctic Preserve to others. Most of us call it the zoo, or the tourist trap." Ten-foot-tall ice walls curved off into the distance. Wynter opened a door as they came to a stop with all the other visitors. "I've arranged for you to meet a powerful ally here on neutral ground."

Outside again, shivering slightly as the wind ripped over the flat miles of polar ice, they trooped along with a few die-hard visitors.

"Normally it's packed," said Wynter. "People fly out from all over the world to visit. But since the navy blockade everyone's been leaving. Commercial flights are unwilling to land. Locals are more worried about the nuke, or trying to leave. It's a ghost town."

They walked along the snowy roads inside the complex, hiking up until they stopped at a lip. On the other side of the fence, a hundred feet below them, were miles of winding bergs, blue water, and a cluster of harp seals sunning themselves.

"Think about this," Wynter said, as the wind ruffled the white fur around her neck and stirred her blond hair. "Instead of assuming that the nuclear device was smuggled in to create a terrorist incident, assume that both major events that have happened here are connected. A nuclear device, capable of emitting an electromagnetic pulse and frying all the electronics in Thule, will also be able to fry the electronics of those millions of little floating balls overhead."

They all looked up at the silver sheen of the gathering artificial clouds miles overhead.

"If it's meant to kill the Gaia cloud, then why was it on a Gaia ship?" Anika asked.

"Protective camouflage?" Roo guessed.

"Or a monumental fuck up on the part our contracted delivery services," said one of a pair of tourists standing nearby. They'd previously been looking out across the sanctuary.

"And an even bigger screw up on the part of our security people," said the other.

Behind them, a cable car moved along over the frigid landscape. According to a plaque near the fence, this is how you could pass over the last of the polar bear's territory, all four hundred of them. This demesne, run by conservationists, was not for people to live in.

The pair of tourists pulled back their thick hoods, and Anika recognized them.

Ivan Cohen and Paige Greer. The founders of Gaia.

In the distance several loud cracks sounded. Like ice snapping, Anika thought. But it continued to thud and spray. Wynter turned around. "That's my call," she said.

"What's happening?" Anika asked.

The pale dictator looked over her shoulder. "In light of the blockade, and the realization that there's a nuclear device somewhere in Thule, several demesnes are separating from Thule. That sound was dynamite taking out bridgework, connecting streets, what have you."

A cloud of steam rose off the buildings in the distance near the harbor.

"Sort of literalizes the phrase 'breakaway republics,' I think," Vy muttered.

Wynter pulled her coat tighter around herself. "This is good-bye," she said. "I hope you all can help each other out. But I need to go supervise what comes next for Pytheas."

She walked off down the snowy ramp as the detonations continued, this time from another sector, closer to the edge of the harbor docks.

Thule was literally ripping itself apart.

# 33

Anika took a step back. Then she jutted her jaw forward and stepped right back into place. "My name is Anika Duncan. Several days ago I worked for the UNPG, and I approached the *Kosatka,* a ship chartered by your corporation. Can you explain why that ship fired rocket-propelled grenades at us, killing my copilot?"

Ivan Cohen, on the right, was clean shaven. He had small eyes, a tall forehead, his grayed hair thinning slightly. But he had an athletic build, and an intensity to his movements as he held his hands up in a conciliatory gesture. "We were *not* responsible for that," he said, his voice shaking with controlled anger. "We did charter that ship, but someone infiltrated it. It was supposed to join five other freighters that would release their cargo into the air tomorrow morning. We were just as stunned to find out a UNPG spotter airship had been shot down by it, and that it had released its cargo early."

Paige Greer put an arm on his elbow, calming him. She smiled at Anika. It was a disarmingly effective smile. Anika found herself relaxing.

"Ms. Duncan, is it okay if I call you Anika?" Paige asked. She left Ivan's personal space and slipped right into Anika's. It felt like they were suddenly having a private conversation. Between friends.

"Yes." Anika looked down at the shorter, older, almost motherly woman with silvering hair.

"We talked to Anton, an investigator with the UNPG, about the incident. You know him, I think. He told us a lot about you."

"Yes, I know Anton," Anika admitted.

"He's a good man. We were trying to find out who the crew was that the U.S. Navy picked up, but by last night, they'd disappeared. No one could say where. But one thing we know, thanks to Anton's help and some pictures he took at the interrogation, is that they were not the crew originally on the ship that we chartered."

"Then who where they?" Anika asked.

Paige put an arm around the small of Anika's back. "Whoever it was," she said softly. "You managed to destroy their plans. We have to assume it was someone who wants to destroy the solar shield. And they were hoping to fire the nuke off from sea, on a ship known to be chartered by Gaia. No doubt it would make us look insane, reckless, and divided amongst ourselves. Instead, if they do fire it, it is now clear Gaia didn't do it. We owe you, Anika, for forcing them to change their plans, forcing them to load the missile into a submarine and bring it here."

"You owe Tom," Anika said, looking across at Paige. "And his family. Not me."

Paige had steered her to the rail on the edge of the ice bluff. "Ivan and I have already made arrangements for his family," she told Anika. "They should no longer pay a price for our mistakes. But that matter aside, I still believe we also owe *you*, Anika. And you've come all the way out here for a reason. To see this through, am I right?"

Anika nodded. Paige let go of her and grabbed the rail with one hand, and made a sweeping gesture with the other. "We have a common enemy. I'd like to give you the resources, and the satisfaction, of going after them with us. And stopping them from destroying something I've spent most of my life trying to save."

"The whole world?" Anika asked, slightly cynically.

Paige smiled sadly, a slight twinge of disappointment in the corners of her mouth. "Yes, Anika. The world."

Anika expected Gaia HQ to be *The Green Monster,* the repurposed aircraft carrier so heavily advertised on their Web site. Instead Ivan and Paige led them to an unmarked building near the edge of the polar preserve.

Humorless security guards let them pass a desk to a bank of glass elevators, but only after they relieved them of their weapons. Anika made a face and let a female guard pat her down to check to make sure she'd handed everything over.

Once that was done, Paige pressed her thumb to the control panel of the elevator they piled into, and the party of five descended down a deep ice tunnel.

After four stories, the ice gave way to a series of massive caverns. They dropped through the ceiling of an underground complex, bustling with activity.

At the ground floor, Paige and Ivan passed them through more security: Uzi-wielding private contractors with throat mics and high-tech glasses reflecting a stream of live information against their eyeballs.

On their left was a series of pools of water. Submarines rested, tied up against concrete pilings. Many of them were being offloaded by workers in green overalls with Gaia logos.

"We anticipated being locked out of many countries. Between *The Green Monster* and our facilities here in Thule, the company can continue regular operations even under the current conditions," Ivan said. There was grim satisfaction in his voice.

They passed through a twenty-foot-tall airlock set into a bulkhead in the complex. Once inside this, three-inch-thick metal hatches swung open to reveal a conference room with plastic windows, fifteen feet tall, looking out through the clear blue water. Above their heads floated icebergs, the same ones Anika had seen looking down from the edge far above where she'd met Paige and Ivan.

A seal splashed into the water and drifted down in front of the windows, then darted away.

The conference room had two private offices, doors leading off to suites with windows of their own on each side of the conference room. Twenty high-backed leather chairs surrounded a C-shaped table made of a highly polished Brazilian wood, a high contrast to the functional, clean metal arches overhead.

Touch-pad screens lay on the desk in front of each chair.

"We started Gaia in college making world-class simulation software for governmental agencies," Ivan said, looking out through the windows. "We were gaming scenarios like what would happen if the oceans rose by so many inches, or what if the temperature rose by a certain percent. What we saw was what the scientists saw: dramatic chaos as borders changed, arable land moved north, resources opened up. The Arctic Tigers coming to ascendance. Our clients were mainly military; they had some of the best foresight studies regarding the loss of Arctic ice and global temperature change. They were paying us obscene amounts of money to help them create better simulators."

Paige tapped a table, and the Gaia logo appeared. "I challenged him to figure out how to make money off the simulations. They were long bets. We never expected them to begin paying off so soon, and paying big. Our plays turned us into the largest energy and water company in the world as everything kept accelerating. Just the massive tundra land purchases we made when we were twenty were enough to make us obscenely rich: they turned into prime real estate within twenty-five years. When those investments began to mature, Ivan started the new phase of Gaia."

Ivan turned his back to the windows and faced them through the logo that hung in the air like ghost. "I didn't want to be that right."

Paige leaned against the table. "Ivan and I believe the reduction of pollution and carbon dumping requires structural changes that the world's communities refuse to make."

"It's like when you see a country with starving people in it that has enough arable land and resources to feed everyone. What you have is a systems problem," Ivan said.

"The problem is improperly adjusted externalities," Paige said. "When you purchase a product, the factory put out some small part of pollution into the world. But when you buy that product, you don't pay for that in the object's price. The pollution goes into the world, and then a government gets involved. A government has to clean it up, and they use Superfund cleanup money. So who pays for that? Taxpayers. It comes out of your check, one way or another. But by hiding it as a tax cost, and letting the government clean it up, you're unaware of the real *cost* of the object in your hand. The pollution also causes medical costs: lung disease, cancer. That comes out of your medical bill, and often the government gets involved there, but you as a human don't perceive the cost of cancer as being a portion of the cost of your new laptop. The company also releases carbon every time a new laptop is made, and when it's transported to you. But no one ever *pays* for that up front. We keep punting the question of what that is doing to the atmosphere to the next generation. We're doing it again. It's warmed up enough that we're experiencing all the benefits of global warming: increased land for northern countries, the release of the Arctic's resources, and a whole new shipping lane and ocean to exploit. But now there's a precipice we're perched on. Who goes over it? Not our problem, right? The cost of the problem isn't paid anywhere. The market fails to price properly because you can time-shift a portion of the cost, creating an unbalanced market."

Ivan smiled. "As Paige keeps testifying to politician after politician, until you pay the true cost of the object, you will never make the right consumer choices, nor will the market properly adjust. Until you have a structural situation where one company offers you a widget for less because it pollutes less, destroys other companies' democracies less, and doesn't dump carbon into the air to move an object to you, then you actually don't have a true, market-based economy. A truly market economy is one that properly maintains the environs it needs to exist in because it adds the price of damaging that environ into the bill of its goods. What we have now is a distorted market that rewards anti-conservation, and hides the real cost of the object in your taxes and elsewhere. Ultimately, it's just really, really bad accounting. They keep passing laws and trying to 'educate' people to make better choices. People don't make better choices, and free people don't like being forced to do things. But if you simply price the cost of your object properly, they'll always make the right choice."

Paige jumped in again. "We've been hammering through a lot of power brokers and other corporate groups. No one country wants to jump first, because when you force your prices higher, you give the others an edge. But I think, given time, we might make some progress. Even if you don't believe global warming is real, we hammer the pollution side of this. We hammer energy independence, not having to rely on a foreign country's oil. We hammer the idea that the best use of oil isn't to vaporize it through combustion and then never have access to it again, but to use it in plastics, which are recyclable. Our civilization can't exist without that. Save the plastic, burn something else. And what the politicians keep asking for is time."

"So we're giving them time," Ivan said. "The solar shield can mitigate the planetary warming trend. Whether you believe warming is manmade or not, the trend is on record. From the moment the Northwest Passage became passable by actual overseas ship traffic for the first time in human history at the turn of the century, it's been undeniable that the polar region has warmed. Even the strongest denialist is in the position of saying, sure it's warmed up, but it's not *humanity's* fault. That's when they talk about cycles or the sun or some bullshit like that. When glaciers are something you read about in picture books but can't see anymore, no one is arguing whether it's a real phenomenon or not, they're just trying to assign blame. The cloud can cool the planet again, to give us the time to get to a solution. Help us get that time."

"What is it you want out of us?" Roo asked.

"You three captured someone who knows about the nuke, maybe even about where it is, right?" Ivan asked. "Can you give him to us?"

"No." Roo shook his head, locks swinging. "Not ours to move around anymore. We gave him to the fleet."

Ivan's lips tightened. "*Them*? You gave him to them," he spat. "Fuck. Fuck. Once the shield is fully initialized, we become a voice at the world table. A serious voice. Because then, we're a superpower. The Earth will have a voice. It will be Gaia. They don't want that. They're the ones *behind* the fucking nuke. Unbelievable."

He turned and walked out, lip curled in disgust, the entire cloak of careful geniality dropped.

Paige watched him go, eyes narrowing. "I'm sorry," she said as the doors closed behind him. "He's under an extraordinary amount of stress. The board of directors, they weren't forewarned. They're pushing hard to have us turn over the command of the cloud to the UN."

Anika cocked her head. "That is a good idea. The blockade would stop. We could focus on finding the nuke, yes?"

Paige looked down. "It's hard to trust that they will make the right choices when they've made so many bad ones. And as Ivan points out, it's very probable that they were the ones that put the nuke here to stop the cloud."

"You playing a dangerous game of chicken," Roo observed.

"If it comes to innocent lives or the cloud, I know what Ivan will choose," Paige muttered. "But we couldn't live with ourselves unless we tried. You understand that? We have a chance to turn the world around. Who lets that go without a fight? I'm not going to. Ivan is headed off to keep talking to the Polar Fleet's commanders to buy us some time. We should use it to find the device. Are you still interested in finishing what you came here for, Anika?"

She wasn't so sure now. A lot of that righteous anger had leached out of her. She'd gone off to slay a dragon, in revenge, and now she felt like she was standing in the shadow of something even larger, that blotted out the sun overhead. Huge, implacable, and monstrous.

But Gabriel's assured words, telling her to go home, to stay out of the way, kept floating around the back of her head.

She wasn't going anywhere.

"We'll help any way we can," she said. "But what do you want from us now that we can't give you Gabriel? You have to have more resources than we do."

"You'd think that," Paige said. "But Ivan pulled Gaia Security off the hunt. A needle in a haystack isn't worth hunting. He wants GS ready in case there are any other surprises the G-35 have in Thule for us. We know there was a lot of traffic into Thule via military transport, not just you three."

"He gave up the hunt for the nuke?" Anika couldn't believe it.

Paige nodded. And it didn't look like she agreed with the decision. "There's a lot of data that Thule citizens have generated and are generating. We put out a bounty, and pictures of the men, and all the information we have. We're trying to crowd-source the hunt. Our corporate data services are even paying people to look through Thule's public-archived video feeds to hunt them. I need someone here to sift through all that. I know who you work for, Roo, and that you're good at this."

Roo shrugged. "If your security forces are elsewhere, what happens if we find something?"

"I'd talked Ivan into getting upstairs to meet you all when Wynter called. When he thought you could give us a good lead, he was willing to commit resources. That changed. If things change again, he will do what's necessary."

Violet had been watching Paige very intently since Ivan stormed out. "For a cofounder, you seem a bit cut out of the loop, Paige."

Paige bit a lip. "This is Ivan's baby. He sees this as his last chance to give his grandchildren a better world."

"It's not a bad world, right now. It needs fixing, but we're not dressed up in hand-me-down football uniforms under armor and driving dune buggies. Most people live blissful, comfortable lives in the cities of their choosing," Violet said. "Is he going to be this twitchy? This is a big fucking standoff. We don't need twitchy here, you know that? How much do you trust that man?"

Paige looked Vy straight on. "I've known him most of my life. I trust him with it, as well. Understand?"

Vy nodded.

Paige walked around the tables to the doors. "I will send someone in with food, drinks, whatever you need. Please feel free to use the bathroom in my office here on the left."

In minutes, Roo had all the touch screens lying on the table propped up and displaying information, and instead of the Gaia logo hovering in the air in the empty space the table curved around, he projected a map of Thule.

A few minutes later he chuckled. "We have unlimited access to Gaia's crowd-sourcing initiative. Paige just sent me the passwords and an unlimited bank account. We have ten thousand people across the world using good old-fashioned eyeball 1.0 to look at millions of photos and video from all around Thule for us. Anything they tag as looking like the guys who unloaded that big box in the Pytheas sub harbor gets forwarded to us. We cross-match that to locations that I'll put up on the main projector here. I'm cross-referencing possible hits to nearby buildings that would be good launch points."

Anika pointed at the large chunks of ice artificially calving themselves free of the periphery of Thule, as well as the barges and portions of the harbor drifting away. "What if it's on one of those?"

"They'll have come in deep into the ice," Roo said. "They won't risk being out on the edges near the demesnes that are breaking away."

"Why is that?"

"If it's really a G-35 spy group doing this," he explained, "they'll want it to look like it was launched from Thule. Being on a piece of land getting towed out near the blockade doesn't quite fit that bill."

But that didn't make Anika feel better. "Roo, you work for those people. Why are you still here, really?"

Roo stopped typing and looked at her. "Anegada."

Vy looked at him. "What?"

Anika thought about his home, lying under the

raised water. For her, the rants about global changes seemed far off. To Roo, it was personal. This hit his family, his people. Everything.

They settled in with the screens, scanning results thrown up in a hierarchy of decision-making algorithms and forwarded by teams of anonymous people, scattered all over the globe, tapped by Gaia to work on looking for faces in the crowds and other patterns that might betray their quarry.

Time stretched out, pulled apart, the streams of information broken by bathroom breaks and coffee. Anika was having trouble engaging, she kept slipping off somewhere else.

There was something she had to do, and she wasn't going to be able to truly focus on the waterfall of results until she did it.

"Can I borrow your phone, Roo?" she asked. "I need to call someone."

# 34

Anika got out of the elevator and checked with the security guards to make sure she could get back in, then slipped outside into the cold.

She took a deep breath, then pulled out Roo's phone.

The numbers came to her fingers quickly enough. She'd tapped them into her phone often enough. Except for the last one.

Her finger always remained poised over the last number, though, unable to commit. Unable to push past the resistance of years of silence and habit.

This time she finished the sequence with a slight shudder, a release of some tension inside of her that she hadn't realized was there. It had ridden alongside her for so long it had become a part of her world.

There was a ring, and then a second, and on the third the connection clicked, and a tired voice said, "Hello?"

"Hello, Mother?" Anika asked, her voice betraying her with a slight tremor. "It's me, it's Anika."

There was no response, only a faint scratchiness that sounded like static.

"Hello?" Anika said.

It wasn't static, but sniffling. "I'm sorry," came a gulp in that old, precise English accent that Anika associated with a large, busy, dusty house and comfort and safety, and then heartbreak and confusion and anger. The one she sometimes heard her father listening to, when he would watch her movies late at night when he thought Anika was asleep. "I'm sorry. I never thought I'd hear your voice again."

"All you had to do was call," Anika said.

"After what I had done, I figured you have the right to be left alone," her mother replied. "But when Abazu called to say you had crashed your airship, I was terrified. I started trying to call you, but your phone is cut off. When I called, he said he hadn't heard from you in two days!"

"I'm okay." Shit. She needed to call her father. He would be a mess. "Mother, where is your ship right now?"

She'd retired to a convalescent cruise ship. Somewhere some accountant had realized that the cost of a retirement home in the Western world wasn't too far different from that of the daily cost for a cruise tour. Setting it up on a ship allowed the companies to attract not just the elderly with the promise of seeing the world in their twilight years, but offering the same carrot to young doctors and caretakers.

Ever since her mother's retirement cruise ship hit the polar waters, her dad had been pressuring her to go see her mother.

"My friends and I had dinner at the captain's table last night, and he said we were somewhere north of Ellesmere Island."

Anika relaxed. A bit. "That's good. Have you turned around yet?"

"Well, the captain has been waiting for this whole blockade thing to blow over, to see if we can still visit Thule. I'm rather excited, I've never been to the North Pole, you know."

"It's not going to blow over, Mother. It's only going to get worse. Are you able to get out? Maybe fly somewhere to visit family, or a friend?"

"You know I can't, Anika. I signed over my house and my retirement account to the ship in order to retire here. They own everything, and the only travel I can do is with the ship."

Anika sighed heavily into the phone. "Maybe I can . . ." But she couldn't. Her accounts would be frozen. She couldn't do anything.

"Anika, what's wrong?" her mother asked. "Where *are* you? Are you in trouble?"

"I'm in Thule," she said. "Tell your captain things are getting worse. Tell him Thule is breaking apart, demesnes are fleeing. It's bad here. Warn him away. Be safe."

"Anika!"

She cut the phone connection off. She stared off at the sky and heard distant thuds and clanging. More activity. She should call her dad, and while she was reassuring him she was okay, see if he could pay for a helicopter ride for her mother off the ship and to Greenland.

Vy tapped her shoulder, startling her. "Hi, sweetness!" She had a pack of cigarettes in her hand.

"What are you doing up here, smoking?"

Vy shook her head, put an arm around Anika, and led her even further away from the building. "Told 'em I was out for a smoke. Wanted to see if you were okay."

They walked back up to the overlook, then Vy glanced around.

"What's wrong?" Anika asked.

Vy pocketed the cigarettes. "So, do you think everyone at any software company headquarters in Silicon Valley walks around with submachine guns?"

"It's like a military base down there," Anika agreed. "But most software companies don't have half the world's navies circling around like angry sharks. You think they don't want to find the nuke?"

"No," Vy said. "They want to find it. But we still need to be careful, okay? People with guns have a habit of using them."

"And we're going to need their help, and protection," Anika said.

Vy looked over at her. "Thinking that far ahead?"

"If we secure and disable the nuke, then whoever put it out here is going to be angry with us. And who is that? Some sort of intelligence agency. We will be criminals."

"Roo will be safe, he has the connections," Vy said.

"And do you trust him still? He's really taking to the whole Gaia song and dance down there. That stuff hits him hard, because of his home."

Vy shrugged. "I trust him as much as I can trust anyone I've known for several years. But yes. He's good people. He'll be okay. As for me, this won't change things too much. I'm already a minor criminal. Grass is legal, but you know I dabble in moving other products. You're the one who's hit the major career change."

Yes. She was right. Anika looked down. Her quiet, stable, life: ripped up and torn apart. Everything she'd slowly worked toward. Gone.

Vy moved closer and turned her around. "You have a place, with me. If you want it."

"What'll I do?" Anika asked, looking into Vy's pale eyes. The wind tugged at her hair.

"Shit, are you kidding me? I'll keep you in a style you're not accustomed to: living under an alternate identity in some non-extradition country! Don't tell me you didn't grow up dreaming someone would sweep you off your feet and tell you that."

Anika laughed, and pulled her closer. "Okay," she said. "I guess I'm stuck with you for a while, then, Vy."

They kissed, a faint brush of the lips. And then a deeper kiss, pulling each other closer together so that they existed in a tiny world of warmth in the cold.

Their breath steamed the air between their faces when they pulled apart.

"You're a pilot," Vy said. "If you come with me, there will always be work for you."

"Not flying airships, though," Anika said, a tiny note of sadness creeping in.

"That could be a problem. But never say never." Vy smiled.

"It was a childhood wish anyway," Anika admitted. "And I got to live that dream for a while, anyway. I have no regrets."

"That's the spirit," Vy said. Then she pointed. "Look!"

A shaggy, beige polar bear ambled its way along a floe, then jumped into the water. It paddled its way to the ice shelf underneath their vantage point, then clambered on.

It sat down and looked up at them.

The two of them stared back, quiet, only the sound of snapping ice in the distance.

Then Vy's phone rang.

The moment broke, and the bear began to paw the air. "He's hoping for a ham sandwich," Vy said sadly. "The tourists probably toss him food from here."

She turned back away and answered the phone. "It's Roo. He says he thinks he's found a good lead. He's on his way up, and Gaia Security is coming with him."

# 35

Paige Greer arrived at the surface and waved them over. "We're scrambling men," she said breathlessly as they raced down the sloping road with her.

"Where's Roo?" Anika asked.

"Up ahead."

Three armored cars braked to a stop at the entrance to the polar preserve and Gaia's underground facility. Roo opened one of the doors and waved them in.

"How'd you find them? That was quick, wasn't it?"

"I'm that good," Roo grinned. "It was lead."

"For shielding?" Anika asked.

"They didn't want another scatter camera to hunt them down, so they purchased sheets of lead. Gabriel mentioned that they would be shielded and hard to find. So far most of the hunt has been for the radiation. But I went hunting for lead. Once I found the lead, I found four possible locations. This is as close as we can get this quick."

"We'll get teams out to each building," Paige said. "See if we can secure local help to check them out. See if anything turns up."

"They won't give up easily," Anika said, thinking of Gabriel.

"I know," Paige said.

They stopped a block away from the target, near a cluster of dome-shaped silvered buildings jacked up on piston stilts.

"This is the Peary demesne," Paige said. "We secured the right to place our men around the building, but volunteer community police are insisting they accompany us."

More Gaia flatbed trucks ripped up ice as they braked to a halt.

"Not a dictatorship here, then?" Anika asked.

Paige brushed hair out of her eyes. "Peary's modeled after Brazilian participatory budget and radical municipal democracy, with a few variants. People committee-vote on all municipal budget matters and draw up the budgets and where tax money goes; municipal employees serve as expert consultants, but have no say in the budget or projects list, they are contractors that execute what the voters decide every quarter needs done. Stops backscratching and corruption. These guys take it a step further: there are no municipal employees, municipal spots are volunteer positions. If you can't find the time, then you can pay to have a subcontractor do your duty. But it means you're stuck with waiting for damn amateurs to run out here."

Several Peary citizens were indeed showing up, pulling on bright red-and-blue vests over their bulky cold weather gear and waving at them.

"Location two is clear," one of the security detail reported.

One of the Peary volunteers walked over and introduced himself as the on-duty sergeant. He wore large goggles, and Anika could see information was scrolling across his field of vision. Probably some sort of software package that let the volunteer police link up with each other.

"We have a hundred community protectors moving in," he said. "Thirty are in full riot gear. Nonlethal instruments. I have four snipers that should be in position within twenty minutes. Twenty of my regulars are armed with low-caliber pistols. If you need more manpower, we can call in other Thule citizens from neighboring demesnes."

Paige nodded. "Okay. My force will go in strong, are you okay with hanging back? We want you to catch anyone who bolts."

The volunteer nodded. "How hard are you going in?"

"They're possibly sitting on a nuke, how hard do you want us to go in?" Paige looked carefully at the sergeant.

He grimaced, and looked upward, accessing some piece of information from his goggles. "We're in a hard spot," he said. "Because my fellow police want to remind you, legally, that you have not proven without a doubt the people you're hunting are the ones inside this building. You could be going in full force . . ."

He never finished his sentence—the sound of gunfire erupted from the building in question.

"We found them!" someone shouted, unnecessarily.

Everyone ducked behind one of the large pylons holding up the nearest building.

"They're shooting up the block," someone shouted.

Roo shook his head. "We should have gone in without asking the demesne for help," he chided Paige. "All they needed to do was grab a volunteer policeman and hold him hostage, let him tell them when any alerts came for him to assemble . . ."

Paige opened her mouth, then closed it. "Shit."

"We should have done a person-to-person communications-are-compromised routine," the sergeant muttered. Then he whispered into the palm of his hand, "Snipers: fire when targets present."

"Sergeant, they're going to be in there trying to arm that thing," Roo shouted. "Time is *not* on our side."

"We're going to rush the building with you," the sergeant told Paige. "We're all in."

"Glad to hear it." Paige tapped an earpiece. "The Peary volunteers are following you in. Give them five minutes to assemble, then break down the doors."

"Paige, I can use a weapon," Anika said. She'd given hers up to get into Gaia headquarters, but not retrieved it.

Paige put a finger up to her lip and shook her head. "You've come far enough, Anika."

The gunfire slowed, and Anika watched Peary volunteers in a wide assortment of winter jackets keeping low, advancing over the snow, dodging around the metallic forest of pylons underneath everything.

Three and a half minutes passed in what felt like a handful of held breaths in between pauses in the gunfire, and then the attack began. Anika left the cover of the pylons to watch.

Gaia Security used clear bulletproof riot shields to protect themselves as they stormed up stairs. Door rams were deployed, and after three swings, the doors crumpled back.

Men and women poured inside, and the sound of gunfire increased. A full-on fusillade of distant firecracker pops of varying tones and frequencies, shouts, and more door cracking.

And much like popcorn, after a while, it slowed down. An occasional shot sounded, randomly. Then quiet.

Roo started walking toward the building.

"Mr. Jones," Paige said sharply.

But he ignored her and kept walking. Anika stood up and jogged after him, and Vy joined them.

"They didn't have a chance to fire it," Anika said. "Right?" She hadn't seen anything. She'd been looking for that flash of smoke, the contrail of a missile, or a rocket, or whatever it was.

But all there had been was gunfire.

"Right?" she repeated.

# 36

They ran up the stairs, boots clanging on metal, and rounded the doors. A body lay at the foot of steps that led up to the next level, blood continuing to expand out in a steaming dark pool.

In the corridor that ran past the steps, three men sat against the wall as one of the Gaia men checked their wounds.

"Up," Roo said.

They stepped carefully over the dead man and ran up, with Paige not far behind.

Two flights of stairs, three more bodies, including one Peary volunteer being carried down the stairs in a stretcher, a raggedy-doll-like hand flopping over the edge.

Had the price been worth it? Or had more people died in vain?

The top floor was dominated by a skylight and ruined walls. They'd been knocked out by sledgehammer. A hastily boarded up gap covered in a blue tarp in the side of one major wall allowed chilled air into the entire upper floor.

In the center of the mess, Anika saw more dead men from both sides sprawled around. But it was the center of the room that drew her attention. There was a muddy white missile, with a fat, red-tipped nose, pointed skyward in the middle of the room. The tip of the missile was just a foot away from the glass of the skylight, fifteen feet above the overly open-spaced third floor. It sat in a hastily constructed cradle of two-by-four timbers that raised it up into launch position. A crude wooden crane had been constructed out of more wooden planks to pull the missile up into position.

A glance out through a small hole in the tarp showed that no one had noticed the missile being cranked up because this side of the house was hemmed in by a large water tower and several more industrial-looking buildings, most likely automated small-scale factories.

Anika turned around.

So here it was.

A fucking, honest-to-goodness, nuclear missile.

They all gathered around it, like mystics around some obelisk.

"Did it get armed, is it going to launch?" Paige asked a grizzled-looking man sitting near a laptop and table filled with cables leading back to the missile.

"*Nyet*," he said emphatically. "Prelaunch system check only. And yes, it was aimed at the solar shield. It takes off to detonate, it is not for the ground."

Paige turned back to look up at the missile. "It's not really that big, is it?" she said, wonderingly.

"All it had to do was knock out the shield with the electromagnetic pulse," Roo said. "It didn't need to be."

"We're safe for now," Paige said, visible relief on her face. "We stopped them."

Anika felt her legs weaken a bit. It was from relief, as well. She'd been carrying tension since she stepped foot in Thule, imagining that, at any second, a flash would be the last thing she saw before some detonation just above her.

That was ridiculous, they now knew for sure. This missile looked like it would climb fairly high. Its job was to get above the shield and then detonate. It wasn't a terrorist's device, intended to destroy people and civilians on the Arctic ground.

Vy had grabbed her gloved hand and squeezed it really hard. "Jesus, Anika. It's over. We got it."

"You're damn right we got it," Paige said. "Come on. Yuri's a Russian military ordnance specialist, he'll work with some contractors by phone to make sure it's turned off properly. We're going to head back to HQ. I want to talk to Ivan about what we do next, but I also want to make sure we take care of you guys for helping us out."

"I need tickets. Anika and I need to get out of the area," Vy said.

There was a weary satisfaction in the air on the drive back. Paige, in particular, leaned back against the seat with a private smile on her face.

"Now we only have one big problem to face," she said.

"The blockade." That was still a massive problem, Anika thought. And she didn't want to be in Thule as all that continued to play out. The retreating demesnes probably had the right idea.

"Yes."

Back at the top of the elevator they were waved through security. Anika noticed Roo frown. "What?" she asked him in a quick whisper.

"Look at the submachine guns," he whispered back.

The men had them slung over their shoulders, at the ready, even though they were standing behind the desk.

"They weren't doing that earlier, the guns were out of sight."

Roo nodded, and Anika really wished she'd slipped something past security. A knife would do.

Down the elevators, back into the Gaia complex's heart, then across to the conference room, where an ebullient Ivan Cohen waited with a twenty-person retinue of dark-suited, older men from a variety of countries.

Something didn't quite feel right, though. They looked nervous. Eyes on the ground, shuffling. They did not look like the normal boardroom of a trillion-dollar corporation.

Then again, what did Anika know about what these sorts of people *should* act like.

Certainly, she felt it shouldn't be like nervous servants, waiting for their employer to find something wrong with their work.

There was champagne on the tables. Ivan passed a glass over to Paige. "We've stopped them from destroying the most important public engineering project of this century," he said. His eyes were wide, almost dilated. Flushed with success, Anika thought. "Congratulations."

Paige set the slender glass down on the table. "Ivan, we still have a problem. . . ."

Ivan shook his head. "I took care of it."

Feet shuffled throughout the room. They were like nervous birds, feathers ruffling as they were disturbed.

Anika was getting a bad feeling.

"Ivan, what do you mean by that?" Paige asked slowly and calmly, as if he were a child.

He waved at all the board members. "They all finally grew a pair—collectively, that is. They came down here to demand you and I step down as CEOs so they could negotiate a surrender with the blockade. They're worried about the impending invasion. Can you believe that? Step down. Now? Here we are, on the brink of quite literally saving the world, and they're going to try and pull some bullshit procedure and give up."

"They're scared," Paige said. "It's understandable. We didn't think there would be such a strong military reaction. Or nukes. Or any of this. Look, if anyone here wants to leave, they should get out now. It hasn't been the first time I've encouraged you."

One of the suits next to her fumbled with his hands. "We can't leave now. Ivan gave an ultimatum."

Paige looked confused. "A what?"

Roo glanced over at Anika and pointed at the door. Get out, he mouthed. But as they turned to leave Gaia Security stepped forward blocked the door.

Vy grabbed her arm. "I don't like this."

Ivan raised his hands and pressed a button on a small controller in his hands. The windows looking out under the polar waters darkened to be replaced by screens showing virtual clocks.

"All of the Earth's systems have checks and balances in them against damage. But for hundreds of years we've shit out pollutants and dumped carbon into the air. Even today archeologists are finding that, as far back as history goes, we have scarred the land that gave us life. We're a cancer. A virus. A problem. Paige says, give us properly balanced markets, and we can be good. But that's not true. The world's religions know it. Man is sinful, dark. We are capable of great evils. Just ask the fucking whales. The Earth needs a protector, not more arguing, not more markets, not more products. It needs a solution. It needs Gaia."

"Ivan, we talked about this. We're playing in the realm of nation states now—not just trying to influence policy, but actively challenging them," Paige said.

"Nation states have done a shitty job as stewards of our world, Paige. Eventually, someone had to challenge them. I know it will be dangerous, but we've been simulating a showdown like this for two years. We've used our most powerful resources to crowdsource possible scenarios, used multiplayer online games to test responses. We know it's ninety percent likely that we'll win here. We can't wait any longer, and it's too late to back down now. We're playing our cards."

"Jesus, we've got to get out," Vy whispered. They edged closer to the door and the grim men with submachine guns.

Paige had been stepping closer and closer to Ivan as he spoke. She put a hand on his shoulder. "Ivan. You really did it? The ultimatum? We didn't agree together . . ."

He grabbed her hand and held it. "The blockade has *ten minutes* left to turn around. It is within Thule national waters, and has crossed sovereign borders. If it doesn't leave, Thule will be forced to protect itself. After that, we get on with the business of saving the world. Paige, I've waited all my life for this, I've seen too many attempts to do things thwarted. There've been billions of dollars spent convincing everyone the Pole wasn't melting, that doing *anything* meant it would cost people money, so that oil companies could keep doing what they were doing. It is time for *action*, now. Our time is finally here. The planet's time. We can defend it now. The moment they said you had the nuke, I've been waiting for that moment my entire life."

Ivan breathed heavily, sweat beading his forehead. He was nervous, and shaking. Paige grabbed his other shoulder and looked him right in the eyes.

"Ivan, what happens when that ten minutes finishes up? Our simulations said there was a chance they would decide to escalate instead of negotiate."

"You know the scenarios," he said, turning for the table.

Paige pulled him back. "*Ivan*, it's one thing to run simulations. It's another to actually do these things. We can't. It's not you."

"Oh, but this *is* me," Ivan said. "I'm scared. I'm angry. But more than that, I'm tired of the long fight. I want to see something get done. And quickly."

Roo had moved through the milling crowd to stand on the other side of the open door from Anika and Vy. He clearly intended to get out past the two men blocking it from the outside, but he was waiting.

What are we waiting for? Anika mouthed.

He shrugged and held up a finger. Just wait.

Ivan shoved Paige back. People gasped. "Don't try to stop me, Paige. Not after all we've done together." He was trembling.

She recovered her balance and strode forward. "You're letting them get to you, Ivan . . . you and me, we don't split apart. Not after all we've built together."

"You let them get to you," Ivan said sadly. "You're the one taking your eyes off the bigger picture. I'm so sorry." He sat down in front of one of the screens that, just hours before, Anika had been using to scan for leads on the missile.

Roo held up his hand. He wanted to see what was going to happen next. Up on the glass the countdown faded away, replaced by video of the recognizably flat-topped shape of an aircraft carrier.

It was flanked by two destroyers.

The countdown hit all zeros and flashed, and Ivan tapped a virtual keyboard on the table. "The sun is the most powerful source of energy in the world," Ivan said. "We hardly use it as a tool. It's a shame that I have to harness it like this, but maybe after this demonstration they will understand. Those hundreds of millions of floating spheres can reflect the energy of it back out into space, cooling the planet and stopping the warming trend.

"They can also refocus the reflected light anywhere I want."

A pure line of light stabbed out of the sky. As it touched the ocean's surface, water boiled and flash-vaporized into steam that hung in the air.

The beam of light continued to move across the water, and Anika could see the carrier begin to tilt, turning as it tried to get out of the way. Spray from the backs of the destroyers kicked up as turbojets engaged and shoved the boats up onto their hydroplanes as they tried to scatter.

Moving implacably on, the beam of light, so bright it almost washed out the video feed, struck the carrier amidships. It slowly sliced through the upper decks, boiling metal splashing and pooling. Secondary explosions ripped through the carrier as the light struck something deep inside.

Like a welding torch wielded by a god, it continued to burn the carrier's structure, ripping deeper and deeper, until the telltale steam blew up out of the horrible crack in the ship's center.

The focused beam of light snapped off as Ivan tapped at the computer.

For a moment, Anika thought that the carrier might be okay. It was still moving forward, after all, pulling itself out of the massive cloud of steam created by the mirror's attack. Smoke still poured out of the crack, and she thought she could see movement. People running to put out the fires? She hoped so.

Then the crack widened. And kept widening.

The two parts of the carrier began to slowly, torturously, split apart. The further it ripped, the more of the massive ship's insides became visible. The edges of the inside decks glowed cherry hot. More smoke gushed out. Debris tumbled into the still-boiling water in between the two halves.

Water kept flooding into the cracked-open parts, and pieces of the carrier started settling into the ocean while vomiting smoke into the air.

# 37

Paige launched herself at Ivan, trying to shove him away from the keyboard. Neither of them said anything but, for a moment, just grunted and scrabbled.

Then Ivan reached down.

"Gun!" Roo warned.

Instead of moving to help, the men in suits shoved each other to get back out of the way as Anika, Vy, and Roo ran toward the table, no longer worrying about trying to escape.

Ivan kicked Paige back and then pulled the gun free and shot her, point blank, in the stomach.

Blood splattered all over the clear polished shine of the table and Paige dropped to the floor clutching her side.

Ivan stood over her, gun raised but not pointed at her anymore. The trembling had turned into a sort of horror. "What did you make me do?" he asked. "What did you make me do?"

Paige stared up at him, pain and anger fighting their way through, and then finally pain winning as she gasped and look down at her bloody hands.

"*What did you make me do?*" Ivan demanded again, and seeing Anika, Roo, and Vy close in, pointed the gun at them. "Don't."

Roo raised his hands. "We just want to help her, man."

"We need to get her help, now," Anika said forcefully, getting Ivan to look at her instead of Roo, giving him another chance to edge even closer. "How long has she been your friend, your ally? You can't leave her bleeding to death on the *floor*!"

"She's . . ." Ivan half turned back to Roo. "*Stop!*"

"Ivan!" Anika shouted, clapping her hands. His eyes flicked toward the sound, gun moving back in her direction.

Roo took advantage of the offered distraction and struck smoothly, grabbing the gun, twisting it up, snaking a hand around, and spinning behind the CEO. Vy dropped to the ground beside Paige.

"The guards," Anika snapped at Roo. Two men armed with submachine guns pushed through the door, guns up at shoulder height.

"I see them," Roo muttered.

"Release Mr. Cohen," the man on the right shouted.

"And then what?" Roo asked.

Three golf-ball-sized metal balls struck the ground and rolled in from outside the door. Roo threw his hands over his face as the world exploded in light and smoke. Anika's ears rang, and she staggered around, blind to the world around her. Flash-bangs. With a touch of tear gas.

When her sight returned she saw Ivan on his hands and knees being dragged across the room by several board members as three more members of Gaia Security in gas masks spilled into the room.

She dropped to the floor as Roo shot the three guards. Her eyes were tearing up, and she could feel the camera-fooling makeup clumping and streaking on her face.

From on the floor, she could see that the first two guards lay dead just a few feet away from her.

"My office," Paige gasped at them as scared board members fled out the door, jamming it up to the frustration of the security detail outside. "You'll all die out here."

"Go," Roo shouted.

Anika rolled over and grabbed a submachine from the nearest dead guard, then helped Vy pull a screaming Paige across the floor into her own office.

Roo slammed the door as the last board member cleared the room. Anika heard the loud *thunk* and looked at him. "That sounded like metal."

Paige scrabbled and got her back against a wall with Anika's help. "Inch-thick steel," she said. "The boardroom and offices are as much bunker as usable space. Ivan and I have been worried about attacks for a long time. What we do has been controversial, ever since the mist boats."

Anika looked around the office. A lot of wood paneling. A pseudo-nautical theme dominated, including a giant, faded wooden ship's wheel mounted to the back wall. The wall was dominated by pictures of Paige and Ivan shaking hands with presidents and politicians.

Vy stood up and stretched. "On a scale of kinda fucked to pretty fucked, how fucked are we?"

"Very, very fucked," Roo said as he locked the door with a large, old-fashioned bolt system that clicked heavily into place.

Paige laughed, then groaned. "It's not that grim, Mr. Jones," she said, and pointed at the large ship's wheel. "It's not a good idea to build a bunker with only one way in."

"They'll be moving someone to cover the exit," Roo said.

"No they won't," Paige said. "It doesn't go to the surface. It's my own moon pool, and my own submarine. Vy, please, my upper right pocket, there's a keychain."

Vy leaned over and fished out a black plastic oval with a rectangular microchip key hanging from it.

Paige grabbed Vy's hand. "That allows you control of the sub, and of my personal yacht, *Tellus*. It's docked in Section A-B of the Gaia docks in Thule's harbor. I promised you transportation. This is me delivering it, okay?"

"Okay," Vy said. "Thank you."

"No," Paige sighed. "I'm sorry I have gotten the three of you into this mess. I should have seen this coming. Ivan and I have been running plans and scenarios for so long. He's focused on all the bad things that have happened, all the deaths from ecological collapse, for so long. All the failures of politicians to do anything. All the denials. The money spent by oil companies to deny anything was happening. All his life he's fought and fought. And now he has a tool that he thinks will let him achieve his life's goals. Who could turn away from that?"

"You did," Anika said.

"Did I? I wanted to use it to bring nations to the negotiating table. The only difference between Ivan and me is a degree."

Roo squatted next to her. "You don't sound like you coming with us," he said.

Paige looked up at him and brushed aside stray hair. "No, Roo. I helped Ivan develop the solar shield. I have access to its guidance system. Help me up into my chair, and from here, I can do my best to degrade the performance of the shield if he tries attacking more ships. I want to see this through. To be honest, I think we need the shield. We've let the genie out. But I refuse to let him stain his gift to the world with more blood. I can't have that on my conscience."

Anika shook her head. Paige still believed in Ivan, deep down. She still was trying to help him, after she'd been shot by him. That was a friendship born of a lifetime of understanding each other on a level Anika wasn't sure she'd ever seen.

"Let me look at this thing first," Roo asked, pointing at Paige's bloody hand, still pressed hard against her stomach. "I have first-aid experience."

"No, Roo, you're wasting time," she said, in the same sort of tone of voice a teacher scolded a misbehaving student with. "Get me up to my chair. Hurry."

She grunted in pain as he got an arm under her and pulled her up. Anika got the other side, and they set Paige on the oversized executive chair in front of the desk.

Anika saw more blood spill from between her fingers as they moved her. She wiped Paige's paling face free of sweat with the corner of her jacket.

"A lifetime of being ignored," Paige said. "A lifetime of knowing that everything we worked for would always be able to be subverted by millions pumped into whisper campaigns that said doing nothing was safer, easier. He thinks the only way to balance the field is by playing the same game they are: use force. He wants to use the same language. Please, don't think him evil. He was twisted into this by larger forces. Forces that refuse to back down or negotiate. You understand, right?"

Anika wiped Paige's forehead free of sweat again. She didn't really understand, and she wasn't going to tell Paige she was wasting her life on a man who'd snapped and was a danger to everything around them. But then she thought about her father's tales of "big men." Men who inspired people to follow them as they outlined great visions and pulled power to themselves. They were always seductive, her father said. Bold visions, powerful statements. Here was someone who stirred your spirit. And after they swept into power, that animal charisma was still there. And long after absolute power corroded, people still believed that vision. Wanted to believe. It was hard to think that a person could change from the person you believed in to something more horrible. "How do we pilot the sub?"

"You're a pilot, you will figure it out quickly enough." She opened another drawer and handed Anika a phone. "But if you do have problems, call me. It's the only number listed in the phone. It should work, I think, as long as you're inside our headquarters. I'll talk you through it. Now go," she hissed.

Roo spun the ship's wheel, and with a puff of pressurized air, the wood-paneled door rolled aside.

They walked through the small corridor, barely wider than their shoulders. At the end was a small moon pool. The blue water slapped against metal grating, and the ceiling overhead reflected blue rippled waves back at them.

The tower of a midget submarine broke the water, close enough to the grating that they could step into it and climb down the ladder. The front of the submarine was a large convex viewing bubble. The main body of it was a long cylindrical tube of metal, painted bright yellow. A cage of struts surrounded the cylinder, with equipment bolted onto it. Anika recognized none of it, though she assumed some of it was their air, some of it ballast.

"How simple does it look?" Roo asked as Anika settled into the cockpit and looked around at the unfamiliar panels and controls.

"Give me a minute," Anika said. She grabbed a plastic handbook dangling from one of the joysticks on either arm of the chair.

Attitude, thrusters. She looked down. The pedals by her feet controlled the up and down vectoring of thrusters, oddly enough. Things were not laid out like a plane, but she could figure it out, as long as she kept thinking about what she was doing.

Paige had left a handbook with labeled steps. Power on, air scrubbers, pressurizing, and ballast.

Anika looked back. There was barely room in the bench seat behind her for Vy and Roo to squeeze together. This was really a *personal* submarine.

"Hatch closed?" Anika asked.

"Yep. I also untied us," Vy said.

"Right." Anika followed the steps on Paige's handbook. Lights flickered on, including bright spotlights on the cage outside. They lit up the metal dock in front of them. Fans hummed inside, and relays clicked as different control mechanisms came online.

The next step startled her, as the sub blew a mist of air and leftover water out of its tanks, then a faint thrumming started as they filled.

They slowly sank away from the moon pool, falling into the dark blue of the deeper ocean. Anika set the small handbook aside after one last quick flip through, then grabbed the two joysticks and eased them forward.

Somewhere behind her, on the cage, propellors kicked into motion and thrust them forward.

When Anika glanced back up, she couldn't see where they'd come from, just miles and miles of ice and upside-down mountains, the peaks descending down toward them.

# 38

They surfaced several miles from Thule's docks, and Anika cut the power. They bobbed in place, half submerged, waves slapping at the top half of the craft and crashing over the structure.

Anika turned around and looked at Vy and Roo. "What are we going to do now?"

"Find that ship of hers and get the hell away," Vy said, holding up the microchipped plastic case Paige had given them. "We have the keys to her ship."

"No, about *that*," Anika said, pointing upward. From her half-submerged position in the cockpit's bubble of glass, she could see the roiling silver sky.

"Leave it," Vy said.

Roo leaned forward. "So far Ivan only threatened the blockade. He's just asking to be allowed to deploy the device and . . . turn back years of disaster."

"The people on that carrier died," Anika said. "They had families and friends."

"And how many millions are going to die as things get worse out there because we're fumbling around with the world?" Roo said. "Worse weather. More heat. Higher oceans, more flooding out in South Asia. That's millions of lives, Anika. Weigh those lives against those of a handful of soldiers, people doing their jobs who know it's risky."

"Like me?" Anika asked. "Or Tom? Casualties? Collateral damage?"

"*Gabriel*'s people shot you two down," Vy said. "Not the company."

"Does it matter?" Anika asked. "Ivan's refusal to create the shield in a way that involved everyone got them crazy about this plan to nuke it. Secrecy, power, how is he any different than any other? *That mess* was what got me and Tom shot down as well. And it is *not* the way to go about it. He's going to get many more people killed. And what if it escalates? One carrier has already been destroyed: what if the entire blockade attacks, and air forces are drawn in? Thule dies. What if the nations decide that it is okay if everyone knows they attacked with a nuclear weapon and Thule is destroyed by Russia, the U.S., and China for its super weapon? This has the potential to get much, much uglier. What's your feeling then, Roo? Still worth it?"

"Versus the tens of millions that pay the price of losing their coastlines, dying in floods, dying from crop failures? What am I supposed to say to that?" Roo snapped. "Predict how many *might* die in this exchange compared to how many we know will continue dying? You're thinking you'll be able to get back through Gaia Security, and what? Fire that missile on your own? No. You can't. You can't finish what Gabriel started. And Gaia has the rest of the team that was going to launch the missile locked away. There is nothing you can do, Anika. Let it go."

"God damn it, Roo." Anika turned back to the controls.

Vy reached forward and squeezed her shoulder. "I'm sorry, Anika. I see your points. Seeing Thule torn apart like this is horrific. Everyone's lives get turned upside down if the Arctic goes back. But I think Roo is right."

Anika didn't say anything, or even acknowledge Vy. After a moment Vy let go of Anika's shoulder and folded her arms. She seemed to get lost in thought as Anika stared ahead and piloted the sub toward the harbor.

Anika threaded them around the giant wind turbines that powered the harbor, and got them close enough to a dock. They'd called ahead and warned the harbormaster, worried that there were mines or something protecting the harbor.

Vy jumped to the dock, slid on some ice, and then caught herself. She tied the sub off as Roo got out and helped her.

Anika clambered out and took a deep breath of cold, fresh air.

"It doesn't just go away, Roo," Vy said softly as they both crouched over a large cleat. It sounded like she didn't want to say that, as she stuttered. She hadn't stopped mulling over their argument in the sub about what to do next, apparently.

"What you mean?"

Anika glanced across the water at them.

Vy twisted to face Roo. "I've been thinking: technology doesn't just go away. It never has. You can slow its growth, you can try and stop it. But once it's made, it escapes. Some places have slid, some countries have locked it down, like Japan and guns, or North Korea. But worldwide, once it's out, it's out, right? Technology just doesn't go away."

Anika hopped onto the dock. She saw exactly where Vy was going with this. They had to make Roo see it, too, before he walked off down the dock. "Vy's right," Anika said. "Roo, someone else will make more of these spheres. Someone with a desktop fabrication printer. Maybe millions of people. Or someone with a small factory in their garage. There are enough spheres floating around; someone will pick them up. Or leak the instructions online. Or just imitate the result. This can't die."

Vy smiled. "The question is control."

"I'm not saying the shield isn't necessary, Roo. The shield is, *something* is. The question is, who controls the shield? Do we make a choice, or do we have it forced on us by one single person. One of the reasons geo-engineering sucks for solving these issues is that whoever controls the project has this . . . huge fucking end-of-the-world James Bond villain-device thing. It's as much a military problem. Who voted on this? Who got to decide? Yeah, there are too many people—what's better, killing off a bunch of them or building better farm techniques and density? Who gets to decide? I fucking prefer democracy to one person with a vision. Because sometimes you're safe in that person's vision, and sometimes you're an acceptable casualty. Get it? Who do *you* want in charge of that thing: an aging old rich dude who's convinced the ends justify the means? Or some other solution, maybe even something like one of the government systems here in Thule?"

Roo held up a palm. "You crazy," he said.

But Anika pressed him. "We can save lives, Roo. And you know it. You have the contacts. Who else besides us can make this happen, right now?"

"We need the nuclear missile. And we'd need the military to turn Gabriel back over to us. Even harder: we need to convince Gabriel to help us. And I'm thinking, after what the three of us did back there, he won't be interested in that, yeah?"

"He'll help," Anika said forcefully. He needed to set that missile off, even if meant working with the three of them.

"We'll need to convince people to risk an attack on the missile, when Ivan all but owns the sky," Roo continued.

"And when we attack," Vy added, "Ivan will try to evaporate us."

Anika hadn't thought about that. She swallowed and looked forward. "I'll go alone," she said. "Give me Gabriel, other military volunteers. I can't ask you two to do this, just to help me get ready."

"Oh bullshit!" Vy said. "I don't like this idea. I think we're going to get ourselves killed. But damnit, Anika, I'm coming with you. There's no way you're doing this by yourself. Roo?"

Roo let out a deep breath that hung in the air between them all. "You asking a lot, Vy. Joining you two on a suicide mission . . ."

The silver cloud overhead flashed, light rippling through it, bouncing around, getting redirected, and a beam stabbed out of the sky into the distant ocean.

Anika flinched, and she saw Roo do the same.

"There are people dying, Roo. Right now. Out there over the curve of the horizon."

The beam of light abruptly sputtered, split into several different beams that wandered aimlessly around, then fizzled.

"Paige is trying to blunt him," she said. "But it's only going to get worse."

Roo was shielding his eyes with a hand and looking up at the silver sky.

"Fuck," he said. "Fuck y'all. Fuck duty." His shoulders slumped and Vy started chuckling.

"Who ever thought we'd be working together helping those guys," Vy said, pointing out toward the blockade.

"You a Southern girl. Always had that flag-waving thing in you," Roo said as he pulled a phone out of his jacket and pointed at Anika. "We see what we can assemble. We reach out to whoever running the blockade, coordinate with them. We do this correct and official, right?"

"Correct and official," Anika agreed, as the lightning danced around the artificial clouds overhead.

## 39

Thule harbor had become a ghost town. Even the massive wind turbines, skyscrapers in and of themselves, had frozen in place, as if the wind had decided to flee with everyone else.

Large parts of the harbor had ripped free: docks attached to floating barges towed out to sea, only their debris left behind. Around the harbor, bridges had been severed, and large chunks of the superstructure cut by high-powered welding torches or detonated in order to free demesenes.

Anika could see, here in a conference room in one of the harbor's taller buildings, that huge chunks of ice had been dynamited free. Large chunks of Thule, calving off and headed for the open sea, much like the free ice had once done twenty years ago. Headed for the Northwest Passage.

Whole cities out floating around the polar sea, keeping a nervous eye on their refrigeration cables.

Turning around in the large conference room, she

could look out one of the corner windows, where she could still spot a few buildings on ice slipping away to open sea under the silver-gray sky.

"Ms. Duncan?"

Anika turned around. A young man in U.S. Navy uniform stood at the door. It was a wet uniform, and the young man was still shivering. The U.S. polar navy-wear was supposed to be some high-tech clothing that sealed the cuffs and trapped body heat and kept water out, not all that different from a dry suit used by scuba divers, but apparently even that still hadn't kept him toasty. "Yes?"

Three more navy types walked through the door, with Roo following. And behind him, Gabriel in handcuffs, his usually carefully brushed hair disheveled, a glassy look in his eyes. He didn't seem sure where he was.

Anika stared at him for a long beat, and he looked past her, out the windows.

He seemed drugged. "Roo, what's wrong with him?"

The man standing to Gabriel's right answered her. "He's mildly sedated right now. He's claustrophobic; the submarine ride over was stressful."

She looked at him, and he finally met her eyes. "It has been a long few days, Ms. Duncan," Gabriel said, his voice scratchy from a deep weariness that made Anika twinge. His mouth tightened. "Please, let's hurry this up."

"Commander Alexandra Forsythe," said a no-nonsense officer with a shaved head, as she shook Anika's hand, introducing herself. She pulled Anika over to a window. "The U.S. military has had plans for an orbiting solar mirror array for over forty years. The army in particular wanted to be able to concentrate solar light to solar stills and panels from orbit, in order to allow for better mobility. If there's one organization on this planet that is aware of the mobilization limitations having to ship fuel around creates, it's people who are faced with having to mobilize hundreds of thousands and keep them moving and using their equipment. However, other than demonstration tests, it was determined that anything bigger would be a default weaponization of space and a treaty violation. Whoever did it first would trigger a rapid arms race over our very heads. So now we're in the middle of that very real mess and, guess what? Most of our response plans are completely inadequate for this scenario because they all assumed actual orbit, not high altitude floating bubbles controlled by an actual U.S. corporation instead of some foreign country."

"So are you going to help us?" Anika asked.

"Some old Brit colleague from a war-gaming conference I attended five years ago calls me up and says I have to talk to Prudence Jones, like right now. And suddenly I'm finding out about nuclear bombs being in place at the site. So here's the problem: my superiors are dealing with politicians losing their minds. The solution to this problem, an ordered attack, will cost the lives of a lot of my people, and a lot of people who're left on Thule. So yes, Ms. Duncan, I'm going to help you set off a nuclear bomb. I shouldn't be helping you, I'm not under orders to do so. But it's clearly the right fucking decision, and it's going to be a hell of a lot easier to ask forgiveness than permission here."

Anika sagged from relief. "Thank you."

Commander Forsythe leaned in close. "But Ms. Duncan, the reason I'm up here is this: we're going to be ghosts, you understand? I'm not here, you're not here, and the SEALs I'm lending you, they've all volunteered and will swear they were never here. We would have tried to get a special operations group from the CIA, but that requires presidential approval, and time to fly them out. With that cloud overhead, we don't really have that, so we're making do the best we can." Forsythe held out a pad.

Anika looked down at it again. "What's this?"

"A very tight, very dangerously written nondisclosure agreement that swears you to silence, quite literally on pain of death. And please take it seriously. You fuck up, and I'm spending the rest of my life in jail as well."

"More paperwork," Anika said.

"I take it you haven't spent that much time in the military?" Forsythe asked.

"I'm not shocked," Anika said. "UN Polar Guard was not any different. I'm just . . . never mind."

After she pressed her thumb on the pad, Forsythe slid it away. "Good. I'm assured by experts who've looked this plan over on the way here that the fallout will be minimal here on the ground. The citizens here are in no more danger than observers at many bomb sites last century, and most of the cloud is over the water, and not Thule. So I had Mister Prudence Jones sign this earlier, and Violet Skaegard signed it in the hallway. Time is not on our side, so let's get started."

. . .

Within the hour Forsythe was shaking hands with clean-cut men in off-duty wear standing on the dock. Some of them were still pulling on newly purchased Thule cold weather gear as they stuffed their old gear into plastic buckets that were then tossed back into the small dinghy tied up to the dock.

Any personal effects that made the men identifiable were also sent home.

"Forsythe said these were volunteers," Roo commented, looking on as the SEALs checked over their weapons. "But this is a full SEAL platoon. I doubt any of these sixteen were capable of saying 'no' when asked."

"Isn't a platoon larger than sixteen men?" Anika asked.

"Not these guys, no," Roo said. "Sixteen should be enough against Gaia Security. Any more: we lose the element of surprise."

"Okay. I see."

"Maybe." Roo turned back to a small case full of weaponry he'd wrangled. They were all snugged nicely away against foam inserts. Anika figured that meant Roo was going to be joining this attack. "You should go talk to Vy."

Anika took a deep breath, ready to harass him for telling her what to do. Then she realized she didn't even know where Vy was, and had been caught up in mentally preparing herself. "Where is she?"

"Inside that pickup." He pointed. Roo had hunted down three winterized Indian Tata pickup trucks converted into ice plow trucks. They'd lined the doors and bed with extra bulletproof vests, and the three trucks would be their lightly armored, rapid transportation in.

"Thank you."

She found Vy sitting in the passenger's side of the indicated truck cab. She had wrapped her arms around her knees and was staring out of the windshield at nothing in particular.

"You know what I fucking hate about the polar circle?" she asked, shivering from the gust of cold air as Anika crawled in next to her and shut the door.

"What?"

"That." She waved her hand at the windshield.

Anika looked out through the frost rimming it at the buildings. "What are you pointing at, Vy?"

"The light. Always the light. It feels like I've been up for three months, and never got to go to bed. And when the winter comes, it'll feel like I'm living in a twilight dream. It eats away your insides and leaves you wondering if it's seeping into your decisions. I'm sick of it."

Anika leaned against her, snuggling in closer. "I don't like it either. It feels unnatural. But then again, who am I to say what is unnatural. I can't even wrap my head around seasons. Whenever I was outside Africa, away from the equator, the idea that the world could grow cold felt . . . alien. Like I'd flown to another planet and was out of my place."

Vy leaned her head on Anika's shoulder. "Between that and the cold, that was why I bought into The Greenhouse. Baffin's little piece of tropical paradise in the middle of the grim. I know it can be beautiful out here: the blue water; clean, stark ice; the purifying wind. Jim Kusugak told me he spent some time in New York and couldn't stand it. No open vistas, too warm, *too fetid*, he said. I think some people just imprint on where they grow up, and I'm one of them. It's not the cold, it's the light. The constant, fucking light. And it doesn't needle at me until I get stressed, and then it's always there, burrowing back behind my eyeballs."

Anika hugged her closer. "Someone should find that boat Paige told us about and get it ready. We're going to have to leave really quickly once we set the missile to fire. And we want to disappear after this. We should disappear somewhere that isn't the North. Ask Roo for help—maybe he can help us escape to the Caribbean?"

"Or a nice, mid-sized little city somewhere on the California coast? With its own municipal nuclear power station and a water desalinizer. Normal day and night cycles, and t-shirt weather all year round," Vy sighed. "I'd been saving up for that."

"It sounds beautiful," Anika said wistfully.

Vy grabbed her cheek to turn Anika to face her. "There's no fucking way I'm sitting on that ice queen's boat and waiting for you and Roo to risk your damn lives without me. Don't disappear on me again."

"Okay," Anika said. They pressed their foreheads together. "I promise. I promise I won't ask why either." It was time to just accept that Vy was there. That she wanted to be there. Anika didn't need to sabotage this by second-guessing. She didn't need to wonder why Vy wanted this, or what it was she had to offer.

She'd pushed enough people away with that before. Excuses about the job. Believing that she couldn't possibly be everything someone else thought she was.

But for now, Vy was the second leg that helped her stand up that much straighter. It felt good. Like here in this small cab, they were a team, with the outside world something they faced together.

And she liked that.

Someone knocked on the window and Vy looked up. "The very nice Marine outside looks like he'd like to talk to us," she said.

"SEAL," Anika said.

"Whatever."

It was time to go over the plans with Commander Tyrone Gallo one more time. If there was anything Anika was learning about the SEALs over the last half day, it was that they believed in preparation.

Meanwhile, reports trickled in of two more ships destroyed by the mirror swarm for pushing too close to Thule. The G-35 navies were standing clear, but a standoff like this wasn't going to last forever.

# 40

The first pickup rolled down the road toward the building, shoving snow out of the way as it went. The spray of ice and flakes thrown up clumsily ahead of it shielded three SEALs running up the street, then ducking behind nearby buildings.

Fifteen minutes later the first truck was parked on the far side of the building.

The three men reported in a few moments later, and Anika watched as Commander Gallo pushed pins into the most recent satellite printout of the surrounding area and updated her. "Lookouts have been disabled," he said. Then he asked, "Is the weapon still in position?"

After listening, he looked back at Anika. "They can see the missile in the upper floor from their positions. Time to go. Let's roll!"

They took off down the ice street.

As planned, one street over, the other pickup truck would be speeding down it. Up ahead, coming down the street at them, the third would now join in as well.

There were four teams, the commander had explained: the small sniper team of three up on the roofs, giving them eyes and cover fire, much like the volunteers had given Gaia earlier; two teams of four each would take the stairs, while a third would hang back to provide support.

Although armed, Vy, Anika, and Roo were, as Gallo said several times, to stay the fuck in the trucks. Vy was in the bed of this one, her back against the rear window.

Fair enough, Anika thought, as one of the SEALs gunned the pickup along. These guys moved with oiled precision and every other trained-to-the-nth-degree, band-of-brothers type of cliché you could think of. She'd unleashed them like dogs on Gaia. Let them do their thing, she thought.

But she still cradled an assault rifle. Another Diemaco C11. Familiar, sturdy. Known to her. Along with a few extra clips she slipped under her waistband.

Just in case.

She also found yet another pistol to tuck into the back of her jeans, under the jacket. It made her feel better.

The three trucks slid to a halt and everyone leapt out. The SEALs moved quickly, each member sweeping a zone around him with a rifle, ready for an attack from any quarter.

For a split moment, as Anika watched them ghost their way through the pylons under the buildings, she felt a slight twinge of déjà vu. Roo took the wheel from the commander—who'd slipped on out—put it in reverse and backed them around underneath a nearby building, out of easy range.

The sense of déjà vu disappeared in a gut-punching series of explosions. They both turned around to look out the back of the truck. Vy had crouched lower, and she turned to look at them through the glass. "What was that?"

"Mines," Roo said. "Shit."

Anika couldn't see any SEALs—they'd found cover as the firefight suddenly ripped the streets open. Bullets cracked into the street surface, throwing up sprays of chipped ice with every single shot.

And the *fizz-schwish* of an RPG filled the air. Orange flames exploded underneath a nearby building. A pylon splintered, and the entire structure slumped slightly over to its side.

"Get down, Vy!" Anika slouched down, patting the bulletproof vest she'd acquired, just to reassure herself it was still there. Glancing at the rearview mirror she saw that Vy was lying down in the bed of the pickup. Good.

"They're ready for us," she said, a cold lump in the back of her throat.

"Very ready," Roo agreed, as Gaia Security began to pour out the doors of buildings all around. "Looks they've moved out the civilians, maybe purchased the surrounding buildings and taken over the whole area. Shit."

One of the SEALs, fifty feet away, was dragging a body back through the pylons at them. Anika kicked the door open, getting low, Diemaco slung under an armpit, and made her way over. She ducked from pylon to pylon and grabbed the wounded SEAL's shoulder.

Vy dropped the truck's tailgate and helped them get the wounded man up. Anika winced as she realized the man's right leg was hanging more by cloth than by leg.

"You need to get him to the hospital," she said. "It's by the harbor."

"Someone needs to drive," the SEAL said, ripping a pants leg apart and pulling open a medical kit. "He's going to bleed out if I leave him."

Roo tapped Vy on the shoulder. "Get him there, you've been in Thule before."

"There'll be others who get hurt," she said, leaping down and getting inside the cab.

"Maybe, but we have other trucks. Go." Roo slammed the door shut and slapped the window.

Vy looked over at Anika. "I'll be right back," she mouthed.

"I know."

The pickup peeled out, sliding underneath the buildings and dodging pylons, and Roo and Anika got to cover.

Gallo joined them a minute later, slipping in low and shoving his back against the thick concrete pylon they were favoring. "Goddamn it, I told you guys to stay in the trucks."

"Violet took your guy to the hospital. You're stuck with us."

"That was Ricardo that stepped on the mine," Gallo said. He tapped his earpiece. "Neil says he's got him stable, but he might lose the leg. They really moved quickly to secure this area, Jones."

Roo sighed. "They're more prepared than I could have anticipated. I looked through their files, only a few of them have Special Forces experience."

"Well, this is a case where the numbers matter as well," Gallo grunted. "We've got fifty or sixty Gaia Security spread through the surrounding buildings, and ten or fifteen in the target building itself."

The clatter of bullets died. Their side had their positions and wasn't wasting ammunition. The other side couldn't see any movement.

In the lull, Gallo continued, his voice level and calm, and almost oddly reassuring. "If I knew for sure I could get Gabriel into that building, I would order my men to cross the roads, risk the mines, and head up those stairs. But I guarantee you we're all going to die in the crossfire from these occupied buildings. We just don't have the tools to do this right."

Anika looked across at the scuffed ice. The house that had been hit by the RPG finished settling one corner onto the ground. They were so close. They were within a couple hundred feet. She crouched over the assault rifle, pulling it close to her. "What tools?" she asked.

"We need air support," Gallo said. "But the bubble cloud's in the way, and Thule has filled the air with antiaircraft mites that choke the inlets. Very effective nontraditional air warfare. We could try for missile strikes if we pull back, but that still leaves the mines. . . ."

"What if I can get you air support?" Anika asked. "Is it still doable?"

"What?"

She was already on the phone Paige had slipped her back in the office before she'd gotten on the submarine. Anika clenched her free hand. Please, please, please still be there, she whispered to herself quietly. Still be in partial control of the cloud.

"Yes?" hissed a strained, brittle voice.

"It's Anika. We need your help, Paige. I can stop Ivan. But in order to do it, you'll have to help me destroy the cloud, so that it can be rebuilt somewhere else, controlled by all of us, not just Ivan. You can't hold him back for very long. What happens next?"

There was a long pause. "What are you doing, Anika?" Paige whispered. Anika could hear her cough wetly through the phone.

Over the occasional burst of gunfire, the crack of nearby bullets as the lull faded away and the Gaia fighters pressed them back, Anika explained.

"Anika!" Roo shouted. "They're going to push up on us now. Is time to leave."

Anika shook her head and held a hand up. "Paige. I talked to an officer from the blockade in town. They will attack, and when they do, it will be the blockade, and everyone left in Thule, who pays the price. We detonate this nuke high up, over the water, the shield goes down. We can end this."

A long moment stretched out so long Anika checked the phone to make sure the call hadn't been dropped.

Finally Paige coughed and croaked, "The moment he knows you've overrun them there, he'll focus the shield on that building and vaporize you all."

"Can you hold him back?"

"Not for very long anymore. He's almost locked me out. You will have to move quickly . . . if I agree." Then suddenly Paige's voice changed sharply. "*Wait.*"

There was more silence. And then one of the Gaia men shouted. They stopped firing, and several of them leaned back and looked up into the sky.

From their position under the building, behind the safety of a pylon, they couldn't see what they were pointing at.

A solid beam of light descended and struck an empty square three blocks away. Steam hissed and boiled over, and the façade of a nearby building slumped.

Distant screams reached them.

Paige returned. "He's trying to destroy the building you're talking about, and the nuke. He must have just gotten the news that you're attacking and doesn't want to risk you getting the nuke."

"We're beaten back; he has to know we haven't taken the building," Anika protested.

"He won't take the chance. He'd rather sacrifice them than risk you taking it." Paige sniffed.

"Paige, you can't support this," Anika said.

"I know. I know. Give me the coordinates you want attacked, and then get ready to move. I'll bake the street. I will not fry my own employees, but I can startle them and make the buildings they're in intolerably hot but survivable. They'll be more interested in getting away than in you, I'd bet. That's the best I can do."

"Thank you, Paige. Thank you."

She didn't say anything.

Anika pointed at the phone, and then repeated the situation to Gallo. "Knowing that, are you still in?"

He looked thoughtfully around. "So we'll have to move the missile. Mr. Jones, is the equipment still up there?"

Roo nodded. "When we initially captured it, they'd knocked out a wall, then put tarp over it to stay warm. The tackle is still there. We can lower it over the side into a pickup and drive like hell to a better location."

Gallo looked at the phone. "How much time will we have?"

Anika met his eyes. "As much as she can give us."

Gallo tapped the butt of his gun against the trampled snow underfoot and thought about it for a second. "Let's do it," he said, and took a deep breath.

"We're all on board," Anika told Paige. "We're ready when you are."

"Then here we go," Paige said, and Anika heard a click.

The world exploded in light.

# 41

The silvered cloud split, and a focused beam of light struck the street in a twenty-foot-wide swath of fury. It swept southward, mines detonating and throwing their debris into the already violent explosion of steam.

Anika, Roo, and Commander Gallo huddled against the pillar as the hot steam blew past them.

The white-hot beam of light faded, and a strange, creaking silence settled in.

"Okay, I'll give you ten seconds, and then I hit the houses," Paige said, her voice so hoarse Anika had to strain to hear it.

"Ten seconds," she shouted to Gallo.

"Ten," he repeated. "Go!"

It took five seconds to run through the pylons. Anika was counting down under her breath. She hit four as she slipped and slid out onto the road. The heat had boiled off a strip of the street, turning it instantly to steam. The rest it had merely warmed, leaving them a slippery river to cross.

She spotted scared Gaia Security forces running away underneath other nearby houses out of the corner of her eye.

But at the count of three, bullets started slapping the standing water around her. At two, her legs were soaking wet with still uncomfortably hot water. At one, the world lit up again: a curtain of light that surrounded the three-story house with the missile in it.

The other houses with Gaia people in them weren't being vaporized, but they were being heated. People were throwing their hands up, then retreating inside. Smoke was curling off the outsides, but that was it.

But it was enough. The SEALs had the house surrounded, and all they had to focus on were the stairs in front of them. Four SEALs were at the main entrance, waiting for Gallo.

He nodded and gave the signal to go in.

Grenades were tossed inside, and the SEALs went in through the door, rifles covering every angle, firing.

"Clear."

From the other side of the first floor came another series of shots. "Clear."

Anika had the Diemaco trained up the stairs, but there was already a SEAL covering them. The third team went up the stairs, a fluid concerted movement that resulted in more brief bursts of fire, then the calm call of "clear."

"Third floor's clear," they called a few seconds later.

When she got up there Anika saw why. The snipers had already taken care of any threats on that floor by getting positions that let them fire down in through the skylights. Five Gaia men lay in pools of their own blood around the missile.

One of the SEALs saw her looking at them and nodded. "Hooyah, ma'am."

"Dee: get on the windows for the counterattack," Gallo growled.

"Sir."

Two SEALs ripped the tarp off the side of the wall and kicked out the rough timber frame that held the tarp in place, while down below one of the pickup trucks pulled into position, the paint on the top of the cab blistered from the quick drive through the heat. One of the snipers hopped out and waved.

The long timbers that made the crude crane, tackle still on the end, were quickly hammered back into place by five SEALs so that they stuck out of the side of the house. Roo pitched in.

They slid the missile down out of the cradle onto the floor. Then, using plain brute force, muscled it onto a wooden sled.

Gallo used wax from a kit to lube up the floor, and they shoved the sled out onto a crude rope sling hanging from the crane. As they were doing that, the curtain of light surrounding the house snapped off.

Anika called Paige. "What's going on?"

"He's figured it out," Paige said. "Get out of there. There's not much I can do . . ."

A massive blast of light struck a nearby house. They could feel the heat wash across the street as the house slumped into a pile of fused rubble.

"Get on top," Gallo snapped, shoving Anika and Roo onto the missile. He handed her the cables and laptops and gear, all shoved into a large duffel bag. "Gabriel's in the pickup. Go!"

Figures flitted around the pylons of nearby buildings. But just as quickly as Anika noticed them, short gunfire sent them scurrying back for cover.

She held the rope as they were lowered, looking up at Gallo and his men slowly easing the missile down.

At fourteen feet long, six feet of the missile still hung out over the edge of the bed. As the missile slowly settled in, the pickup truck's springs groaning, Anika and Roo grabbed spare straps to secure the tip.

Every slip seemed to be a catastrophic mistake, and every second stretched into an eternity Anika didn't feel she had.

"Get the truck clear!" Gallo shouted from overhead as he leaned out over the side of the house on the crane.

The truck lurched into gear, tracks clattering and slipping in the water and slush underneath. Anika crouched down and grabbed ahold of the lip of the bed. They'd gotten halfway across the street, when the light struck the house.

Anika covered her face with the crook of her elbow as heat washed over her. She could barely breathe, or think, and when it snapped off, she gasped and started coughing.

As her eyesight slowly returned, she stared at the gaping, bubbling pit where the house had once stood.

"Jesus," she whispered.

Someone was screaming, and she realized it wasn't

her: it was the SEAL driving the truck. He was punching the dashboard and swearing, but keeping them on the road as they trundled farther and farther away from the glowing hot debris behind them.

Shadowy figures ran along the pylons, trying to keep up with the truck as it sped up. Some of them started opening fire, but both Roo and Anika braced their backs against the cab and started firing bursts at any movement.

Three blocks later, and the attacks stopped.

Anika's phone buzzed.

"Paige?"

"You're alive. And you have the missile?" Paige's voice sounded even fainter, more papery, with a faint gurgle.

"Yes." Anika decided to spare her the casualty details.

"They're cutting through the door with a torch of some kind," Paige said. Anika heard several shallow breaths. "So, I want you to remember something really important. Do you have a pen?"

Anika patted herself down. "Roo! Pen?"

He shrugged.

"Forty-five, sixteen, seventy-nine, twelve," Paige said over a loud crackling and spitting sound in the background.

"What? What's that for?" Anika asked.

"Forty-five, sixteen, seventy-nine, twelve," Paige repeated. A loud crack sounded. "They're coming through."

Forty-five, sixteen, seventy-nine, twelve, Anika said to herself. Then again. She rapped on the glass window, and when Gabriel slid it open for her, she leaned through and grabbed a pen off the seat, where Gallo had left it.

She rolled her left sleeve back and wrote the numbers down on her forearm.

"Good luck," Paige said.

The sound of a single gunshot made Anika jump.

On the other end, someone picked the phone up. "We're hunting you. And when we find you, we will quite literally *smite* you," Ivan Cohen said, then cut the connection.

For a stunned, long moment, Anika sat with the phone in her hands, staring at it.

They passed a streetlight, and Anika looked at the tiny camera mounted at the top. She raised a fist and flipped it off as they passed underneath.

# 42

They'd ducked the truck under some buildings for cover, hoping that Ivan's ability to ferret out their location wouldn't be as rapid as Roo's.

Roo ducked his head into the back window. "Gabriel, how are we going to launch this thing?"

"The more important question is where," Gabriel replied slowly. "Anika said Ivan is hunting for us via public cameras. The moment he figures out where we are he'll use the shield against us. Mainly what we need is a pit. We can slide the missile into it and get it pointed. The four of us can do that from the truck."

"We have a ship," Roo said. "Can we get it aboard Paige's ship and launch it from there?"

"We need to be quick," Gabriel said. "And we don't have time to build a cradle for the missile on a ship."

Anika had been thinking about this since she flipped off the traffic camera. It was highly unlikely

Ivan had seen that, or if he did, he was probably just now collating the footage to try to retrace their footsteps. "Was all of the Pytheas demesne ripped apart from Thule, or are there any pieces left? There won't be cameras there. We can set the missile up in the open."

Gabriel tapped the surviving SEAL, he'd told them his name was Weirs, on the shoulder. Weirs put the truck back into gear and they clattered along again, leaving the perceived safety of their hiding spot.

The gaping ruin of tangled metal and ice where the core of Pytheas had ripped itself away from Thule stretched for a mile, looking out onto the open sea.

Sewer lines dribbled brown water. Bridges drooped, half their span severed, leading out into midair. Jagged road edges just stopped before the ocean.

In the distance, beams of light coalesced from the cloud to stab at the ocean over the horizon. Each blazing, eye-dazzling explosion meant another ship had been attacked. As she watched, the beam slowly moved from point to point.

And in the distance, near the cloud's edge, a steady stream of explosions. It looked like someone was testing regular munitions out on the cloud.

The war had truly begun.

Walking as close to the brink as she dared, Anika looked down thirty feet to the water below. Clumps of ice bobbed and smacked against the cleaved-off edge. A mile away, Anika could see Thule's harbor. The hospital was near there. Vy would be as well.

A few hundred feet away, a large chunk of ice creaked, groaned, and then slipped off the jagged fringe of Pytheas and into the water.

Not a good idea to stand here, she thought, and turned back for the truck.

Gabriel and Roo had found a raised walkway in front of a set of five-story apartments and driven the truck up onto it, then turned the truck and backed it up until the rear tires were on the edge of the walkway.

From there they'd all used the spare ropes to slowly, carefully, lower the missile down to the ice road seven feet below.

The missile sat on its fins pointing straight up into the air, with several pieces of rope around its midsection to brace it.

All they needed to do was cut the ropes as it launched. Low-tech, but hopefully workable.

Roo handed her his phone as she approached. "Violet."

Anika pointed at the cables leading away from the missile toward the cab of the truck. "How far away are we?"

"Gabriel says we have telemetry. Power is good. We're getting close."

Anika nodded and answered the phone. "Vy? How are you doing?"

"They came in by helicopter and took them both away. They told me I should leave with them, because they were going to start the invasion. I refused." Vy sounded tired. "The airborne attack will begin shortly."

Anika didn't know what to say. She was still processing that bright, burning flash.

One moment those men had been there, fighting alongside her. Fighting because of something she'd set in motion.

And then, in a flash, they had been edited out of the universe.

"Roo said you were on the edge of Pytheas. Do you want me to come out there?" Vy asked.

"No," Anika insisted. "Roo says we're almost ready to launch. I think it would be better if you could get to Paige's boat, get it started and ready?"

"I'm already working on it," Vy said. "I'll see you soon."

"It . . ." won't be long, she was going to say, but Anika noticed a furtive movement in the distance. Someone ducked behind a building. "I have to go, Vy. I will see you at the boat."

She cut the connection and reslung the Diemaco from her back down to across her front. "Roo."

He turned around from leaning into the cab and caught the phone as she tossed it back to him.

"I think someone's at the end of the street," she said.

Roo stepped up onto the edge of the door panel and looked over the top of the cab. "I don't see anything," he said, looking back down at here. "Where?"

The window of the cab exploded and Roo dropped to the ground, swearing. Gabriel calmly slouched deeper into the seat, still looking at the laptop balanced between his stomach and the wheel of the truck. "I really was hoping they wouldn't find us so quick," Roo said, moving to the back of the pickup and grabbing a rifle and pocketing several grenades.

Weir joined them, walking in a crouch. "They're coming from the other side as well."

They had their backs to the open sea, the truck facing the apartment complex, and Gaia now moving in from either side. Gaia's forces would be calling back the coordinates to Ivan Cohen any second now.

"Shit," Anika said. "Roo, how long do you think it takes for the shield to reposition the mirrors and attack?"

"Minutes? It can't be a *quick* process," he said, looking up into the sky.

Anika ignored the impulse. When the flash came for her, she didn't want to be looking up.

Gunfire rattled out, smacking into the ground around them. This attack was coming from their unprotected side. Weir returned fire and moved behind a concrete balustrade that decorated a set of apartments.

"Vy said the invasion began. If that's true, we may have longer, if Ivan is trying to shock and awe them into not continuing." She stabbed a finger at the horizon where light danced and cracked.

Roo shrugged and smiled sadly. "Gabriel?"

He raised a hand. "Just hold them off while I start the launch sequence." He looked at Anika. He'd been avoiding looking at her, visibly tensing whenever he saw her. Now those old, cold eyes narrowed. "I wonder, have you thought about the lives we could have avoided wasting had you not remained so focused on your quest for revenge?"

Anika bit her lip. Fuck *him*. Now it was her turn to tense and hold something back. He was here. That was more than she would have done. And right now, they needed him to finish what he'd started. "I have."

Roo grabbed her and pulled her back along the bed. "Keep fire on them," he said. "You have you back covered by Weir."

"Where are you going?"

He pointed at the road the missile sat on. "If I was them, I'd be crawling along the lip or under this walkway. Now, keep an eye on the apartments. They'll be getting up into those windows up there to get a good shot down at us."

Anika glanced upward. Now the dark windows looked shadowy and menacing.

"Shit," she muttered.

"Seen," Roo agreed, and then sprinted for the edge of the walkway and jumped down onto the road below.

The pop of gunfire started.

For the next few minutes Anika fired off quick bursts at any movement up the street while she used the apartment building's concrete stair banisters for cover, just like Weir. She wasn't sure half of the movement she shot at wasn't shadows, but if it moved, she pulled the trigger, pausing only to slip out a new clip from her waistband and slap it into place.

If this worked, she half imagined she was going to die protecting the missile.

If it didn't, either the people attacking would shoot her, or the sky would flare up and vaporize her at Ivan Cohen's direction.

At least vaporization would be instantaneous, she thought.

She was on her last clip when Gabriel threw the laptop out of the car after yanking the cables out that led to the missile. "Weir: get ready to cut the ropes."

"Is it ready?" Anika asked.

"I started the launch sequence. In two minutes it'll fire. You don't want to be standing here," Gabriel said. "Give me your gun."

"Why?"

Weir jogged their way, pulling out a large hunting knife.

"I'm going to shoot that laptop so that if they rush us, they can't plug back in and stop the launch. And I'm going to hold them back from damaging the missile."

A foot away, Weir jerked as a hail of gunfire slapped the vehicle's far side, the ground near them, and the rails near the missile.

For a second, Weir looked like he was taking cover with Anika and Gabriel, who got down. Anika fired back over the top of the truck bed. But Weir didn't stop running—he clumsily spun to his left and staggered sideways, out into the open, and collapsed.

"Weir?" Anika shouted, horrified. Another life on her hands?

Gabriel shook his head.

Weir was sprawled out, looking up at the sky, a red mess of brain and blood leaking out of the side of his head onto his jacket. He was dead.

The burst of fire faded. Part of the natural rhythm of the firefight.

"Anika? The Diemaco?"

Anika handed Gabriel the Diemaco and, zombie-like, pulled out the pistol from the back of her jeans.

He looked down at it. "You still don't trust me, Ms. Duncan?"

She shook her head. She was still numbed. "No."

"Why?"

The death of yet another man just a few feet away chewed through her like an acid, and the words that tumbled out were bitter, and not even aimed at Gabriel but at the messed-up situation. "Men like you use words like 'preemptive' and 'just' and chew through lives. You even destroy countries. You run around, playing your games, imagining you are gods moving the little people around on boards like game pieces. And you are right, you are not human, you are something else. But it is not gods. I flew enough of your kind into conflict zones to know the type. You know why natural resources are the curse of a developing nation? Because the rebel army meets someone like you, who parachutes into the jungle, and they say when they get control of the resources, they'll cut you a deal. And so you give them arms, or a loan, because maybe you don't like the current government. And the brutal flip-flopping of overthrow, violence, and overthrow continues. I know you, Gabriel. You're the kind of man who thinks it makes any sense to smuggle a nuclear missile around the world to kill an engineering project."

Gabriel shifted the Diemaco. "You ignore the very simple fact that I was right, though. What *exactly* is wrong with you that you can't just accept that?"

"A broken clock is correct twice a day," Anika said. "You are correct now. But you will always be doing things like this around the clock. That is how you are. Regular people, we are reactive. Hit us, we hit back. But you walk around looking for people to hit ahead of time. You see?"

"You would just let Ivan Cohen dominate you all, then?" Gabriel sighted down the rifle and fired off a full burst at the laptop. Pieces of plastic and circuit board flew off into the air as it was destroyed.

"No," Anika said. "Your people and him, they are the same. They dictate from on high. They are always convinced that they, and only they, have all the answers. They have to force the issue. The ends justify the means. Get rid of your masters and him, the rest of us get on with living. But since we're stuck with each other, we have this mess. Right?"

She looked at him. She'd gotten a reaction of some kind, but she wasn't sure.

Gabriel spotted movement and used the rifle to quickly force someone back into cover.

When he crouched back down, Anika grabbed his shoulders. "Who *do* you work for, Gabriel? Because the military types who picked you up, they all kept hearing back that you were retired. So who are you contracting out to?"

"I work for a group whose interests are harmed by the ice returning," Gabriel said. "And that is all you need to know."

"I'm about to die helping you," Anika spat. "The least you can do is give me this satisfaction." The satisfaction of knowing more about the forces that had turned her life upside down and led to her crouching here, wondering how many more minutes she had left.

"You're wrong," Gabriel said. He reversed the rifle. "About a lot of things. In particular—"

"What?"

He smacked her in the face with the butt of the rifle. Anika's vision went dark, and she staggered backward. She had the pistol up, but as she opened her eyes, she realized he had the Diemaco trained on her. She wasn't going to be able to shoot him. "Gabriel? What are you doing?" She was thinking about double betrayals. Wondering if he'd really set the missile to launch.

Gabriel smiled sadly. "No one's going to miss an old spy who did horrible things no one wants dredged back up," he told her. "But you have someone waiting for you. So you're wrong: you're not going to die. I'm going to hold them off, so that they don't shoot the missile, or damage it. You, on the other hand, have about two minutes to run for safety. Do it, or I'll shoot you."

"Really?" She wasn't buying it, and besides, she was still wearing her bulletproof vest. She took a step forward. He tightened his stance, grinned slightly, and shot her in the upper left shoulder, just clear of the vest.

Stuffing flew out of her jacket and hung in the air while the impact of the bullet smacked half of her body backward. Anika staggered another step back, clutching the top of her arm as blood seeped out. "You *fucker,*" she spat, the pain trickling down through her.

The bullet had hit shoulder flesh and exited. Gabriel had damn good aim. Her eyes narrowed and his smile faded. "Run," he repeated, and shifted his aim at her temple.

"Where?" she responded. "We're cut off. There's no 'away,' Gabriel."

"Take two more steps backward, and look over your shoulder." He gestured with his rifle.

Anika took the steps and glanced. At first, she saw nothing but the ruined edge of ice, road, structure, and the ocean out past it. Then she saw it. A small antenna, rocking back and forth, hard to spot when the angle made it look like part of the jumbled mess the demesne had left behind when tearing itself away from Thule.

She turned back to Gabriel and threw him the pistol. "You'll need that more than I will."

"Ah, now you trust me," he said sadly.

After one last look, Anika sprinted for the railing. The movement prompted more gunfire, and she could hear the slap of bullets against the walkway as she slid off the raised section and dropped to the road below. She was standing right next to the base of the missile.

"Roo!" she shouted, looking around at the wall the raised walkway created on this side of the road. There were a few bodies in Gaia Security uniforms, but no Roo. "Roo!"

"*Ras*, woman, keep quiet. Over here." He was slumped on the ground near the lip of a half-destroyed bridge on the other side of the road. All she could see was a hand waving her over.

Anika ran across the street, drawing fire again, and hunkered down behind a twisted steel beam.

Roo'd been shot in the leg. He had ripped up an undershirt to create a makeshift compress, and tied that on tight with a piece of electric wire.

"This it," he said to her. "Can't hold them back much longer. I think, hearing them talk about what Ivan wants, they will kill us even if the missile goes off and they realize they lost."

"He said he would smite us," Anika said. "Gabriel's holding them off, the missile's going to launch any second. Roo, do you trust me?"

He glanced over. "We come this far and you asking me that?"

From his position in the cover of the ruins of half a bridge, they couldn't see the sea next to the ragged edge. "We have to jump," Anika said. "I think Vy's here."

Roo leaned around her and looked at the water. "You *think*?"

"Someone's here. I saw them, they're right up against the edge. We're going to jump."

"In water this cold, without survival suits, we'll live for minutes," Roo shouted.

On the road across from them, the missile began to hiss and vent.

It was going to take off any second now.

"Death by water or death by Gaia?"

Anika got Roo up on his good leg, and they hopped awkwardly along the remains of the bridge. Out over the cold water, the bridge groaned and shifted from the extra weight, protesting the indignities forced on it.

The missile fired, a hot roar of exploding gases and a deep thrum of motive power. Anika shoved

Roo harder, and at the very edge he glanced over at her.

"Jump," she said, and shoved him over first as she jumped back away from the bridge.

The last thing she saw, just before the bridge flashed in front of her, were the ropes springing off from the missile as Gabriel cut them away.

# 43

Anika hit the water. For a moment the cold and shock narrowed the world to a faint pinprick, then her vision returned, and she was looking up at the surface of the water. It looked like a mirror over the world, out of reach far over her head.

She kicked off her shoes, shed her bulky jacket, and kicked for the surface.

It was so cold, it felt like the water burned her skin and face. Already she'd started shivering violently, and when she broke the surface and gasped air, it also burned her lungs and throat.

She floundered in place for a second, looking for the ship and Vy, but stopped when she saw the missile.

It rose, vomiting smoke and fire behind it, speeding up faster and faster as she and Roo watched, breath steaming the air. "It's off," Roo said, a note of wonder in his strained voice.

At the edge of the road, Gabriel limped to a stop, looking up at the missile.

"Jump!" Anika shouted, though it hurt to shout and seemed to take almost all of her energy. "Jump!"

Gabriel raised a hand, as if to wave, and then the sky flashed and a pillar of pure light smacked the road. There was no Gabriel, no apartments, no nothing. Anika's eyesight was washed out by the sudden attack from the sky.

But it hadn't gotten the missile; she could still hear its roar in the background, even as the crackle and explosions of the heat ray destroyed the entire block she'd just been standing on.

It was okay, she thought, that the cold had sapped so much heat from her body that she was starting to feel warm, at least they'd gotten the missile off.

But instead of slowing down and slumping into the water, she was feeling strong. Warm and strong.

Roo grabbed her shoulder. "Swim for the colder water," he hissed. "We're too close here, it's warming up."

She wasn't dying. The solar shield's beam wasn't just chewing up the block, but the waste heat, bubbling out from the destruction, was also warming up the nearby water.

Roo was right: without their sight, they'd have to swim for colder water. It was the only way to know they were swimming away from Thule.

"This way!" he shouted.

She followed his voice out into the bitter chill, but someone else shouted from behind them. "No, this way!"

It was Vy.

Anika swam toward the voice as the ocean began to scald her. Then Vy grabbed her hand and hauled her onto a swim platform, with Roo hauling himself up right behind her.

Anika's vision began to return as she blinked and looked around to see that she stood on the back of a very luxurious forty-foot motor yacht. She shielded her eyes and looked back toward Thule as best she could. They floated just a few hundred feet away from the ripped up, and now mostly slagged remains of it. They were just far enough away that she could feel the heat on her skin. Had they delayed by just half a minute, they would have been cooked in their skin, she realized with a shudder.

Vy left them to run up to the enclosed cockpit above the main cabin. The water started to boil as Vy gunned the engines all the way up into a full howl and got the large boat up to speed, headed back into the cold Arctic Ocean.

Anika crawled up onto the bridge with a limping Roo.

Vy looked back at them. "I heard the gunshots," she said. "I was already near the boat when you called, when I heard the gunshots I knew you'd been found, so I took the boat out."

Anika grabbed her in a big full-of-warm-sea-water hug, and Vy reached up to hold her hand, while still keeping them on course.

"How long?" she asked Roo.

"Anything we can hit up ahead?"

"No."

"Then close your eyes," he said.

The motor yacht surged on ahead. Anika closed her eyes and held on to Vy as the deck shifted under their feet.

Then the backs of her eyelids briefly lit up.

At the same instant, the engines died, the electronics burned out by the electromagnetic pulse far overhead. They surfed to a slow stop on the waves.

"Okay," Roo said softly. "Let's see it."

They walked outside and looked up at the troubled sky. Far overhead, a glowing, multihued fireball of apocalypse continued expanding, punching its way through the silver cloud that dominated overhead.

"Holy fuck," Anika said, squeezing Vy's hand.

"Yes." Vy nodded her head. "What the hell did we just do?"

Punctured silver spheres dropped out of the sky like a strangely light hail as they floated, dead in the water. Vy asked Roo about the risk of radiation, but he shrugged. "They said it was 'clean,' yeah. We should be okay as long as it doesn't rain. Most of the spheres that drop will fall because of the pulse." Then he left them to hop his way down into the palatial main cabin, looking for tools that might help repair the EMP damage. Anika and Vy remained outside the cockpit near the railing, watching the skies.

"I'm done," Anika said, leaning against Vy. "I don't have anything left. I don't care who Gabriel worked for, I don't care about Ivan Cohen or who caused the people on that ship to shoot me down. I just want a life again. And I don't need to worry about my standing in the UNPG anymore because of being with you, because I'll be on the run now. Will you come with me?" She wanted to visit her mother, then see her father again. In person. And then after that, she and Vy would find somewhere where Anika could pilot for money. They could make a life.

Vy laughed. "I'm broke, they took all my money. I'll go anywhere you go, as long as it's warm and has a proper day and night cycle."

They kissed again, and with no interruptions or worries Anika could just close her eyes and feel Vy, warm against her still soggy clothes.

Anika looked up at the large gas ball in the sky. "I thought nuclear explosions looked like mushroom clouds," she murmured.

"I think it has to be near the ground for that," Vy said.

"Do you think we did the right thing?" Anika asked, running a hand over Vy's cheek.

Vy flinched slightly. "We have to hope."

Roo limped up to them and held up a sphere he'd swiped off the deck. "I think we did the right thing. You were right; we'll do it better the next time around. We can reverse engineer these things, given time. It'll happen. Listen . . ." Roo started to say, but Vy cut him off.

"What are you going to do, Roo? After all this?"

"Go back to my old life. Right now, I think, once I get a new phone and some equipment back, I'm going to see if I can get these seceded parts of Thule to consider coming down to the Caribbean. Tourism died off due to the overactive hurricane seasons these last decades, but we strong still. We have sea walls, solar and wind to stay energy independent. But we still need factories and greenhouses, yes? Get them down to the Caribbean where it isn't the Wild West like up here. If I can get some seed money rounded up, and a new boat, I'll be going from floating demesne to demesne to convince them to get towed down south. Once they build up on barges instead of ice, right."

Anika smiled. "It sounds good. Messy, democratic, and good."

Roo shook himself back to the present. "Look, while I was down there I peeked at the engines. They're shot, but I went up to the forecastle. There's a parasail packed and ready for deploy. I imagine Paige used it to cut fuel costs. It's not very big, but it will be enough for us to sail on out. We don't have to be dead in the water long."

"That's great news, Roo," Vy said. "But what about the blockade?"

Roo smiled. "Oh, I'm sure I can pull a few strings to let us through without problems. After everything we've been involved in, they're going to want us to disappear just as badly as we want to."

"I don't think I'll rest easy until we're well clear of it," Vy said.

"I understand. Hey, there's something else you two should see downstairs, though," Roo said.

"What?"

"Come look. You'll want to see this."

The main stateroom of the lower cabin was dominated by what looked like a custom-installed bank vault. It had been squeezed in, and was not part of the original build at all. The legs had been bolted and then welded to the back bulkhead, and the grim, bulky, square metal surface matched none of the silvered and modern curves of the interior decor of the yacht.

"Did Paige tell you anything about this?" Roo asked.

Anika shook her head. "No."

"It's a very particular safe," Roo said. "I've seen a few of these models in the intelligence community. If it is what I think it is, it's rigged."

"Rigged?" Vy had a curious smile. "As in: explosives?"

"Yeah. That thing would take this whole ship down with it if someone without the code tried to force their way in. And if Paige has some sort of time-delay check-in code for it, it may yet go off with us on board."

"Wait," Anika said, straightening and walking forward to the giant safe. She had a feeling she knew what this was about. And then at the same time, she sighed. She'd jumped in the water. Had the ink held? "It won't do that. She gave me the numbers."

"Numbers?"

Anika rolled the sleeve of her shirt back up her arm and looked down. The ink had mostly run. It was all an illegible stain of blue smudges on her brown skin.

They all stared at the blue ink for a moment.

Anika reached up and grabbed the large dial. "Forty-five, sixteen, seventy-nine, twelve," she said as she rotated it through the numbers.

With a loud thunk the thick safe door swung open, and the three of them stared inside.

"Well now," said Anika, as the extra reflected light from inside the safe dappled her face, "that changes . . . everything."

## ACKNOWLEDGMENTS

I have two people to initially thank in a big way for encouraging me to create *Arctic Rising*: Karl Schroeder and Paolo Bacigalupi. Karl and I collaborated on a short story back in 2007 called "Mitigation" about a mostly ice-free Arctic. It appeared in the anthology *Fast Forward 2*, edited by Lou Anders, and was also reprinted in one of the *Year's Best* anthologies shortly after. The idea to do something like this book has been stuck in the back of my head ever since spending that weekend in Toronto with Karl brainstorming the geopolitical intrigues of a new, seventh ocean. Both Karl and I lamented the lack of fiction in this sort of setting, and we wished to write more near-future explorations ourselves.

I had also come to know Paolo well through shared time at the novel workshop Blue Heaven. His infectious enthusiasm for probing all manner of around-the-corner ecological futures and similar milieus (to amazing success and acclaim, as we were all to soon find out) also lit a fire under me to do more of this when I met him, leading to my writing a novella and another short story in this vein.

In 2008, when my editor, Paul Stevens, asked if I would do something different for my next book after *Sly Mongoose*, I already came prepared with a rough idea for *Arctic Rising* thanks to conversations with Paolo and Karl.

Due to a genetic heart defect that took me out of the game for a while in late 2008 and early 2009, getting a full draft took a lot longer than expected. In a way, it's been quite a marathon for me, but one I'm glad to have finished, even if it was mostly by walking. My thanks go out to the folks at Tor, particularly my editor, Paul, again, for being patient as I put my life back together. I also have to thank Eddie Schneider and Joshua Bilmes, my agents, for being patient as I limped my way back into finishing this project.

Another round of thanks goes to the crew of Blue Heaven 2009, who read and critiqued the first fifty pages. Big thanks go to Greg van Eekhout and Paolo Bacigalupi, who helped me brainstorm pieces of the last third of the book.

More big thanks go to the various branches of the military that release publicly funded studies and foresight materials online where greedy little authorial minds like mine can hunt them down for future idea mining. Most of the ideas and scenarios in this book came from reading about what *those* dudes are worried about. The amount of time they spend worried about peak oil and how to run armies on solar power, you'd think the armed forces were a bunch of hippies who wanted to run their Humvees on fry oil. Certainly, one thing I came to find is that there is a massive disconnect between people who study the future, whether it be scientists, weather experts, or military strategists and brass, and politicians and talking heads who seem to think there aren't some challenges around the corner. When I started writing this novel in 2008, the navy reports I was using in regards to Arctic ice didn't include ice-free scenarios in the possibility charts; by the time I was done with a draft it was on the worst-case plot, and now it looks like ice-free summers are a given very soon. I hope this book comes out before my "science-fictional" plot idea of a generally ice-free Arctic isn't quite so shocking.

Lastly, I'd like to thank all the readers who've waited so long for the latest book. Thanks for sticking with me—it won't be so long until next time!

## ABOUT THE AUTHOR

Tobias S. Buckell is a Caribbean-born US author. He spent much of his younger life growing up aboard boats in Grenada, then on boats with various family members in the British Virgin Islands, and again in the US Virgin Islands.

Since 2006 he's been a full time author and freelancer. He also works for the excellent independent publisher Subterranean Press where he looks after their e-Books.